Impending Love and Madness

by

Laura Freeman

Impending Love Series

Impending Love and Madness

Cover Art by *Debbie Taylor*

The Wild Rose Press, Inc.
PO Box 708
Adams Basin, NY 14410-0708
Visit us at www.thewildrosepress.com

Publishing History
First American Rose Edition, 2018
Print ISBN 978-1-5092-2060-1
Digital ISBN 978-1-5092-2059-5

Impending Love Series
Published in the United States of America

"Mister Ravenswood is ill
and isn't receiving guests."

"But we traveled all this way," Cass said. "Isn't there going to be a sale?"

"A gale?" The old woman looked at the sky and pointed at a dark cloud. "It looks like rain."

"We were asking about the horse sale!" Ethan shouted.

"The sale is on Saturday. You should return then." She pushed the door closed. The clank of a bolt locking the entrance echoed from inside.

"Well, I never." Cass stared at the wooden barrier, willing it to open. "We're here to see Zach! If he's ill, I can help!" Her shouts were unanswered.

"Come on." Ethan pulled her away and helped her into the buggy.

She turned. A curtain moved. Someone was watching them.

Harry took the reins and glanced at the sky. "She was right about a storm. We better hurry to the village. We can try again tomorrow."

Ethan relaxed against the back seat. "Any of you buying that fairytale the old witch was telling?"

"No, but what can we do?" Harry asked. "We've been thrown out of the castle."

"Old witch," Cass repeated Ethan's description.

Harry slowed the horse. "Are you all right, Miss Cassie? You look pale."

"Don't you remember the fortune teller's prediction? I think Zach is in trouble, and he needs our help."

Ethan leaned forward. "How do you propose we sneak past the crazy doorkeeper?"

Praise for Laura Freeman

"A romance you will not want to end. Great characters and plot keep this book fun and you wanting to turn the pages. This author knows how to write a great story."

~Barbara H., Reviewer

~*~

"Good romance setting and story line set in the midst of war and survival. This is the first book I've read by this author and will be looking up the rest of the series."

~Dawn M., Reviewer

~*~

"This was a saga of love conquering all when all things conspire to prevent it."

~GumboMom

~*~

"This was a great historical romance set in the Civil War. It is really well written and very believable."

~Poppy

Dedication

To my dad, Bill, who encouraged my dreams.

Chapter One

Cassandra Beecher snatched the silky fabric of her gown and rushed through the bedroom door and into the hall, peering over the banister to the foyer below. "Is Zach here?"

Her sister, Jem, ascended the staircase at a snail's pace. "Logan is taking the children to the Mermaid's Mirth and bringing Sergeant Ravenswood back to Pierce House. Promise you won't gallop down the stairs when they arrive."

Cass gasped for air. "I doubt I could run without fainting in this corset." She must have been insane to torture her body with the stiff undergarment emphasizing an hour-glass figure beneath the evening gown, but she wanted Sergeant Zachary Ravenswood to realize she was more than a nurse. "Are we going to see *Aladdin*?"

"I'm sorry. Logan couldn't obtain tickets to Grover's Theater," Jem said. "*Aladdin* was sold out, but Ford's Theater is having a special showing of the British comedy, *Our American Cousin.*"

A stuffy British play. She would have preferred a tale about magic and adventure. Zach would be disappointed.

"Don't pout," Jem said. "Laura Keene is starring in it."

Who was Laura Keene? She didn't want to appear

ungracious. "I'm sure it will be lovely."

"I read in the afternoon paper the President and Mrs. Lincoln along with General Grant and his wife, Julia, will be attending Ford's Theater to see it."

"The president!" Cass twirled the four yards of fabric in a dizzy spin. "Zach and I would love to see Lincoln. We've memorized some of his speeches."

"Did Zach meet Grant before he was made general-in-chief of the Union armies?"

"I don't think their paths crossed," Cass said. "He served under Hooker at Chancellorsville and Meade at Gettysburg before he was shipped west to serve under Sherman."

"I hope he wrote about more than the battles he fought in."

Cass had met Zach at her home in Darrow Falls, Ohio, while he was on furlough in January of 1864. They had exchanged letters during the past year, and she had arrived in Washington City a few weeks before Zach broke his leg and was sent to Mermaid's Mirth to recover.

A member of the Twenty-ninth Ohio Veteran Volunteer Infantry, Zach had been crossing a bridge in North Carolina in March when a sharpshooter's bullet hit the man marching beside him. Zach had grabbed his comrade, but the dead man's weight had pulled both of them over the side and into a rocky gulch. A broken leg was better than a bullet in a limb. Usually amputation was the only option when a lead ball smashed bone and left a splintered mess no doctor could set.

Their reunion had confirmed her belief that Zach was the man she wanted to marry, but her parents and four older married sisters considered her too young.

The chaperoned visit to the theater was the first social event they had been allowed to attend together. Cass was determined to make the most of it.

"You look beautiful." Jem returned with her to the guest bedroom.

Cass examined her appearance in the full-length mirror in the corner. The elegant silk was a sharp contrast to the work dresses she wore to care for the wounded or help with the chores at her sister's home. The green material shimmered in the gaslight, and the off-the-shoulder bodice displayed a wide-expanse of creamy smooth skin. The bone-ribbing pressed her breasts upward, and the low-cut gown proved she was no longer a child but a woman of seventeen.

Cass smoothed the green silk over the bell-shaped crinoline. The gown and matching satin slippers were perfect for a ball. "Too bad we're viewing a play instead of attending a dance."

"I doubt Zach would enjoy sitting along the wall while you dance with other men," Jem said.

"Zach has nothing to be jealous about." Cass searched for her long gloves.

"You've set your heart on Zach, but don't let it muddle your thoughts," Jem said. "I've seen too many women marry the wrong man because they didn't take time to look beyond a uniform or flattering words. You choose your husband, but you don't want to regret it."

Was her sister hiding trouble in her marriage? "Do you regret marrying Logan?"

"Don't be a goose. I love Logan." Jem smoothed her gathered skirt over her rounded belly. She was beginning to show her pregnancy. "But you're young. And with the war nearly over, you have all the time in the world to enjoy life. You don't have to rush into marriage."

Jem meant well, but she was treating her like a little girl. Cass was second from the youngest of the six Beecher sisters, and they found it difficult to treat her as an adult, let alone an equal.

Jennifer, Colleen, Jessica, and Cassandra had journeyed to Washington City where they had used their nursing skills to help with the wounded. And fortunately, for Cass, Zach was one of the wounded.

The Mermaid's Mirth hotel belonged to Zach's commanding officer, Captain Blake Ellsworth, who was married to Colleen or Cole as she was known to her sisters. Trained as midwives, Cass and Jem had spent last night delivering a baby boy to their sister, Jess. Her husband, Confederate Major Morgan Mackinnon had surrendered with General Robert E. Lee at Appomattox Courthouse on April 9 and had returned yesterday on the thirteenth. Normally, she would have helped with the care of the newborn, but the reunited parents didn't want to be disturbed.

Cass could only imagine the poetic phrases and gentle caresses that passed behind closed doors. Her ignorance frustrated her. But that could change. Zach would no longer be a soldier, and she planned to steer the conversation to more personal topics. Jem was right about one thing. Talking about the weather or how pretty her gown looked would not help her decide if Zach would make a good husband. But what would convince her that she should spend the rest of her life with him?

Cass examined her coiffure in the mirror, turning to see the back. Jem had arranged her dark hair in a thick braid at the crown of her head with smaller intricate braids looped in the rear and threaded with green and gold ribbons. "Thank you for doing my hair."

"I always enjoyed braiding your hair when you were little."

Did the braids make her look too young? The door opened below. Cass gathered her gloves, reticule, and wool cloak and hurried to the staircase.

"Walk," Jem reminded her.

Cass paused at the newel post at the top of the steps. Zach leaned against his crutch as he waited in the foyer. His dark blue frock coat fit snugly against his broad shoulders and tapered to a narrow waist. The light blue trousers were creased, something no soldier in the field worried about. He wore a thick sock on the foot of his broken leg, but his single brogan was polished to a shiny black. He had removed his kepi and rotated it in his gloved hands.

The winter had faded the tan he had acquired marching across Georgia last fall under the command of General William Sherman, and miles of hardship had transformed his lanky build into hard sinew that convalescing had failed to soften.

He turned. The gaslight emphasized his blond hair, but his eyes were his most attractive feature. He had sour apple green eyes that sparkled as she descended. A lopsided grin expressed his pleasure. She paused on the bottom step and tugged on her gloves, allowing him to survey her appearance. Although a novice at impressing men, Cass had paid attention to her sisters and their interactions with their husbands.

"You look lovely." His deep baritone caused her body to vibrate in response.

Zach and his friends had joined the Twenty-ninth Ohio in late 1862. Zach was twenty-one now, but age wasn't measured by years when life required killing to survive.

He had fought in the Twelfth Corps before traveling to Tennessee to become part of the Twentieth Corps. The Union forces had fought Confederate General Joe Johnston in Atlanta and across Georgia to Savannah before moving north, whittling away at his stubborn forces. Johnston had yet to surrender.

Zach missed his friends and sometimes withdrew, haunted by the dark memories of the battlefield. Although her sisters had protected her from the worst images of the war, she was no stranger to the horrific results of battered bodies and shocked minds. Cass had witnessed the men in the hospitals struggling with nightmares from the violence and mutilation of the war. Both sides prayed for a quick end to the Civil War that had been waged across five Aprils.

"I'm looking forward to the evening," Cass said.

"It's a beautiful night," Zach said. "Most of the houses between Mermaid's Mirth and Pierce House are lit with lights. You can hear people singing on street corners."

"The town wants to celebrate Lee's surrender," Cass said. "Aren't you happy the war will be over soon?"

Zach's laugh was rich and masculine and sent tremors radiating along her spine. "I'm not going to miss living in a tent and trudging through mud."

"I'll be grateful no Johnny Rebs will be shooting at you."

His smile was wide and eager. "Will you?"

She took a deep breath to steady her reply. "Enough men have died in this war." She should have said something more personal.

"Too many." A shadow darkened his handsome face. "Victory can't raise Pax from the grave."

Paxton Ravenswood had been Zach's older brother. He had been shot at Cedar Mountain and died at Mermaid's Mirth. Most families had been touched by death. Her cousin Jacob Donovan had been killed at Antietam, and Darrow Falls neighbor Ed Herbruck had died at Gettysburg. "Let's not think about death tonight." She smiled. "Let's enjoy the celebration."

Logan Pierce offered his arm to his wife. Jem wore her dark red hair in a braided chignon laced with blue and white ribbons. Her matching blue gown possessed sheer off-the-shoulder sleeves and a white lace-edged bodice. A woman expecting a child normally didn't appear in public, but the full skirt hid her pregnancy from social criticism. Her due date was in late August, and she would have to suffer through a humid, hot summer. Cass would complete the chores and tasks that would allow her sister to rest in the coming months.

Logan wore a black suit with a lace trimmed white shirt and black tie. His white vest had been embroidered by Jem with a colorful flight of birds across the silk. He worked for the Department of the Treasury and was acquainted with most of the political and military leaders who had guided as well as thwarted President Abraham Lincoln's years in office. "Good news for the economy," he said. "General Grant stopped orders for supplies for the army, saving the country four million dollars a day."

"Four million dollars?" She couldn't imagine four

million of anything let alone money. "How could we spend so much?"

"A lot of men to feed and clothe," Zach said. "And pay."

"After four years, the debt has grown to nearly three billion dollars," Logan said. "The national debt was a modest sixty-five million dollars in 1860."

Cass shook her head, her braids dancing with the motion. "Why did we ever go to war?"

"It was going to be over in three months," Jem said.

Jem had lost her first husband at the first Battle of Bull Run. But she had met Logan, and they had built a home and family during the war. Logan had purchased the boarding house before marrying Jem. It had belonged to a Southern patriot who idolized Lee. Logan changed the name of the Southern Belle to Pierce House. Ironically, their daughter Chauncy Theodora had been named after two Southern soldiers who had befriended them at the beginning of the conflict.

The war had not been able to separate North and South completely. Cass had attended Lincoln's second inauguration, and he had talked about reconciliation. Many were ready to put the last four years behind them and work toward rebuilding a united nation.

The Beecher sisters had done their part healing and not only through nursing the wounded. They had family on both sides of the conflict. "Morgan is at Mermaid's Mirth. Did you meet him?"

Zach blushed. "No. He's been with Miss Jessie and their son since he arrived."

"I hope he realizes she just had a baby and needs to rest," Jem said.

Logan placed a wool cloak around Jem's shoulders. He changed the subject. "Looks like we might have rain again."

Cass handed her cloak to Zach who draped it around her bare shoulders. "Thank you." Her lips were inches from his face. Their eyes met in unspoken desire. He turned away, and the spell was broken.

Logan looked at his watch. "The carriage is waiting, and we don't want to be late. The play starts promptly at eight."

Cass took Zach's free arm, her fingertips resting on hard muscle beneath his sleeve.

The ladies boarded the hired carriage, and Zach hopped on the steps and plopped onto the leather seat beside Cass. Logan sat beside Jem and instructed the driver to take them to Ford's Theater.

The carriage traveled west on Pennsylvania Avenue and turned north on Tenth Street.

Cass waved at all the lights in the windows of the homes and buildings along the path. "You were right, Zach. The town has so many lights; it looks magical tonight."

Hotels, restaurants, and shops were decorated with red, white, and blue bunting with candles or oil lamps in the windows. Citizens filled the streets, and musicians formed bands on the street corners. The excitement in the air was contagious. Cass recognized the tune as the music grew louder and sang the familiar words, "*The Union forever, hurrah, boys, hurrah! Down with the traitor, up with the star.*"

The others joined in and had finished a verse and another chorus by the time they passed Taltavul's Star Saloon, and the carriage stopped in front of Ford's

Theater. The front of the brick building had five decorative archways. The street was muddy, and someone had placed boards to form a ramp to the center entrance.

Logan paid the driver to find a place to wait along Tenth Street. Zach hopped to the ground and placed his crutch under his arm. He offered his hand to Cass and escorted her inside to the lobby where the ticket booth was located. Logan had already purchased tickets, and a boy offered them programs. They removed their cloaks and hats, and Logan gave them to a young man who stored them with other patrons' belongings. A staircase led to the second and third floors of the theater, but they were seated on the main floor on the right side near the presidential booth. Logan entered the row of straight back cane chairs so Jem and Cass could sit next to each other. Zach took the aisle seat, which gave him extra room for his splinted leg.

Patrons murmured in their seats, glancing toward the empty corner box overlooking the stage. The president was late, but productions at Ford's Theater were punctual. The gaslights dimmed at eight p.m. as the play began.

Lincoln had not been popular because of the war. Even victories at Gettysburg and Vicksburg had not guaranteed his reelection, and he had changed his choice for vice president to Andrew Johnson who was from Tennessee. But time and victory had softened the opinion many had of the gangly, homely man who had been born in a log cabin, studied law by candlelight, and was elected twice as president of the nation.

Cass and Zach could recite the *Gettysburg Address* and lines from Lincoln's other speeches. His words contained a beauty and inspiration rarely uttered by politicians.

She stared at the empty booth reserved for Lincoln. The tall arched openings were framed with gold and white draperies and standing flags. A loose flag was draped across the front of the balcony in thick folds with a portrait of George Washington in the center. "Maybe the president decided to see *Aladdin.*"

Zach laughed, and even though the play was a comedy, he received a few harsh stares from those concentrating on the actors' lines.

The low lights allowed the actors to see the audience, and some of the thespians spoke directly with those seated in the front rows as the play progressed.

Zach took her hand into his and squeezed her fingers. Even with both of them wearing gloves, it was scandalous public behavior, but they weren't famous enough for gossip to ruin their reputations.

"I don't mind missing the president when I can spend time with you," Zach whispered.

Her heart raced at his compliment. But did his words mean he enjoyed her platonic company or he considered her more? Did a romance require a declaration of love before it became official? And how would she find the courage to say *I love you* to Zach? What if he laughed at her tender feelings? What if he didn't feel the same way? Thankfully, the play prevented her from speaking.

The play was twenty minutes into the first act when Laura Keene said the word *president*, a cue that signaled Lincoln's arrival. The audience turned toward the back balcony, and the orchestra played "Hail to the Chief."

The audience stood. Cass helped Zach balance on one foot. She rested her hand on his back, ready to grab his coat if he faltered. Zach put his arm around her bare shoulders and grinned. His bold smile frightened her. Had she encouraged him too much? Would he take liberties if alone with her? And how did she discourage him if he did? Instead of medical training, she should have sought courting maneuvers from her older sisters.

Lincoln surveyed the crowd and entered a hallway before emerging in the presidential box. Cheers echoed in the theater as Lincoln acknowledged the audience and actors. Mary, whose short stature contrasted against her husband's tall frame, sat in a red chair near the railing. Ulysses and Julia Grant were missing.

"Who is that?" Cass whispered as an officer and young woman took seats to Mary Lincoln's right.

"He's no general," Zach said under his breath.

"That's Major Henry Reed Rathbone," Logan said. "The young lady is his fiancée, Clara Harris, the daughter of Senator Ira Harris of New York."

"What happened to Grant?" Zach seemed disappointed.

Logan shrugged. He was a secretary, and although it was his job to know important people, he wasn't privy to decisions made by superiors. But Logan was friends with Lincoln's primary secretaries and had been to the White House on numerous business occasions.

Lincoln nodded in their direction, and Cass turned to Logan. "Lincoln acknowledged you."

"Wishful thinking," Logan said. "He could have been nodding at you, Cassie."

Lincoln bowed a second time to the audience and took his seat in a rocking chair on the near side of the balcony. A curtain hid him from view except for the times he rocked forward and peeked at the audience.

Cass removed her fan from her reticule and waved it in front of her face. The crowd of warm bodies and late hour were making her sleepy. The third act had started at ten p.m. The play would be over soon. She covered a yawn. "I'm sorry."

"I think a funny part is coming up," Jem said.

"Have you seen the play before?"

"A year ago, but the president wasn't attending and neither were you."

Cass looked at her program. Actress Helen Muzzy stood and said, *"I am aware, Mr. Trenchard, you are not used to the manners of good society, and that, alone, will excuse you the impertinence of which you have been guilty."* She departed, leaving Harry Hawk, who was portraying Asa Trenchard, alone on the stage.

"Don't know the manners of good society, eh?" Hawk demanded. *"Well, I guess I know enough to turn you inside out, old gal, you sockdologizing old man-trap!"*

"Sockdologizing?" Zach repeated amidst the loud laughter of the audience. He turned toward the presidential box. "Was that a gun shot?"

Chapter Two

Zach pointed at two men wrestling in the state box. "What is the major doing?" The other man was dressed all in black. He leaped over the railing of the box toward the stage but caught his right boot in the thick folds of the decorative flag and landed on his left leg and hands. "Who is that?"

"It looks like John Wilkes Booth, the actor," Logan said.

Booth rose to one knee and shouted, "Sic temper tyrannis! The South is avenged!"

Zach turned to the others. "Is this part of the play?"

"He was speaking Latin," Cass said. "Thus always to tyrants."

"You said you heard a gunshot?" Logan looked toward the balcony.

Major Rathbone pointed to Booth who was limping to the back of the stage. "Stop that man!"

"Won't somebody please stop that man," Clara Harris cried from the box.

"What is the matter?" a man shouted from the audience.

"The president has been shot," Clara said.

Silence answered her declaration. Then murmurs.

"Why would anyone shoot President Lincoln?" Cass looked at Jem. "Are you sure it isn't part of the show?"

Logan and Jem's stricken faces revealed the horrible truth. "I should do something." Zach stepped on his splinted leg and winced. His mobility was limited, and he carried no weapon. He was useless.

A Union officer climbed over the orchestra pit and footlights to reach the stage. Booth had disappeared in the shadows.

"I don't have my medical supplies, but I could help." Jem stood.

"This crowd will trample you. Stay here, and I'll see what I can find out." Logan turned to Zach. "Protect the ladies."

"Yes, sir." Zach braced himself against his crutch, ready to defend them. He saw the fear and shock on the ladies' faces. He'd seen the same look on men facing battle and afterward when surrounded by the dead and dying. "I'm sure the president will be fine. He's strong," he reassured them.

While some of the men ran toward the stage to pursue Booth, the crowd surged against them and headed for the back, away from the stage, away from the last sighting of the shooter. Zach blocked a man heading heedlessly toward them. "Go around."

"Stay here, and you'll be shot." He knocked over several chairs in his struggle to pass the sea of retreating bodies.

Zach searched the crowd for suspicious characters. "I don't think he had any accomplices," he reassured them.

Cass gripped his arm. "I hope not."

The presidential box was crowded with soldiers and civilians. Sobs echoed in the theater, an expression of utter desperation. It had to be Mary Lincoln.

Cass twisted her handkerchief in trembling hands, her gaze on the box. "I hope someone in the balcony is a doctor. They have to save him."

Zach choked back his own grief. Lincoln had suffered insults and verbal attacks by his enemies yet returned their viciousness with wisdom and kindness. He had fought to unite the nation torn apart through a horrible war. He had freed the slaves. "It's utter madness."

He maintained his post and guarded the end of the row while Jem and Cass waited for Logan to return. They whispered prayers, begging for a miracle. A few clusters of tearful patrons remained on the main floor of the theater, their gaze focused on the activity in the presidential box, waiting for news. Most of the crowd had surged outside, overturning chairs and leaving crumpled programs trampled under the fleeing mob. Gawkers crowded the second floor, hoping to catch a glimpse of the president if and when he was carried out.

Zach looked at his watch. It was after eleven p.m. The presidential box had only a few people moving in the shadows. Where had they taken the president? Logan approached from the back. He carried their cloaks and hats.

"Are we leaving?" Cass asked as Logan distributed their belongings.

"Soldiers are carrying Lincoln outside to his carriage." Logan's voice caught in his throat. "The doctor said it was a mortal head wound."

"Is this doctor experienced?" Jem asked.

"Yes, and the other doctors agree with his prognosis." Logan arranged a cloak around Jem's shoulders. "The president was shot with a derringer at close range. The major was stabbed with a Bowie knife in the arm but will survive."

Zach helped Cass put on her cloak. Tears glistened on her lower lashes. One broke over the fragile barrier and streamed over the smooth skin of her cheek. He reached forward and brushed the droplet away. More followed.

"It can't be true," she whispered.

Zach pulled her against his chest and offered comfort. A man going into battle prepared for the chance he might not survive, but this crime, a shot from the shadows while his victim enjoyed a play in the company of his wife, was a violation of all that was decent.

Logan took Jem's arm. "A crowd is gathered outside. We should leave before the road becomes impassable."

"Could we wait for news?" Cass looked at Jem. "Head wounds can be unpredictable."

Logan looked worried. "Are you sure you want to be in a crowd?"

"I'm not ill," Jem defended.

"But it's raining."

"We could sit in the carriage," Cass suggested. "I couldn't go home until we know what has happened to the president."

Zach looked at the two sisters. Although trained as midwives, they had worked as nurses. "Is there a chance he could survive?"

"We can pray and hope until there is none," Jem said. "I've seen miracles at the bedside of gravely wounded men."

Logan's expression was grim. He was not as

hopeful.

It would be better to spare the women the crowd and anxiety of waiting, but Zach would not sleep until Lincoln's fate had been confirmed. He hobbled toward the door as Logan led the way.

They found the hired coach, but the driver was missing. Logan looked at his watch. "He's probably waiting in one of the saloons. He should return soon."

Logan helped the women enter the carriage. Zach hopped onto the step and paused, surveying the scene over the roof of the vehicle. News of the shooting had spread, and the crowd had swelled, filling the street.

From his perch he counted six soldiers carrying Lincoln on a long board. They paused in front of the entrance, their forms outlined by the eerie yellow light from the tar torches in the front of Ford's Theater. A soldier returned from the saloon next door and shook his head.

A doctor pointed across the street, and the soldiers gripped the board with the president's body and stepped into the muddy street, shouting for the crowd to clear a path.

"They're taking him across the street, but they'll never get through that mob." Zach waved his crutch over the roof of the carriage. "Make way! Let them pass!"

The soldiers bearing Lincoln pressed against the crowd but made little headway.

"Can you help them?" Cass asked.

Zach cursed his broken leg. He was helpless because of his injury.

Logan patted Jem's hand. "I doubt I can make much of a difference, but I can try."

"Wait." Zach pointed toward mounted soldiers. "Cavalry heading this way. They're Ohio boys," he added. "They'll part the crowd."

The Seventh Independent Company of Ohio Volunteer Cavalry used their horses to make a path, and the soldiers carried a motionless Lincoln across Tenth Street.

"Bring him in here! Bring him in here!" A man waved a lantern in front of a row house.

The soldiers bore Lincoln up the steps and inside. Among the soldiers and doctors was Mary Lincoln sobbing into her handkerchief.

As soon as the door closed, the crowd rushed forward and waited for news of the president's fate.

Logan turned his coat collar upward and addressed Zach. "If there's any trouble, take my wife and Miss Cassie home."

"Yes, sir." Zach entered the carriage and sat next to Cass. They peered out the window facing the street as Logan pressed his way through the crowd toward the boardinghouse. He spoke to a soldier outside and headed for the alley.

Cass turned toward Jem. "Logan is going around back."

Jem stared out the window by her seat, her gaze following the fading figure of her husband. "The president can't die. Not now. He's guided the country through horrible years of death and destruction, but his work isn't finished. We need him."

Cass grabbed Zach's hand. "I'm so glad you're here."

Zach wanted to be with Logan. He was a soldier, a man of action, but he resigned himself to the mission of comforting the women. He stared at their tear-streaked faces. How did he offer support? He'd spent the last two years with fellow soldiers. He was ignorant of women, but Cass had smiled at his jokes and listened attentively to his comments the past few weeks. Besides being clever and talented, Cass was the most beautiful woman he had ever met.

He wanted to impress her, but he was little better than a cripple until he shed his crutch. He was a helpless spectator in this drama. Could he have done anything to save the president's life? He hadn't seen Booth moving toward his prey. But why? Why now when the end of the war was so near had Booth taken the life of the man who had promised reconciliation instead of revenge? Booth needed to be caught. The public needed to know that the heinous act of murdering the president would not go unpunished.

The driver opened the door and peered inside. "Did the play end early?"

"Where have you been?"

The man backed away at Zach's shouting. "Having a drink with an old friend." He surveyed the crowd. "I heard outlandish rumors on my way here. Do you know what's going on?"

"Lincoln has been shot," Zach informed him.

"It's true? But who would shoot the president?"

"It was John Wilkes Booth," Jem sobbed.

The driver frowned. "The actor?"

Cass dabbed at her tears. "Do you know him?"

"He was drinking whiskey at the Star Saloon."

Zach leaned toward him. "When?"

"It's been an hour or…"

"Was he alone?" Zach asked.

"Yes, with a look on his face that didn't invite company."

Zach ran his fingers through his damp hair. "Doesn't Lincoln have a bodyguard?"

"Yes," Jem said. "They were chosen from the police officers."

Zach shook his head. "How could one man get past an armed guard?"

"John Parker is his bodyguard," the driver said. "He was drinking with Lincoln's carriage driver at Star Saloon."

"What? He should have been outside the presidential box!" Zach shouted. "What sort of man is this Parker?"

"Parker is a lazy drunk," the driver said. "He must know someone in authority to keep his job."

Cass pressed against Zach. "How could he leave Lincoln unguarded?"

"It's dereliction of duty," Zach said. "A soldier would never leave his post. Is Parker in the saloon?"

"I think he left during the commotion," the driver said. "Do you want me to drive you home?" He looked around at the people surrounding the carriage. "I don't know if I can get through this mob."

"No, we'll wait," Zach said.

"Here comes Logan." Jem pointed across the street.

He squeezed through bodies and acknowledged the driver who held the door. Logan brushed the rain from his coat before sitting next to his wife. His face was grim. "The Secretary of War Edwin Stanton is with Lincoln along with Mary and their son, Robert. Tad was at Grover's Theater."

"Thank goodness he wasn't with his father." Jem

took Logan's hand. "Poor Mary. Losing Willie and now this. It's too much for one woman to bear."

"The doctors have made him as comfortable as possible, but I'm afraid there's nothing that can be done," Logan said.

Cass leaned toward Jem. "I'll understand if you want to return to Pierce House, but I'd like to remain here."

"I'd rather wait and hear the news," Jem said. "I couldn't sleep until I knew. I pray the doctor is wrong."

Logan conferred with the driver, who agreed to stay where he was while they awaited news of Lincoln. He provided blankets to keep them warm. Cass covered Jem and tucked her cloak around her shoulders. "Are you warm enough?"

"I'm the big sister. When did you become my caretaker?"

"I learned from the best."

Jem stroked her cheek.

Zach stared at their intimate tenderness. Jem and Cass had a special bond he had not known even with his brother, Pax. He was an intruder. How could he ever think that Cass would love him more than her family? Why would she leave them for him when he had nothing to offer but his soldier's pay? He had attended a year of college before enlisting but doubted he would return to school. His grandfather wanted him to take on the responsibility of running the family horse farm as soon as he was mustered out. Even though he was heir to Ravenswood, he would have to earn his inheritance. It would be years before he could marry.

In spite of the drizzle, the crowd grew through the night as word spread of the attempt on Lincoln's life.

Most waited in silence while others prayed or sobbed. Those who carried umbrellas, shared them. Others preferred the rain, washing away the tears that flowed in grief.

Cass stared silently out the window, whispering prayers. "Please spare Mr. Lincoln. Please let him be all right."

They maintained a vigil all night, waiting, praying, and crying. Jem napped, resting against the shoulder of her husband. Cass snuggled against Zach, but she never slept. She recited one of Lincoln's speeches. He joined her. Even if Lincoln died, his words would live on.

It was nearly seven-thirty a.m. April 15 when a man stepped outside of the boardinghouse and announced Lincoln had died. The news rippled through the crowd. At first no one reacted. The truth was too horrible to accept.

President Abraham Lincoln could not be dead. He had laughed along with the rest of the audience during the play. The soldiers had called him an ordinary man, one they would follow into the darkest hours of war. The former slaves, who had escaped their masters and plantation life, called him Father Abraham. Emotions, kept at bay with hope, broke into wails and cries of distress.

"Noooo!" a woman mourned and fainted into a man's arms.

Others denied the message. "He can't be dead. He can't."

Cass buried her face in Zach's shoulder. He embraced her, turning to Logan, who comforted his wife. Logan was crying. Afraid his grief would overcome any fragment of self-control he still possessed, Zach turned to anger. "What did this man think he would achieve?"

"He was a Southern sympathizer," Logan said.

"The South lost the war," Cass said. "Couldn't he accept that?"

"Now he's changed history." Zach stared at the crowd. "Whatever his intent, he has set in motion events that will alter the future. For everyone."

Chapter Three

Logan motioned to the driver who eased his way through a crowd numb with grief. He urged the team away from Ford's Theater to G Street and then back to Pierce House using Seventh Street to Pennsylvania Avenue.

They passed homes decorated to celebrate Lee's surrender. "We hung red, white, and blue bunting yesterday." Cass sobbed. "Now we'll have to replace it with black crepe."

The driver stopped at Pierce House. "The children are at Mermaid's Mirth," Jem said.

"You need to rest," Logan said. "And I have work to do." Logan would report to the Treasury Building and help sort through the chaos of the aftermath of the assassination.

"I'll stay with Deidre and Chauncy at Mermaid's Mirth so you can sleep," Cass said.

Jem tenderly stroked her sister's cheek. "You could use some sleep, too."

Cass looked around as morning sunshine filtered through the clouds. It didn't match the heaviness in her heart. "I can't stop thinking about what has happened. We were so happy with the birth of the baby and Morgan's return."

Logan helped Jem descend and leaned inside the carriage door. "You need to warn Morgan to stay inside. Retribution could turn ugly for any Southerner." He paid the driver. "Take them to Mermaid's Mirth on Maryland Avenue."

"Yes, Mr. Pierce."

Cass twisted the dry handkerchief Zach had given her. "How will I tell them what's happened?"

"Don't worry about it," Zach said. "I'll tell them."

It was her responsibility, but she was willing to share the burden. "We'll tell them together."

They were a short distance from the hotel when soldiers stopped the carriage and peered inside. Zach shielded Cass. "What do you want?"

"The president has been shot."

"We know. We were at Ford's Theater last night."

"What were you doing there?"

He grabbed a program Jem had discarded on the vacant seat and waved it in his face. "We were watching the play."

"Why are you returning home this morning?"

"We waited with the crowd to hear news of the president."

"Who is that with you?"

Cass leaned forward. "I'm Cassandra Beecher. I live at Pierce House."

The soldier removed his kepi. "Sorry to bother you, miss, but we have orders to search for the assassins."

The soldier sent them on their way before his words registered. Assassins. Booth had not acted alone.

Cass took Zach's hand as he helped her descend from the carriage. The Mermaid's Mirth was a three-story hotel that offered beds to wounded Ohio soldiers. A sign near the road identified the hotel and was painted with a mermaid who bore an uncanny resemblance to her sister, Cole.

When they entered the foyer, the aroma of maple syrup and cornbread drifted from the dining hall and kitchen at the far end of the hallway. The staff was awake, preparing breakfast for the boarders. Some were soldiers like Zach, recovering from wounds, but most worked in the city. Those who worked on Saturday had already departed for their jobs.

They avoided the guests and climbed the staircase to the second floor. Cass waited at the newel post as Zach hopped on each step to reach her.

Cole was chasing her son, Jake, in the hall. The soon-to-be two-year-old was naked.

Cass caught him, and he struggled. "No, no, Aunt Cassie. Put Jake down."

Cole wrapped a towel around him. "It took me forever to bathe him."

"Don't you usually bathe him at night?" Cass ran her hand through Jake's damp ginger curls.

"He poured maple syrup over his head instead of on his johnnycakes this morning."

A wide grin creased his chubby cheeks. "Jake cakes."

"You're sweet enough without syrup," Cass said to her nephew.

Cole stared at their evening clothes. "Have you been out all night?"

Cass fought any outbreak of tears. "Yes."

Zach put his arm around her trembling shoulders.

"If you think you can compromise my little sister without a proposal of marriage, you are in for a rude awakening, Zach Ravenswood." Cole turned to Cass. "Why wasn't Jem chaperoning?"

Her resolve to be brave failed, and Cass burst into tears.

"What's wrong?" Cole clutched Jake. "Did Jem lose the baby? She had a difficult time when she was carrying Chauncy."

"No," Cass gasped. "President Lincoln is dead."

Cole stared, her face pale. "What do you mean he's dead? How can that be?"

"An assassin shot him at Ford's Theater during the play," Zach explained.

Cole pulled Jake against her breast. "You saw it?"

"We should warn Morgan," Zach reminded her.

"Is he with Jess?" Cass headed for her sister's room.

"Since he arrived." Cole followed with Jake in her arms. "What does Morgan have to do with this?"

Zach rested on his crutch. "He's a Southerner."

"But Grant pardoned him at Appomattox Courthouse."

Cass paused at the door. "The man who shot Lincoln was a Southern sympathizer."

"John Wilkes Booth," Zach added.

"I know that name," Cole said.

"He's an actor," Zach said. "Who would be suspicious of an actor in a theater?"

"Wait." Cole placed Jake on the floor, snatched the diaper from her shoulder, and pinned it in place around her son. "The actor John Wilkes Booth shot President Lincoln during the play?"

Cass nodded. "We waited in the carriage all night, but the doctors couldn't save him. He died this morning." She knocked on the bedroom door. "Are you awake?"

"What is it?" Jess called from inside the room.

"May we come in?" Cass shouted through the door.

"It better be important," a man growled. She was about to meet Morgan Mackinnon. Because he was a Confederate, only a few family members had met the big Scotsman who had captured her sister's heart.

Cass opened the door and stepped toward the bed. The heavy draperies in the window blocked the morning sun from the room where Morgan and Jess were nestled in bed. Jess was two years older than Cass and opposite in coloring with wavy blond hair cascading around her shoulders. Morgan was bent over their newborn son nursing at his wife's breast.

Morgan turned. His dark red hair framed a face that had seen the horrors of war. Jess had cared for Morgan after he was wounded in the Wilderness. Nine months ago, he had returned to Richmond and waited out the siege by the Union forces. Once the Southern capital fell to General Grant on April 3, Morgan had marched with the Army of Northern Virginia's dwindling forces to Appomattox Courthouse where General Robert E. Lee surrendered. Forced to wait three days for the formal ceremony, Morgan had rushed to join Jess at Mermaid's Mirth. His battered gray uniform lay discarded on the floor.

Morgan shielded Jess when he saw Zach. "Who are you?"

Zach saluted. "This is Mrs. Blake Ellsworth, Miss Cassandra Beecher, and I'm Sergeant Zach Ravenswood. I'm in the Twenty-ninth Ohio Veteran Volunteer Infantry."

"I know Colleen and Jake." He looked from Cass to Jess. "Another sister?"

"She helped deliver your son." She pressed a finger against her breast to release the suction of her son's mouth on her nipple and closed her gown. "Jem trained Cass to be a midwife."

He turned to Zach. "Blake's regiment?"

"Yes, sir."

He looked at his crutch. "Wounded?"

"Broken leg, sir."

"Broken leg?" Morgan shook his head. "What did you do, trip over your long pants?"

Zach snorted at the reference to his boyish appearance. "A sharpshooter took out the man next to me, and I grabbed him. His weight pulled me over the side of the bridge we were on…"

Zach stopped his narrative when Morgan sat on the edge of the bed. The coverlet fell to his waist, exposing his emaciated upper body. His ribs poked through his bruised skin from months of starvation. The scars of bullets and cuts from past injuries marred his fragile flesh.

Morgan reached for a tattered shirt discarded on the floor. His arms and chest rippled with muscles forged from long marches and four years of battles. "I hope this isn't a family tradition."

"A what?" Cass looked at the others for an explanation.

He slipped the shirt over his head. "Are you planning to greet us every morning in bed?"

Jess paused in burping the baby. "Something has happened."

Cass shook her head in agreement. "Something awful."

Jess grabbed her husband's arm. "They've taken

away Morgan's pardon."

"No, but he may be in danger," Zach said. "President Lincoln was assassinated last night."

"Assassinated?" Morgan and Jess mirrored the same emotion—fear.

"At Ford's Theater during the third act," Cass said. "He was shot by a man who entered the presidential box."

"But Lee surrendered," Morgan said. "He said go home."

"This wasn't a soldier," Zach said.

"A Southern spy?" Morgan demanded.

Cass shared the details she had learned from Logan. "John Wilkes Booth entered the presidential box and shot Lincoln in the back of the head while the audience laughed at a joke in the play. Then he wrestled with Major Rathbone and stabbed him before he jumped to the stage and escaped out the back."

"It sounds like a theatrical stunt," Morgan said. "Are you sure the gun was real?"

Zack nodded. "A derringer."

"A one-shot derringer? Who uses a toy to kill a man?"

"An actor," Cass said. "We didn't realize it was real at first. Booth appeared to be part of the show. Something special for the president. But he wanted people to know he did it. He gave a speech when he landed on stage. He wanted to be famous."

"He's probably at a saloon bragging about his greatest performance." Morgan stared with golden eyes that penetrated like a hawk. "Are you sure Lincoln is dead?"

"We waited for the announcement," Cass said. "He

died this morning."

Morgan ran his hands through his thick curls. The movement revealed a jagged scar on the side of his head. A near fatal wound. "I liked Lincoln. He wrote a fine speech about Gettysburg."

"I memorized the words," Cass said.

He smiled, and the years of war fell away to reveal the handsome Scotsman who had won her sister's heart.

Morgan's sister, Tootie, and her husband, Sid Wilson, pushed open the door. Sid had lost the lower part of his leg at the battle of Antietam and used a peg leg for mobility. He removed his spectacles. "Lincoln has been killed." He slid the back of his hand across his eyes.

"We delivered the horrible news," Cass said.

Tootie grabbed the edge of her apron and swiped at a tear. She had dark hair and a face full of freckles. Her resemblance to Morgan was minimal even though they shared the same father.

"The rest of the family has arrived." Morgan stood. The long shirt covered most of the worn-out sections in his short pants. He grabbed a battered gray frock coat from the floor.

Tootie snatched it from him. "You can't wear your uniform. I'll find something for you."

"I walked into Washington City wearing my uniform," Morgan said. "Waving my pardon under the nose of every man who stopped me."

"Soldiers are searching for Booth and arresting any Southern sympathizers," Zach warned. "They stopped our carriage on the way here."

"You wear that uniform, and they'll arrest you," Tootie said.

"Wasn't it one man?" Morgan said. "Why arrest others?"

"It was a conspiracy," Sid said.

"The soldiers who stopped us said assassins, but we were at the theater," Zach said. "Major Rathbone was wounded, but only Lincoln was killed by Booth."

"I've been talking to people all morning on the way back from the market," Sid said. "Secretary of State William Seward and his sons were brutally attacked at their home in Lafayette Park a little after ten p.m."

"But that's when Booth attacked Lincoln," Cass said.

"This assailant wasn't Booth," Sid said. "His gun misfired, and he beat Frederick Seward with his pistol before using his knife. He stabbed a sergeant guarding Seward and attacked a courier who had arrived at the door before he ran away."

"Morgan had nothing to do with those attacks," Jess said. "He's been in bed with me since returning home."

"We know that, but mobs are forming," Sid said. "People are angry. They want someone to pay."

Cole adjusted Jake on her hip. "No one is going to harm a guest under my roof."

"I'll stand guard at the front porch," Zach said.

Cass stifled a yawn. "You've been awake all night."

"I'll take first watch." Sid looked at Zach. "You get some sleep. You can take over guard duty after you rest."

"No one needs to guard me." Morgan searched his haversack. "Grant allowed officers to keep their side arms."

"No more shooting!" Cass raised her hands in the air. "President Abraham Lincoln is dead, and all he wanted was unity. Can't we have a little peace?"

Cole put her arm around her. "Let's put you to bed. You were awake Wednesday night delivering the baby and now all night again. You must be exhausted."

"By the time anyone recognized Booth was a threat, it was too late," Cass said. "All we could do was witness Lincoln's death."

"It happened so quickly," Zach said. "One lucky shot. If Lincoln had rocked forward or the gun misfired, he might have survived."

"As a soldier, you know you can't dwell on what could have been." Morgan turned to Sid. "What happens now?"

"Vice President Andrew Johnson is being sworn in this morning," Sid said. "He'll decide what's next."

Chapter Four

Signs of mourning couldn't be ignored. Flags were lowered to half-staff, and black crepe was draped over windows, balconies, and doorways.

Zach, Cass, and the others gathered in front of Pierce House on Wednesday afternoon. The sun was shining on April 19, a day too beautiful for the solemn occasion. Logan had spent the previous day at the Treasury Building where six-hundred ticket holders gathered before attending the services in the East Room. This afternoon, crowds lined Pennsylvania Avenue waiting for the body of Abraham Lincoln to be transported from the White House to the Rotunda of the Capitol.

A funeral service had been conducted by several clergymen before the procession began at two p.m. Pennsylvania Avenue had been cleared the entire route. Bells in church towers tolled, and minute guns fired to signal the start of the march of mourners.

Members of the cavalry, artillery, and infantry wearing badges of mourning on their left arms escorted the president's body to the steady beat of muffled drums. Footsteps echoed on the cobblestones in a slow, solemn walk to the newly renovated Capitol.

Jake pointed at the horses and men as they passed. "Parade!"

"It's for President Lincoln," Cass said. A hollow

spot couldn't be filled as the magnitude of the loss struck her. She had only seen him from a distance, but he had been the leader of the country, a symbol of hope. Now the future was full of uncertainty.

The procession included newly sworn-in President Andrew Johnson, senators, congressmen, and wounded veterans.

The funeral car was large with the base high enough above the ground for the people lining the street to see the coffin placed below a canopy. Six gray horses, each one with a groom, pulled the car.

Morgan snapped his heels and stood at attention, his hand saluting the fallen leader. Zach and Sid followed his action. Jake looked at the men and raised his small hand to the brim of his baby bonnet in a salute as the coffin passed.

The rest of the parade was a blur through tears. Cass clung to Zach's arm, her sobs muffled by her soaked handkerchief. With Lee's surrender, hope for a normal future had seemed imminent, but now a shadow passed over the dreams for tomorrow. Morgan was reunited with Jess, but what if there was retribution for serving in the Confederacy? The Ohio boys were heading home, but what if their journey was delayed because of Booth's crime? And most importantly, Lincoln's work of reconciliation had yet to begin, and many doubted if Johnson had the ability to lead the country toward a peaceful union as fractures gaped wider with distrust and suspicion in the wake of the conspiracy.

"We better go inside," Jem suggested as the street filled with civilians. They retired to the dining room where the women served sandwiches, fruit, and raw vegetables.

Cass poured iced tea. "What happens next?"

"The president will lie in state at the Capitol until Friday, and then Lincoln and Willie's bodies will be transported by train to Springfield, Illinois," Logan said. "The route will be the same one he took when he arrived in Washington City."

"I can't believe he's gone." Zach slammed his fist into the palm of his other hand. "We chose him as our leader, and no one had the right to end his life so violently."

"They'll catch Booth and the rest of his gang," Sid said.

Logan shared several papers. Copies of the images of the wanted men had been in the newspapers and on posters nailed to buildings throughout the area. "General Grant is helping Secretary Stanton track him down. They're offering a hundred-thousand-dollar reward."

Zach showed Cass one of the newspapers. Lewis Powell, who violently attacked Seward and the others at his home, was arrested at the Surratt house on April 17 along with the owner of the boarding house, Mary Surratt.

Cass reread the last paragraph. "A woman helped Booth?"

"They're arresting anyone connected to the conspiracy," Logan said. "I'm sure the truth will come out in the trial."

The next day as thousands of people solemnly walked through the Capitol's Rotunda to view Lincoln's body in an open coffin, the newspapers printed the news that George Atzerodt, who had been assigned to kill Johnson, was arrested.

The same day the train pulled out of the station for the long journey to Springfield, Illinois, with the bodies of Lincoln and his son, news arrived that Confederate General Joe Johnston had surrendered to General William Sherman. A celebration on the tail of the president's funeral was difficult to comprehend, but for Blake and the Ohio boys, the war was over. Relief and joy filled the empty void that had followed in the days after Lincoln's assassination.

Cass and her family gathered in the large parlor at Mermaid's Mirth to have a quiet toast to Blake, Harry Herbruck, and Ethan Donovan's homecoming.

Zach threatened to throw his crutch away. "I don't want Harry and Ethan to see me limping around."

"You walk on your leg too early, and it may not heal correctly," Cass warned. "Give it one more week before you put weight on it. Then you can start *slowly* regaining strength in it."

"Well, when they march into Washington City, I plan to march beside them," Zach said.

"Papa is coming home," Cole explained as she hugged Jake.

"Papa?" he repeated.

"The last time Blake saw him, Jake was six months old," Cole said. "They barely had any time to bond."

Morgan looked at his son cradled in the crook of his arm. "Blake won't waste any time getting to know him."

Jess leaned against Morgan on the sofa and stared at the life they had created. They had been man and wife for one day before the war parted them. Morgan doted on his wife and son. Jess was recovering quickly from childbirth, and with Tootie's help, they had combined their efforts to restore Morgan's health.

Cass offered a clean diaper to Jess when the baby spit up. "Have you settled on a name?"

Morgan and Jess shared a smile, a secret between them. "Jess wanted to name him Jackson Morgan Mackinnon but we changed it to Jackson Lincoln Mackinnon."

"Jackson," Zach repeated as he sat across from them with his broken leg perched on a stool. "Little Stonewall. Only had to face your general once. At Chancellorsville."

"Can't blame the Yanks for his death." Morgan frowned. "I fought under his command for nearly three years. We missed him at Gettysburg."

"I was glad he wasn't there," Zach said. "We had a tough time as it was. And I wouldn't mention Gettysburg to Harry Herbruck when he arrives. His brother was killed in that battle."

"Ed Herbruck." Morgan kissed his wife. "Jess shared the news about Ed being shot at Culp's Hill. I won't broach the subject."

Jake pressed against Morgan's leg and pointed at Jackson. "My baby."

"Cousin to you," Morgan corrected. "Do you want to hold him?"

"No!" the women echoed in unison.

Morgan laughed. "You don't trust your little angel?"

"Do you?" Cole asked.

He pulled Jake onto his lap but far enough away from Jackson to protect his son. "Have you written Blake that I'm part of the family?"

"No," Cole said. "I wasn't sure how to explain your presence in Washington City nine months ago."

Morgan looked at Jackson. "We're not getting rid of the evidence."

****

The news that the Army of Tennessee formally surrendered April 26 in Greensboro, North Carolina, was overshadowed by reports John Wilkes Booth had been shot and killed in a barn in Bowling Green, Virginia. Some people were angry he had died so quickly. They had wanted a trial and justice for the murder of the president.

The next day the steamship *Sultana,* which had been overloaded with nearly two-thousand paroled Union prisoners of war at Vicksburg, sank near Memphis. The boilers exploded, destroying the pilothouse and a large section of the boat. Flames engulfed the wooden structure. About seven hundred survived. The rest were killed in the blast, burned by the fires, or drowned in the cold swollen Mississippi River. Many were boys from Ohio.

Jem marked the names listed in the newspaper that were familiar.

Cass sat beside her on the sofa in the parlor. "Why is this happening? The war is over, and men keep dying."

Tears splattered the page. "It was an accident," Jem said. "A horrible, senseless accident."

"The boat was overloaded," Cass said. "Those men survived Andersonville and Cahaba prisons. They earned a safe passage home. Someone is to blame."

"I'm sure there will be an investigation," Jem said.

"Investigations, trials, and executions," Cass said.

"When the war began, abolitionists wanted to abolish slavery. It was a noble idea. How could it result in the death of so many?"

Jem spat in her kerchief and wiped the ink on her fingertips left by the newsprint. "Logan blames the politicians. If they had done their job, if they had abolished slavery, there wouldn't have been the need for a war."

"Then why didn't they?"

"Avarice." Jem's voice was bitter. "We live in a capitalistic society where wealth is admired, and the sins of greed are overlooked."

Cass pulled away and studied her sister. "When did you become a cynic, Jem?"

"Logan has not spared me from the stories of bribery and corruption." She crumpled the paper in her fists. "Perhaps I've lived in Washington City too long."

The Pierce family had worked in politics for generations. "Would Logan leave?"

"We've talked about returning to Ohio since Chauncy was born, but these tragedies have convinced me we have to move. I've barely seen Logan since Lincoln's death, and when he returns home, he's exhausted." Jem took her hand. "I never valued an ordinary life until now."

Ordinary life. How long would it take for life to return to normal? "My life had no impact on Lincoln's death or the war," Cass said. "But they are a big part of mine now. It makes me appreciate Darrow Falls more."

"Do you want to go home?"

"No." She meant it. She wanted to see the soldiers return. She wanted to celebrate their victory. It would help make sense of the tragedies.

"Is Zach one of the reasons?"

Zach? "I haven't spent time alone with him since Lincoln's death." Cass pointed at the newspaper. "As soon as something good happens, the headlines announce another awful event. How can we enjoy each other's company in the midst of bad news?"

"Aren't you the Beecher sister who rode a horse to fetch Papa to save Blake's life?" Jem smoothed the wrinkles in the paper. "Cole told me how brave you were. Life can overwhelm you if you think about all the hardships at once. Take one problem at a time. Figure out what you can do to make life better, and then find the strength and courage to do it."

She'd been too ignorant of the dangers on her ride to fetch her father to be afraid. "I couldn't let Blake die." She sighed. "I wish I could have done something to help President Lincoln."

"No one could. The theater was John Wilkes Booth's home territory. No one was alarmed by his figure in the balcony making his way to the presidential box. Logan said he drilled a hole in the back of the wall so he could peer inside. He timed his assault for when the audience would laugh. He had a boy holding his horse at the back door. Booth planned the details to the minute, giving him the advantage."

"Zach says soldiers blame fate when one of their friends dies. The bullet had his name on it. He was meant to be killed. But he keeps wondering what if?"

"What if Lincoln had lived? What if Lincoln was leading the nation instead of Johnson? For better or worse, we prepare for whatever life presents us," Jem said.

"I've always been a spectator," Cass said. "I tend

to watch people and life unfolding as if it's a play. I was distant but fascinated by what was occurring, but I never participated. But I think I need to be a player instead."

"You want to be an actress?"

Cass laughed at her confusion. "No. I mean a player in life. I need to figure out how I can contribute to society. I have to decide what is important to me and pursue it."

"Is Zach Ravenswood part of your future?"

"I don't know." Cass stood and paced across the wooden floor. "There hasn't been time for romance or talk about any future together with all the tragedy."

"You can't let the evil of the world prevent your chance at happiness," Jem said. "I almost missed my opportunity to be with Logan. My world would be dark without him. Find the time to spend with Zach."

"You're my chaperone. Aren't you supposed to keep us apart?"

"I'm a romantic, little sister. And I've seen how you watch him when you don't think he's looking."

"It doesn't matter how I feel if he doesn't feel the same way."

"Then find out if he's a friend, foe, or future husband."

Chapter Five

On the first day of May, Zach's splint was removed. His leg was weak, but he began walking on it to build strength in his mended limb. His walks took him to Pierce House where he asked Cass to join him in his recovery. They had shared the tragedy of Lincoln's death, but guilt about enjoying life had prevented any romantic gestures in the aftermath. Now dark times had passed, and spring was in full bloom. His regiment would arrive soon, and he needed to declare his feelings before his life would be commanded by orders and military duties, before he would return home and have little time to call upon her.

They walked toward the Capitol to view the finished work on the dome and additions. The city had matured in four years, its accomplishments tempered by its tragedies. The Capitol symbolized a great country, but with Southern states returning to its chambers, would they work together or strive to tear the fragile fabric of unity Lincoln had created?

They climbed the steps and turned to view the rest of the city. Cass took a deep breath. "It's a beautiful sight."

Zach had a different vision. "If you overlook the tents, wagons, mud and..."

Cass laid her hand on his arm. "Ethan wrote me. They plan to arrive soon."

"Harry wrote me," Zach said. "He's looking forward to arriving in Washington City and rescuing you from my boring company."

Cass laughed, a strange sound after weeks of tears. "He was teasing."

Zach frowned. Harry was a rival. The Beecher sisters grew up with the Herbruck brothers in Darrow Falls. Jess had nearly married Ed Herbruck. When they returned home, Harry would be able to call on Cass daily. Zach's home of Ravenswood was in the next county. Zach would be lucky to call on Sundays once a month. He needed to declare his intentions and soon.

But if she rejected him, he wouldn't have a second chance. Cass was young. Was it too early for her to consider marriage? What if she had higher ambitions than what he could offer? The Beecher sisters had married successful men. Cory had married Tyler, who was a lawyer, Logan worked for the Treasury Department, and Blake owned three hotels. Morgan had no job, but he had graduated from West Point and was talking about building bridges and roads. He had sold the family store during the war, and Jess had saved the gold and silver for their future.

Zach had dropped out of Western Reserve College. He could return, but would Cass wait for three years? And what would a college education benefit him if he took over the family farm to raise horses? Zach didn't know what his future would hold, but of one thing he was certain. He wanted Cass to be a part of it.

What if Cass didn't reciprocate his feelings? When they arrived at Pierce House, he accepted her invitation for tea and pie. Jem was busy giving a lesson to Logan's ten-year-old niece, Deidre, at the dining room table. Chauncy was taking her afternoon nap. They would be alone in the parlor.

The room overlooked the street, and they sat on the sofa facing the open window. A warm breeze fluttered the lace curtains. Outside, horses' hooves smacked the cobblestones, and drivers shouted to clear a path in the crowded avenue.

"What will you do after you muster out?" Cass bit into the flaky pie crust. Blueberry filling stained her bottom lip.

"My grandfather expects me to help run the farm. We talked about it when I was on furlough last year. I wrote him I was ready to take on the responsibilities."

Her brows knit in a frown. "I didn't think you liked your grandfather."

"He's the only family I have left. He didn't like the fact I dropped out of college to join the army, but when he saw me in my uniform and I shared my battle experiences, he was proud of my choices. We had long talks about Ravenswood." He reached with his napkin and wiped the extra blueberry from her mouth.

She put her pie plate on the serving tray. "I must look a mess."

"Not at all." He put his empty plate next to hers. It was now or never. He leaned forward. She didn't scream. He moved closer, her mouth his target. His lips brushed hers. She tasted of blueberries. Delicious. What did he do with his hands? He gripped her shoulders and lowered her against the soft cushion on the sofa. Would she be repulsed and demand an apology? Her mouth sought his, and her hand caressed his neck. Her touch sent shivers through his body.

It was all the encouragement he needed. He kissed

her again, teasing her mouth with his tongue, parting her moist lips and gaining entry. Her body molded to his, soft and compliant. The blood rushed to parts of his body he never used in battle, and he fought hard to control a mounting desire. He pressed her limp body against the sofa.

A stiff corset formed a thick barrier, and the crinoline beneath her bell-shaped skirt crunched beneath his weight. A primal groan escaped his lips. No dream ever matched the building tension within, seeking release. He paused and opened his eyes. Her cheeks were flushed, and her breathing matched the rapid pace of his own. A loose strand of hair crossed the feather arch of her eyebrow, and he blew against her face to sweep it away. She opened her eyes, confused by his hesitation. She returned his smile, and he pressed forward, bruising her lips with his own.

"Stop canoodling," Cole shouted as she walked through the open door. "I have news from Blake."

Zach pulled away from Cass and fell on the floor.

Cass straightened and extended her hand toward him. "Are you all right?"

Cole looked around and scowled. "Where's your chaperone?"

Cass waved her hand. "Jem is in the other room."

"Jennifer!" Cole turned to Zach, who had regained his feet. "What were you doing sprawled all over my sister?"

"I'm sorry, ma'am."

"Ma'am?" She pointed to the door. "Take a walk. A long walk."

"But what about Blake's letter?"

Cole's face matched her ginger hair. "Out!"

Zach glanced toward Cass, but she was smoothing the material of her skirt. Had he done something wrong?

****

Jem entered the room. "What happened? Where is Zach going?"

"Fine chaperone you are." Cole sat next to Cass. "Our little sister is nearly compromised while you're baking biscuits."

"Biscuits? I was helping Chauncy with her letters." Jem stared at Cass. "Compromised? What happened?"

Cass waved her hand to dismiss any concern, but her hand shook. "Zach kissed me."

"He had her pinned on the sofa with her feet in the air," Cole said.

Jem's mouth dropped. "Cassie!"

"It happened so quickly, I didn't know what to do."

"You tell him to stop!" both sisters echoed.

"But I wanted him to kiss me."

"Baby, that wasn't a kiss," Cole said. "That was an examination, and he was playing doctor."

"A lot of men have kissed you," Cass accused.

"And Jess was always chaperoning." Cole looked at Jem. "In the same room."

"The door was open," Jem defended. "I didn't hear a cry for help."

Cole patted Cass on the shoulder. "It's hard to scream with a man's tongue in your mouth."

Tongue? Cass narrowed her eyes. "Does Blake kiss you with his tongue?"

"He's my husband," Cole said. "He can put his tongue anywhere he wants."

"Colleen!" Jem shrieked.

Cole smoothed her skirt. "An unmarried lady doesn't bestow her kisses freely."

This from her sister who was going to write a book about kissing? "You said you couldn't tell if a man was the right one without a kiss. Remember how you kissed Blake on Grandpa's canal boat?"

Cole shook her head. "I was demonstrating *how* to kiss."

Jem threw her hands in the air. "When was this?"

"Hours after we met Blake," Cass said. "Cole bragged she could write a book about kissing and demonstrated her expertise."

"Get up!" Jem shouted, pulling Cole to her feet. "You shouldn't be giving advice to a young girl."

Cass stood, her hands on her hips. "I'm not a child."

Her sisters ignored her as they turned to each other. "How long did it take you to kiss Logan?"

"I was married when I met Logan."

"So, you never kissed him until after you were a widow?"

Jem hesitated. "Those were special circumstances. The war is over now." She turned to Cass. "You can afford to wait longer before any intimacies."

"I should ask Jess when she…"

"No!" Cole paced the room. "That wouldn't be a good idea."

None of her sisters had practiced the rules they were forcing her to obey. "How can you judge me? I've been writing to Zach for more than a year. I've been his nurse, and the first time he kisses me after months of proper courtship, you send him walking. If he doesn't come back, I'll never forgive you."

Cole looked at Jem and then turned to Cass. "Oh, he'll come back. After that kiss, you'll have trouble keeping him away."

"You need to set boundaries," Jem said.

"But I liked it."

Her sisters exchanged worried looks. "I think it's time I showed her the drawings," Jem said.

"A few more minutes and she wouldn't need drawings," Cole said. "She would have seen the real thing."

Cass had seen the real thing on a couple of patients when volunteering at the hospitals. She wasn't sure whether they were ignorant of her presence or wanted to shock her, but she hadn't been impressed by a dangling stem of flesh surrounded by a mat of hair.

Cole pulled her to the sofa and lowered her voice. "Men are different from women."

"Oh, I know that," Cass said. "I've seen baby boys." And a few men.

"There's more than anatomy." Jem sat on the other side of her. "Men are guaranteed pleasure whenever they have relations with a woman."

"Pleasure? Don't men and women marry to have children?"

"That's part of it," Cole said. "But it can be pleasurable with the right person."

"Is that what all the noise is about?"

"You listen?" Jem's face went red.

"The walls are thin," Cass defended.

"She's right," Cole agreed with a sigh. "Jess and I could hear you and Logan when we were in the room next door. And when we visited Tyler and Cory, nobody could sleep."

Jem had a look of horror on her face. "Why didn't you say something?"

Cass shrugged. "It was educational."

"You can sleep in the room at the end of the hall," Jem said. "As soon as I empty it of all the supplies I've been storing from Ohio."

"Don't get a bee in your bonnet," Cole said. "It would be worse if you silently endured his touches."

Cass turned to Jem. "Why would you do that?"

Jem sat with her back straight and her hands in her lap. "Some women don't marry for love, but they can't reject a husband in the marriage bed."

"Why not?"

"A man can divorce his wife if she doesn't submit."

"Or worse," Cole said.

"What could be worse than divorce?" A husband took the property, money, and the children in a divorce. The wife was left with nothing.

"Beatings or rape," Cole said. "I remember helping Papa treat a woman who had been beaten so badly, she was covered with bruises. Her eyes were swollen shut…"

"Stop!" Jem interrupted. "Cassie doesn't need to hear about that."

Her older sisters didn't realize in their absence, she had taken over duties helping their father with patients. She had seen the results of drunken husbands and fathers. A little boy, not much older than Jake, had been thrown across the room. His father cried and apologized between gulps from a bottle of whiskey. She had learned that not all men are redeemable. She shook the image from her head and concentrated on the voices of her sisters.

"That's why love needs to be mutual," Jem said.

"Men can be with a person they barely know and enjoy it," Cole added. "But a woman needs more. She needs security and love or the physical part means nothing."

"And women have to worry about having a baby. Look at Jess. One night with Morgan and she had Jackson. A woman has to be careful."

Cass dismissed their warnings. "But when he kissed me, it was like being in a wonderful dream."

"Passion is nice," Cole said. "But it has to be controlled."

"By both parties," Jem added. "I'll have Logan talk to young Zach Ravenswood."

"Oh, no," Cass said. "That would be embarrassing."

"Unmarried with a baby is embarrassing," Jem said.

In her experiences as a midwife, an unwed mother was not uncommon. "Did I do something wrong?"

"No, baby." Cole stroked her hair back from her face. "Men have been kissing women since the beginning of time. Most of the time we wipe off their spittle and send them on their way, but when it's nice…"

"It was nice."

"Did he say he loved you?"

"He didn't say anything."

"Were you talking?"

"No, I was eating my pie. He wiped off my mouth and the next thing he was…"

"Devouring you." Cole stood and paced. "You

need to talk more. Men can't kiss you when you're talking. And where's your fan? You can block a kiss with your fan."

"When do I permit him to kiss me?"

"When he vows undying devotion," Cole said.

"And proposes," Jem added.

A knock echoed from the door.

"I'll get it," Jem volunteered.

She returned with Zach, who twirled his kepi in his hands. "I sincerely apologize for my behavior, Miss Beecher."

Cass smiled. "I'm not as upset as my sisters."

"Yes, she is," Cole corrected. "You don't treat a young lady like a camp follower."

"I never visited any hookers," Zach defended.

Jem waved her hand. "Sit down, Zach."

Cass moved to the end of the couch to make room.

"Not there." Cole pointed to a chair opposite the sofa. "That should be a safe distance."

Cole sat on one side and Jem on the other, guarding her virtue. Zach looked nervous. Cass smiled. "Did you enjoy your walk?"

"No, he did not enjoy his walk," Cole said. "He was contemplating the error of his actions."

"Yes, ma'am."

"Don't ma'am me. And don't think I won't tell my husband about this. He's still your commanding officer." Cole shrieked. "My letter. In all this turmoil I forgot about my letter."

"Let's find out what Blake has to say." Jem folded her hands in her lap, and Cass followed her example.

Cole retrieved a letter from her reticule and unfolded the pages.

"We're in Virginia and marched through Richmond. Not much left. My father's hotel was burned to the ground. The Mackinnon store is gone, too. No one seems eager to rebuild. The surrounding land is barren as well. Farms that sold for $5 an acre can't be given away now. We're marching toward Washington City and home. Our gait is long, knowing each step takes us closer to the end of our journey. I don't know how many miles we've marched. I know I've worn out more boots than I can count. This is it, Cole, darling. I'm coming home. Kiss Jake for me.

All my love,

Blake"

Zach raised an eyebrow. "Is that it?"

Cole waved the letter in his direction, the crisp sheets crackling in her fingertips. "There's a note for you on the second page."

Zach leaned forward.

"Tell Sergeant Zach Ravenswood we expect him to join us when we reach Washington City. No need to join us sooner."

"I'm stuck here," Zach said.

Cass stood. "I'm sorry our company bores you."

"Oh, no. You're not boring, Cassandra."

Only her father called her Cassandra. Her sisters called her Cass and others called her Cassie, but it was a little girl's name. Did Zach see her as a grown woman? Finally? Had a kiss made the difference? She walked Zach to the door. Cole and Jem hovered nearby. She extended her hand. "It was a pleasure having you visit today. I hope you will call again soon."

His grin widened, and his sour apple green eyes twinkled. "You can count on it, Cassandra." He kissed her hand, strolled to the gate, and threw a wave in her direction.

Chapter Six

Zach called the next day with flowers in hand and a box of caramels. Instead of the parlor, they sat at the dining room table where Jem helped Deidre form cursive letters on a slate and Cass drew a horse for Chauncy on paper with a piece of lead.

"My grandfather raises horses at Ravenswood," Zach said.

"How many?" Deidre asked.

"Around sixty, give or take a few."

Deidre resembled her uncle with blond streaks in her light brown hair and dimples when she smiled. "Wow, that's a lot."

"How big of a place does your grandfather own?" Jem asked.

"About eight-hundred acres."

"Do you own any of it?"

Zach hesitated. "No, but I'll own all of it one day."

"Inheriting something isn't the same as earning it," Jem said.

"Oh, my grandfather will make me earn it," Zach said. "Raising horses involves hard work."

Chauncy handed him a blank piece of paper. "Can you draw a horse like Aunt Cassie?"

Zach stared at the three-year-old. She had her father's blond hair and her mother's blue eyes. "No, but I can draw a map of Ravenswood."

Jem paused in her knitting. She was making booties for the coming baby. "A map?"

"I drew maps on our marches so we wouldn't get lost. I was promoted to sergeant because of my penmanship."

"What's that?" Diedre asked.

Jem pointed to the chalk letters on her slate. "It's what you're learning. Copy the letters in your book."

Zach drew rectangles for the buildings, slashed lines for the fences, and double lines for the roads and paths on the farm. He wrote *Ravenswood Farm* at the top.

Cass pointed at a large oval. "What's that?"

"The lake." Zach pointed to a square near the edge. "This is the log cabin, and over here is the barn for the older horses. The ones Grandfather sells in the spring."

"Has he sold them yet?"

"He wrote to say he's waiting for me to return home before he advertises for the sale."

"I bet it's exciting." Cass studied the map as Zach inhaled the scent of lilacs in her hair.

"A lot of buyers come annually. Grandfather has a reputation for quality horses."

Her profile formed an elegant line curving in and out to accent her features. His artistic talents were limited, and he doubted he could capture her beauty with pencil and paper. Tomorrow, they could stop at Matthew Brady's photography shop down the road and have their pictures taken.

"Does your grandfather manage all of it by himself?"

Zach focused on their conversation. "No, he has trainers for the horses, and Seymour runs the household."

"Seymour? Who is he?"

"Seymour Woods is the family accountant at Ravenswood," Zach explained. "Pax and I never liked him."

"Why not?"

"He liked bossing us around. We were boys. What if we tracked mud in on the floor or slid on the bannister? We didn't do any harm." Zach frowned. "It wasn't his place. My great-grandfather Gabriel Ravenswood built the main house. Now there was an interesting man."

"Tell us about him," Cass begged. "I love a good story."

Deidre clapped her hands. "Me, too."

"Gabriel was a smuggler before the Revolutionary War. Fought for George Washington and traveled to Ohio when they opened the west for settlement. But before that, when he was a boy in England, he lived on the estate of a wealthy duke. He claimed to be his illegitimate son." Zach reddened. "I shouldn't have said that in front of the children."

Jem put her knitting in a cloth bag and stood. "Chauncy needs a nap."

"I want my horse," Chauncy pleaded.

Cass handed the little girl her drawing. "You can put it by your bed and dream of riding it."

Jem hesitated by the staircase. "Deidre can chaperone while I'm gone."

Deidre paused her writing. "What's a chaperone, Aunt Jenny?"

Jem smirked. "You make sure there's no kissing."

Jem took Chauncy's hand and climbed the stairs.

Deidre wiped her slate. Her dimples deepened. "I won't tell if you kiss," she whispered.

Zach pulled Cass close. She pushed against his chest. "What do you think you're doing? There's a child present." She took a deep breath. "You were talking about Gabriel and his lack of a father."

"I want to reassure you that I would marry you if anything happened." He glanced at Deidre who wrote a letter on her slate.

"What makes you think I would allow anything to happen?" Cass sat rigid. "Besides I don't want a man to marry me because he has to. I want him to marry me because he values me as a partner in life and because he loves me."

Zach ran his fingertips through his long hair. He should have left out a few details about his family, but it was too late. The Ravenswood men had been notorious womanizers, but his father had remained faithful to his mother. They had loved each other, but what was love? How did a man know a woman loved him as much as he loved her?

Cass snapped her fingers in front of his eyes. "Tell me about your great-grandfather."

Zach took a deep breath to clear his thoughts. "When he arrived in Ohio, Gabriel built his own castle and named it Ravens Roost. He used quarry stone for the exterior and local wood for the inside. There's a grand hall and double staircase. My grandfather, Elijah Ravenswood, added the stables and horses."

"Sounds wonderful," Cass said. "You must have loved living there."

"Pax and I lived in the cabin by the lake with our parents. Those were good years. We worked with the horses when we were boys. I can't count how many foals I've seen born. We named a few. While we were attending Western Reserve Preparatory School, our parents died. Influenza," he explained. "When we returned home, our belongings had been moved to Ravens Roost, but it never felt like home. How could it without our parents."

"I'm sorry. I'm grateful I have parents, but sometimes I forget to appreciate them." She retrieved a pen and ink well from a roll top desk in the parlor and arranged a sheet of paper. "I'm writing them."

She knocked the pen against the glass edge of the ink well and made graceful strokes with the sharp nib. "Would you like to write your grandfather?"

Zach took a sheet of paper. "I want to tell him I'd be proud to help him with the sale."

"I'd love to see the horses and Ravenswood, if your grandfather wouldn't mind."

"I think Grandfather would like you, but I should warn you. He has a reputation for charming the ladies."

"Like you?" Cass blushed.

She considered him charming? He was a blundering novice. "When would you like to visit?"

"I'd love to see the horse sale." She frowned and glanced toward the upstairs. "But I can't visit without a chaperone."

"That's me," Deidre said.

"And you're doing an excellent job." Cass pulled softly on her braid.

"Can't Ethan escort you?" Zach asked. "He's your cousin."

"I don't know if Papa would agree. It's a day's journey, and I would have to spend the night." She looked down, and a blush stained her cheeks.

Maybe Ethan would be a lousy chaperone. His fingers fluttered across her hand. "There are plenty of bedrooms. And I'll install a lock on your door."

She faced him. "Why would I need a lock?"

"You're right," he agreed. "It would be useless against the ghost."

"What ghost?" Deidre demanded.

"Every castle has a ghost." He grinned. "My mother talked about seeing one roaming the halls of Ravens Roost. That's why she didn't like living there. She said the cabin by the lake was friendlier."

"It sounds intriguing. Now, I have to visit Ravenswood."

Zach slid the map across the table. "Then keep this until you come."

****

The troops gathered around the capital in late May. Zach found the Twenty-ninth Ohio Veteran Volunteer Infantry camped in Alexandria. The Army of the Potomac was marching through town in the Grand Review on May 23. Although the Twenty-ninth had been part of the Twelfth Corps for three years, they had been transferred to the Army of the Cumberland and would wait until May 24 to march through the streets of Washington City for review by President Andrew Johnson and General Ulysses S. Grant.

Zach pulled on the reins of Romulus and Remus to halt the wagon when he reached the Ohio camp. The pair of draft horses belonged to Blake Ellsworth, but he had given authority to Cole over all his property during his absence. Union soldiers had continued to fight knowing a home and job waited for them when they returned. Desertions had been high in the last year of the war for the Confederacy. Rebels had returned to ghost towns where skeletal women wandered in black, unable to accept the loss.

He handed the reins to Cass and jumped to the ground. He circled around the team and offered his hand to Cole who sat next to Cass with Jake perched on her lap. She didn't move. "Don't you want to go with me?"

"You go first," Cole said. "Tell him I'm here."

"Are you sure?" She had talked about nothing else but seeing Blake.

Cass shook her head. "We'll wait here."

Zach obeyed. He was learning that if a woman set her mind to something, he wasn't going to budge her. What was Cole worried about? Did she think Blake would have a woman in his tent? Hardly. He had seen the looks women gave the captain, and he had seen Blake turn a blind eye to their obvious flirtations. Blake had set a good example for him and the other young men in the regiment, not only as a commanding officer, but as husband, and father.

Other officers had failed morally, and it had tarnished any military success. Once a man chose the path of adultery, there was no turning back. He had betrayed his wife and family. But was he settling on Cass too soon? What if she wasn't the woman for him? Would he be tempted by someone else? He couldn't think of anyone. Women worried about nothing.

Zach entered the officer's tent pitched at the head of a long row of dog tents. Captain Blake Ellsworth was seated at a table filling out paperwork. He dipped a pen into a tin inkwell and scribbled his name at the bottom of the paper in front of him.

"I'm drowning in ink." Blake had dark hair that fell across his eyes as he moved the signed paper to his left and pulled another paper from the stack on his right to sign.

Zach handed him the orders from his doctor returning him to active duty. "Here's one more."

Blake looked up, his stormy gray eyes searching Zach's face. "Sergeant Ravenswood, welcome back." He stood and looked beyond the tent opening. "How is my wife?"

Zach pointed over his shoulder. "She's in the wagon. She said you might miss Romulus and Remus."

Zach stopped grinning and swallowed uncomfortably. The captain did not appreciate his attempt at humor. Zach stepped aside as Blake rushed outside. He followed at a more leisurely rate but quickened his pace when he saw the crowd. In the short span he had been gone, soldiers had surrounded the wagon, and he couldn't see the ladies. He caught a glimpse of red hair.

Cass and Cole were in the back handing out supplies that had been stored at Pierce House for the Ohio boys. Quilts, shirts, knitted socks, jellies, jams, hard candy, and personal items like razors, soap, and housewife sewing kits had been accumulating since they had begun their march through Georgia in 1864.

"Move aside," Blake ordered as he fought to reach the wagon. Zach joined him, pushing against men to create a path. Blake pulled Cole from the back of the wagon and took her in his arms. He ignored the crowd and kissed her, and when she kissed him back, the men cheered.

Zach waved his hat in the air and looked for Cass. She was struggling to hold onto Jake, who stood on the edge of the wagon bed.

"Don't hurt my mommy!" Jake shouted.

"Mommy?" Blake kept his arm around his wife as he looked at his son. "He talks?"

"Fluently for a toddler."

"That's your Papa," Zach said, giving a smart salute. "He's our commanding officer."

Zach had trained the little boy to salute like he had during Lincoln's funeral procession. He stood tall in his white gown and raised his hand to his forehead.

Blake saluted back and grabbed him. "Come here, son." He put his arm around Cole and escorted his family to his tent.

Harry Herbruck shook a box. "What do you have in here, Miss Cassie?"

"Broken jars of jam if you keep shaking it, Harry."

Like all the Herbruck boys, Harry had a high forehead and deep-set eyes. He reddened under her reprimand. Her smile forgave him. "Make sure you share them with the other men."

Harry turned away from Zach. He tapped him on the shoulder. "Don't you recognize me?"

Harry brushed the dust from his coat. "You're too clean and pretty to be Zach Ravenswood."

He ignored Harry's insult and hugged him.

Someone nudged him from behind. He turned. It was Ethan Donovan with ginger curls dangling in a tangled mess beneath his kepi. His blue eyes sparkled. "I didn't think we'd ever see you again."

He hugged Ethan before noticing the stripes on his sleeves. "How did you make sergeant?"

"Someone had to take command while you were convalescing."

Harry coughed, pointing toward the three stripes on his sleeve.

"Both of you?" He shook his head. "The quality of officers has sunk to an ultimate low."

Ethan waved his hand. "Neither of us fell off a bridge."

"I was trying to save a life."

"How's the leg?" Harry asked.

Zach marched around in an exaggerated high and low step. "Good as new."

"If you're going to walk on a hillside," Ethan ribbed.

Zach turned to Cass. "I had an excellent nurse."

"No doubt, but a woman shouldn't have to suffer indefinitely. Thank goodness we arrived in time to save you, Miss Cassie," Harry said. "We were afraid Zach would weary you with tales of his exaggerated heroics."

Ethan offered his arm to help Cass out of the back. "Hey, Cousin, let these privates unload the supplies."

Ethan was her first cousin and had the right to escort her. The obligation. Zach claimed his belongings and followed with Harry, who had claimed a box marked candy.

They strolled through a row of canvas dog tents and stopped at a larger straight wall tent with a fire pit in front. A pot of coffee hung from a hook stuck in the ground. A bed of hot coals kept the container warm.

Zach looked inside where two bed rolls were laid out. A third was tied and placed off to the side. "When did you boys rate these quarters?"

"Since the army began distributing its unused

supplies," Harry said. "If you don't want to bunk with us, you can pitch a dog tent with the rest of the men."

Zach dropped his haversack inside the tent and placed his rifle near the entrance. The Enfield was ornamental. Neither powder nor bullet had been shoved in its barrel, and Zach didn't plan on loading the gun now that the war was over.

Harry grabbed four folding chairs stacked inside the tent and placed them near the fire pit.

Ethan added a folded blanket to the one for Cass. "We have to hide the chairs," he said. "Some of the men think they make great kindling."

"They're good chairs," Cass said. "Why burn them?"

"Some men don't want any memories of the war," Harry said, taking a seat beside her.

Zach claimed the chair on the other side, and Ethan sat opposite them.

"I've had time to balance the good with the bad, but I wouldn't want to do it again." Ethan poured a cup of coffee and filled two more for the others. He looked at Cass. "Have you acquired a taste for the bitter brew?"

"Afraid not, but don't let it stop you from drinking."

"I have cold water in my canteen." Zach offered it. "I haven't touched it."

She sipped and corked the container.

"You missed some grand adventures, Zach," Ethan said.

Harry blew on the steaming coffee in his cup. "Would you like to hear about our travels, Miss Cassie?"

"Blake wrote about Richmond. What happened after that?"

"We marched through the old battlefields," Ethan said. "We had fought at Chancellorsville, but it was strange to see Cedar Mountain where Art and Pax were wounded."

"Pax." Zach sipped the strong brew. Paxton Ravenswood and Art Herburck had been wounded at Cedar Mountain. Art's arm had been crippled, and he returned home to Darrow Falls, but Pax had died of a gut wound at Mermaid's Mirth. Harry had replaced Art, and Zach had replaced his brother. The celebration of the end of the war was tempered by the memories of those who had died. "To Pax." Zach lifted his cup.

"To Ed," Harry said, clanging his cup against Zach's.

"Don't forget our cousin, Jake," Ethan added.

Cass nodded. "Never."

Zach needed to change the somber mood. "What else did you see?"

"We stopped at Bull Run," Ethan said. "The Twenty-ninth didn't fight there, but other Ohio boys did. I wonder what will happen to all the places where men fought and died during the war."

"You can't plow the ground," Harry said. "Too many bodies buried on site."

"Harry!" Zach reprimanded. "Remember there's a lady present."

"Jess wouldn't have complained," Ethan excused.

Cass frowned. "I'm not Jess, but I won't faint. I've seen my share of wounded at the hospitals in Washington City. I've visited the cemeteries. I've read the letters from families searching for news of lost ones.

Clara Barton is gathering information to locate missing soldiers so they can be buried at home or in proper graveyards. Your task may be done, but ours isn't until all the wounded men leave the hospitals and each grave has a marker."

"The first thing I'm going to do when I return home is pay my respects to Ed's gravesite," Harry said. "And Jakes," he added.

"It's strange to finally be returning home," Ethan said. "Do you think they'll recognize us?"

"Not with those mustaches and long hair," Cass said.

Ethan stroked the corners of his hairy mouth. "I worked too hard to grow mine to shave it."

Cass poked at the fire with a long stick. "What will you do when you return home?"

"If Grandpa hasn't retired, I'll probably help on the canal boat." Ethan looked at Harry. "You want to join my brother, Paddy, and me?"

"I'll probably work with my pa doctoring animals," Harry said.

"You don't sound enthusiastic about it."

"You don't make money working for family. Pa figures a room and meals are payment."

"My grandfather might want more help," Zach said. "It takes work to train the horses before they're ready to be sold."

"How many horses do you have?" Harry asked.

"My grandfather has anywhere from forty to sixty at a time. The number varies depending on the number of foals born each spring. Ravenswood is home to about a dozen broodmares. It takes a couple of years to train the colts and fillies for saddle and harness. The older horses are sold annually to pay for expenses," Zach said. "It's a grand affair with traders from all over the country visiting to bid on them."

"Zach invited me to the sale," Cass said.

"Did he?" Harry stared at Zach. "When is it?"

"My grandfather is waiting for me to return home."

"We could help," Ethan volunteered. "For a percentage."

"Horses are selling for a hundred and fifty dollars," Harry said. "Maybe more with the shortage from the war."

"I'll ask my grandfather about giving you jobs," Zach said. "But you shouldn't be hurting with the bonuses and pay we'll receive when we muster out."

"I have plans for my money," Harry said. "I might buy some of your grandfather's stock and start my own farm."

"You'll be broke," Zach warned. "Horses are expensive to raise. Besides shelter and feed, you have to worry about defects and diseases. Grandfather somehow manages to pay the bills, but he's far from rich."

"We've lived without money for two years," Ethan said. "I don't mind being poor, but I'm going to enjoy being rich for a little while."

"If anything, the war has taught me what is important." Zach lifted his cup of coffee. "To friends."

Harry raised his cup. "To a good pair of shoes and a full haversack."

"May the wind be ever to our backs, and our paths cross often," Ethan added.

"I feel like an outsider," Cass said. "The war has made you devoted comrades."

"We were friends before joining," Zach said. "And we welcome you to our pack. We could use some beauty among the beasts."

"We called ourselves the three musketeers," Ethan said. "Have you read the book?"

"By Alexandre Dumas," Cass said. "One of my favorites. I liked d'Artagnan the best."

"Then you can be part of our band," Zach said. *"One for all and all for one, united we stand divided we fall."*

"A girl can't be a musketeer," Harry said.

"Why not?" Zach demanded. "We couldn't have won this war without women providing supplies, taking care of the wounded, and encouraging our spirits."

Harry scratched his head. "I can't fault you there."

Zach stretched out his hand. Ethan and Harry placed their hands on top of Zach's. "Come on," he urged Cass.

She placed her hand on top. "One for all and all for one." They broke apart and laughed. It was a childish gesture, an imitation of characters in a book, but the pledge was real.

"Attention!" Ethan shouted as Blake and Cole approached. The men stood. Jake was asleep and cradled in his father's arm. Sergeant Donovan, you can escort your cousins to Long Bridge and return. Sergeant Ravenswood, you can report to my tent and help with my paperwork."

"I could help," Harry volunteered.

"I can't read your chicken scratches, Sergeant Herbruck. You can remind your fellow soldiers to be ready for tomorrow's review."

Cass grabbed Cole's arm. "Isn't Blake coming with

us to Mermaid's Mirth?"

"I don't have a pass," Blake said. "My orders are to make the men in my regiment pretty with their shoes blackened and brass polished to a shine for tomorrow's Grand Review. No one is going to be ashamed when the Twenty-ninth Ohio marches through the streets."

Blake helped Cass board the wagon and handed her Jake, who stirred and fell back into slumber. He pulled his wife close and kissed her.

Cole had chastised Zach for kissing Cass, but his novice attempt at lovemaking was nothing compared to Blake's silent communication of desire. Jake wasn't going to be an only child for long.

Chapter Seven

May 24 dawned with the sound of bugles and drums in the distance calling the men to formation. The women dressed in their finest gowns and prettiest bonnets to welcome the soldiers through the streets of Washington City.

Sid had placed a canvas awning near the street with benches and chairs and a table for refreshments. Three Beecher sisters stood in front of Mermaid's Mirth to witness the troops marching in from Long Bridge. The soldiers would circle the Capitol and head along Pennsylvania Avenue to the White House for their final review.

Cass and the others planned to take Seventh Street to Pennsylvania Avenue after the Ohio boys passed and see them a second time in front of Pierce House.

Jake sat in a wheelbarrow filled with straw and covered with a quilt. Cole knelt by the toddler and straightened his gown and tied his bonnet to shade his face. "Daddy is coming soon."

"Dada parade?"

"Yes, Daddy is going to march right in front of us with all his men." Cole wrung her hands. "Blake couldn't believe how much Jake has grown. We had so little time together yesterday."

"I was surprised he let you go," Cass said. "There was no order preventing you from spending the night in his tent."

Cole gave her a sly smile. "Don't think I didn't suggest it."

The door to Mermaid's Mirth opened. "Good, Tootie is bringing cold drinks. You might want to cool your ardor so you don't throw yourself at your husband when he marches past."

Sid took the tray even though Tootie balked at his help. Tootie was showing her pregnancy, and Sid was helpful to an annoying level. It would be a close race to see who delivered first, Tootie or Jem.

The Seventh Ohio Volunteer Infantry had mustered out last year, but Sid wore his kepi with the number seven with a bugle on the cap. "You ladies look excited."

Cole brushed away a tear. "I waited a long time for this day."

Morgan placed a baby buggy next to Jake. He peered inside. "Where's my baby?"

Morgan turned to Jess who was carrying Jackson. "No matter how many times I tell him Jackson is my baby, he claims him as his own."

Jess placed Jackson in the buggy. "Don't argue with a two-year-old. They latch onto an idea and never let go."

Morgan offered a finger to his son, who clasped his plump fist around it. "He's doubled in size. You're a good mother, Mrs. Mackinnon."

Jess put her arm around Morgan's waist. "I wish I could keep weight on you."

"You can't see my ribs anymore."

Cass had witnessed the tender care Jess gave her husband, especially when memories of the war haunted him. Zach had his own demons as did everyone who had gone mad on the battlefield and chosen to kill or be killed. It left a mark that only time would fade. But today was a day for celebrating. The war was over.

The sound of a band became louder, and the women took their seats.

Jake stood to see where the music was coming from, and Morgan put his hand around the toddler to steady him. "Patient, young man. They're coming."

"I see Dada!" He pointed at the band leading the way.

"Not every soldier is Daddy," Morgan corrected. "How did Blake look last night when you saw him?"

"A little tired," Cole said. "He's glad to be home though."

"We all are," Morgan said. "Is Blake going to resign his commission?"

"Can he do that?" Tootie asked.

"He's not a career officer," Morgan said. "He's a businessman."

"He said he had to finish all the paperwork," Cole said. "He enlisted Zach to help him."

Sid squeezed Tootie around her expanding waist. "You better sit. You shouldn't tire yourself."

She sat on the bench next to Jess. "I'm not the first woman to have a baby."

Morgan looked at his sister. "It's about time you embraced motherhood. How long have you been married to the Yank?"

"We were married the same day as you and Jessie, but some couples believe in waiting before starting a family," Tootie said.

"You won't embarrass him." Jess adjusted the

blanket around Jackson as he slept in his buggy. "He's proud Jackson is a honeymoon baby."

"A lucky roll of the dice," Sid said.

Morgan winked at his wife. "Luck had nothing to do with it."

"And I thought I cut your arrogance down a notch," Jess said.

"Darlin', you only raised it."

Jess gasped. "Morgan Mackinnon, my little sister is present."

Morgan squeezed her waist. "She's old enough to keep Sergeant Ravenswood pining."

Cass reviewed their playful banter. The words weren't the usual sweet flattering remarks lovers shared in the parlor, but the sensual attraction was palpable. How did her sisters do it?

Cole pointed in the distance. "Here they come!"

The first regiment approached. The flag bearers showed off the regimental colors. The tears and holes were a proud reminder of the battles the troops had carried the banner in without surrendering.

A row of drummers pounded a steady beat and broke into a lively rhythm as the men raised their fifes and played "Marching Through Georgia." The men in the ranks broke into song. *"Hurrah, Hurrah! We bring the jubilee! Hurrah! Hurrah! The flag that makes you free! So we sang the chorus from Atlanta to the sea while we were marching through Georgia."*

Cass stared at the baby sleeping in the buggy. "How can Jackson sleep through all this noise?"

Jess shook her head. "It's not as much noise as he makes when he's hungry."

"That's the Rebel cry," Morgan said.

"I would think you'd call it a highlander shout," Tootie said.

As if on cue, Jackson wailed, and Jess took him into her arms to calm him.

Cass had made a sign with the words *Ohio welcomes her brave boys home* painted on it. She stood and lifted it as the Twenty-ninth regiment approached. "They're coming. I can see their blue flag."

"Up!" Jake stood in the wheelbarrow. "I wanna see."

Morgan swung him onto his shoulders.

Cole stood next to Cass, tears glistening in her eyes. "Don't they look grand?"

Hot tears stained her cheeks. Why was she crying? The war was finally over. The worst was behind them.

The band played "When Johnny Comes Marching Home," and they joined in with the words. *"When Johnny comes marching home again, Hurrah! Hurrah! We'll give him a hearty welcome then, Hurrah! Hurrah! The men will cheer and the boys will shout. The ladies they will all turn out. And we'll all feel gay when Johnny Comes Marching Home."*

Whether it was on Blake's command or impromptu, all the men in the regiment raised their kepis and gave a shout. Cass waved at Zach. Ethan and Harry waved back.

Blake froze when Morgan saluted. Jake copied the hand motion from his uncle's shoulders. The men reduced their stride but kept marching. "What are you doing here?"

"I'm visiting my wife and son."

He stared at Jess and the baby in her arms. "When did this happen?" He turned to Cole, a puzzled expression on his face. "Did I miss a letter telling me about Morgan becoming my brother-in-law?"

Cole pointed down the road. "You're being left behind by your men."

Blake pulled her against his chest and kissed her. "We'll talk later."

"Talk?" Cole pouted. "I was expecting more."

He whispered something in her ear and hurried after his regiment.

"I don't think you have to worry about him resigning his commission," Cass said. "The ink won't even be dry by the time he removes his uniform."

Cole bumped Cass with her hip. "I think you're right."

"I wish I could make Zach look at me that way."

"Baby, he already does. That's what has us worried."

Was Cole right? But was Zach in love with her or only interested in free love? Many women were raising babies on their own after the fathers, unfettered by marriage, abandoned them. Free love was only free for men.

Morgan carried Jake on his shoulders while Jess pushed Jackson in the buggy. They joined Logan and Jem at Pierce House where they had set chairs along the street. Deidre and Chauncy waved small flags and gave one to Jake.

The crowd along Pennsylvania Avenue was larger. School girls in white dresses lined the avenue and sang "The Battle Cry of Freedom" as the men passed. Others threw flowers in their path or placed wreaths around their guns.

When the Twenty-ninth Ohio passed, they broke

into a chorus of "Dixie." Blake looked at Morgan and saluted. "He's still your best friend," Cole said.

Cass remained with Jem and her family while the others returned to Mermaid's Mirth. She wondered if the boys would visit and after eating, glanced out the window for any sign of them.

Logan gathered the leather satchel he used for transporting important papers. "Would you like to walk with me to Mermaid's Mirth? I have some papers Blake will need to sign in order to resign his commission. I'm dropping them off."

Cass grabbed her bonnet from the sideboard near the stairs.

"You might want to remove your apron," Jem said.

Cass looked at her attire and undid the apron. She dropped it on the sideboard and dashed out the door, keeping pace with Logan's strides. "How long do you think it will be before Ethan, Harry, and Zach muster out?"

"As soon as possible. The longer the men stay in the army, the more it costs the government."

"I promised Jem I'd stay to help with the baby. It'll be fall before I return home."

"We're thinking of going to Darrow Falls in a few weeks. Summers are hard to bear in Washington City, and I'm going to look for a job in Ohio."

Jem had talked with Logan about moving home for the past three years. "You are?"

"I arrived in Washington City to serve Salmon Chase like my brother and father did before me," Logan said. "Now that he's serving in the Supreme Court, I'm not needed. I only stayed on at the Treasury Department because of the war."

"That's wonderful news." She would be home when the boys arrived and when Zach stepped off the train. Their relationship would be different in Darrow Falls. The familiar sights and sounds of her home would provide the proper atmosphere for a romance. And her baby sister, Jules, was a lenient chaperone.

Logan joined Blake and Morgan eating at the dining room table. Cass looked around. "Did anyone else come?"

"Only officers were given leave." Blake wiped his mouth.

Cass sighed and gathered their dishes. The boys were in camp.

"If you had graduated from West Point, you would have made major by now," Morgan said.

"The Union army was stricter about promotions, Major Mackinnon."

"Civilian now." Morgan snatched the last slice of bread. "Welcome home, Blake."

"I'm glad we both made it, Mac."

"You don't know how many times I saved your life."

"Saved my life?" Blake shook his head. "When?"

"One of my sharpshooters had you in his sites at Culp's Hill, and a few others wanted to blow the *Baltic* out of the water when she ran aground on a sandbar. I talked them out of it."

"Thanks, but I wasn't the horse thief who stole Romulus and Remus."

Jess served dessert of cake topped with berries. "I was the one he took captive."

"I haven't forgotten." Blake grabbed her hand and examined the ring. "How long have you been wearing this?"

"Close to eleven months." A loud wail from the adjoining room interrupted their conversation. "Jackson is hungry," Jess said.

Blake's eyes widened. "Jackson?"

"Jackson Lincoln Mackinnon," Morgan said. "My son."

"When did you have time to leave Lee's army, marry my sister-in-law, and create a baby?"

Morgan leaned forward. "I was wounded in the Wilderness. Jess found me on the battlefield, transported me to Mermaid's Mirth, and nursed me back to health."

"Must not have been much of a wound."

Morgan pulled his hair back to reveal a long scar on his skull. Blake grimaced.

"You can compare battle scars later," Jess said, calming Jackson in her arms. "Cole has put Jake to bed by now."

Logan gathered the papers Blake had signed. "I'll deliver these to Stanton's office in the morning."

Blake shook his hand. "Thank you. It'll save me a trip back from Cleveland."

"Do you think your boys will be able to make it on their own?" Morgan asked.

"They know the way home." Blake stared at the ceiling. "My room was on the main floor."

"Cole needed more space," Jess said. "Sid and Tootie stay in your former room."

Blake shook his head. "Sid didn't have a problem with you staying here to recover?"

"He didn't know I was a Confederate major."

Blake raised his hand. "Don't tell me tonight. It'll

give me nightmares." He kissed Jess and Cass and grabbed Morgan in a hug. "I always considered you a brother. Welcome to the family, Mac."

Blake and Morgan had been best friends before the war and enemies the past years, facing each other on the battlefields. Now they were glad to be alive.

Cass paused at the foot of the staircase while she tied her bonnet. Morgan carried Jackson and escorted Jess upstairs. She'd been frightened of the big Scotsman, but even little Jake recognized his tender heart and embraced him. Cole shrieked inside her room at the top of the stairs, and Blake's laughter followed. Morgan paused outside the door before Jess pulled him toward their bedroom.

What would life be like with Zach? What happened once the bedroom door was closed? And how long would it be before she found out?

Chapter Eight

The boys were enlisted to help the clerks update the company books and didn't receive passes to visit the town for a week. All three called on Cass at Pierce House. Ethan was family and acted as chaperone. It wasn't necessary. Zach and Harry were in a battle to impress her. If Zach recited poetry, Harry read a passage in a book. If Harry told an amusing story, Zach told a bold tale.

Ethan took a tray from her. "And you thought the war was over." He glanced at his friends arguing over who should read next. "How does it feel to have two men fighting for your attention?"

"It's exhausting." Cass gathered her bonnet and reticule. "Let's go for a walk." Ethan held the door, Zach offered his arm, and Harry claimed her other arm.

Ethan chuckled. "I didn't realize my cousin was so helpless."

Cass froze by the gate. Pennsylvania Avenue was crowded with soldiers, a sea of blue flowing in and out of town. "Maybe this wasn't a good idea. What's it like toward Mermaid's Mirth?"

"Worse," Harry said. "Every open space is filled with tents."

"Where are you camped?"

"Bladensburg in Maryland about five miles outside of town," Zach said. "And we had to squeeze into that patch of ground. Every regiment has to wait upon paperwork before it boards a train and heads home."

"We received a present from Ohio," Harry said. "A new national flag. They stenciled the names of thirteen battles we fought in onto the stripes."

Her head was like a pendulum turning right and left to listen to their warring conversation. Cass was in the company of three handsome young men and didn't want them fighting. "Let's enjoy the day. What do we do first?"

"Unless we want to battle the rest of the Union army, we better avoid the popular sites," Ethan said.

"I need to post some letters," Harry said. "I wrote Ma and Pa I was coming home."

"I wrote my grandfather that I'd be home soon to help him with the horse sale. I hope everyone can visit." Zach's gaze lingered on hers.

"We'll be happy to visit," Harry said. "I'd like to see this Ravens Roost you keep talking about."

Cass turned to Ethan. "Didn't you write your parents you were coming home?"

"I'm waiting until I know the date we're mustered out."

"It can't be long," Cass said. "Why would they keep you any longer than necessary?"

Ethan shook his head. "The army never makes orders simple. They're sending the new one-year enlistments home right away. We veterans have to wait. Shouldn't it be the other way around?"

The boys were at the mercy of the U.S. Army until they were formally mustered out. They delivered the letters to the General Post Office on the corner of E and Seventh streets.

Outside, a crowd gathered around a young black girl dancing on the corner. She had a bright yellow scarf wrapped around her head, and brass bracelets dangled on her thin arms as she twirled for the spectators. "Have your fortune told?" She clicked castanets and smiled at Ethan. "Madame Cherie can predict your future."

"It's witchcraft," Harry said. "They claim to talk to the spirits of dead people."

"Madame Cherie reads the cards," the girl corrected.

"That sounds harmless." Ethan winked at the others. "Let's see what she says about our futures."

"I'm not going to have her predict mine," Harry said. "Ma wouldn't like it."

Ethan pulled him along. "Just watching won't jeopardize your soul."

"Come." The girl led them two blocks away to a decrepit three-story boarding house in need of paint and repair. A poster nailed to a bulletin board near the entrance announced in neatly printed letters, *Madame Cherie, fortune teller, spiritual guide, and faith healer.*

"That covers everything," Zach said.

The girl led the way along a narrow staircase to the third floor. She knocked on a door with a star nailed below the number 303. The room was dark except for a grouping of candles on a well-worn sideboard. Some wax pillars were tall and newly lit while others had burned to the base, a puddle of wax coating the tin holder. A strangely sweet scent permeated the humid air. A scrap of cloth served as a curtain for the single window overlooking the adjoining building, but no breeze offered relief from the heat of early June.

Her eyes burned, and Cass waved her fan against the smoke and odors that assaulted her senses and made her dizzy.

In the center of the room was a round table, the wooden surface nicked and scarred from years of service. Mismatched chairs were placed at spaced intervals. On the far side was seated an ancient black woman. Her white hair was cropped short, and her leathery skin was wrinkled around toothless gums. She bent over the cards spread in front of her. Her gnarled arthritic fingers plucked at one and turned it over. She looked up. One eye was discolored. "Come in, come in."

"This is my great-grandmother, Madame Cherie," the girl announced.

"This isn't a good idea," Harry muttered as he remained by the door.

"He's a non-believer," Ethan said. "Will that ruin the reading?"

"No," Madame Cherie said. "But your disbelief will."

Ethan frowned. "What makes me a non-believer?"

"You can only trust what you see," she said.

Ethan shrugged. "That leaves you two."

"Ladies first." Zach scraped a wooden chair against the floorboards, and Cass sat. He took the seat beside her.

"How much?" Cass reached into her drawstring purse.

"Whatever my wisdom is worth." Madame Cherie shoved a carved figure of a naked woman with a basket upon her head toward her.

Zach placed his hand over her purse. "I'll pay. He

deposited a few coins into the basket. Ethan sat beside Zach, glancing beneath the table, while Harry remained standing in the doorway.

Madame Cherie shuffled the cards and had Cass cut the deck. Then she laid out four cards in a row. "Turn over the first card."

The occult was popular. Those who had lost loved ones in the war sought answers from the dead. She didn't believe in the nonsense. No one could predict the future, but was it wrong for her to encourage the old woman in her game of fraud? Even in fun.

She hesitated. Zach had already paid. She flipped the card over. It was a naked couple. Cass swallowed. Had her thoughts and curiosity about coupling been so transparent?

"Love is in your future," she said.

Ethan's blue eyes danced with merriment. "Anyone could have predicted that."

Madame Cherie raised her gnarled hand. "Silence, non-believer."

"Harry is the non-believer," Ethan defended.

"No, his faith is strong but not in me. You are the skeptical one, muleskinner."

Because mules pulled canal boats, some people called the canal workers muleskinners. How had Madame Cherie known Ethan worked on the canal?

"Hey, I'm a soldier now."

She cackled and pointed at the next card. Cass turned it over. It was the moon.

"Beware of danger, child. A stranger who is not unknown shall return into your life."

"She has no enemies," Zach said. "Don't scare her."

Madame Cherie raised a crooked finger to her sunken mouth. "Hush." She focused on Cass. "Believe in yourself. Your courage will help you choose the correct path."

The next card had a knight on a horse.

"You will go on a journey that will yield danger for you." She looked around. "And others."

The final card had a knight yielding a sword.

"You must risk your life to overcome your foe."

"I think she's predicting *my* past," Zach said. "How many times did I risk my life battling the Rebels?"

"Enemies come in many forms," Madame Cherie said, shuffling the cards.

"You go next," Cass said. "I hope your future is nicer than mine."

Madame Cherie waited for Zach to deposit more coins in the basket atop the statue. He cut the deck, and she dealt four cards in front of him.

The first card had a chariot and driver.

"You will have an argument with another and fall ill."

"He already did that." Ethan laughed. "He fell and broke his leg."

"Do not confuse the past with the future." Madame Cherie pointed at the next card.

Zach turned over a hermit.

"You need to be cautious. Deceit surrounds you."

Zach looked at his friends. "I hope she's not talking about you."

"You mock the cards," Madame Cherie warned. "But they speak the truth to those who will listen." She tapped her crooked finger near the next card.

He displayed the image of five wands.

"You will struggle for your fortune."

"I don't have a fortune," Zach said.

"She wants more money," Ethan said.

"No more coins," Madame Cherie said. "Turn over the final card."

It contained five cups.

"A single decision will save what you love or lose it all."

Zach laughed. "This is all nonsense."

Madame Cherie pointed at his chest. "Beware of the witch. Her brew is poison."

Zach looked around, confusion expressed on his handsome face. "What witch?"

Cass stood. "I don't like this."

The old woman grabbed her wrist. "Do not believe what you see with your eyes. They will deceive you." She released her. "You are his only hope."

Cass shivered. "I want to leave."

Ethan led the way outside. The sunshine dispelled the feeling of doom the woman's words had evoked. "I expected her to tell us we'd be rich or famous."

"It's nonsense," Harry said. "Miss Cassie will have the pick of suitors when she returns home. I only hope I'm one of them."

Cass smiled, but when she turned to Zach, he seemed preoccupied. "Is something wrong?"

"I think I'm becoming ill." He staggered on the sidewalk, clutching his throat.

"Madame Cherie was right!" Harry backed away.

Zach reached for him, gagging, and falling to one knee. He grabbed his ankle. Harry tried to shake him off. Zach let go and laughed. "Don't be so gullible, Harry." He stood and offered his arm to Cass.

"That wasn't funny," Harry said, retrieving his kepi, which he'd knocked off in his retreat.

"Zach is the gullible one, wasting his coins on the fanciful remarks of an old hag," Ethan said.

"It was entertaining," Zach said. "And I liked the part about having a fortune."

"She said you'd struggle for it and lose it if you made the wrong decision," Ethan said.

"Do you remember what she said about me?" Cass asked.

"Love, a stranger, and danger," Ethan said. "That leaves these two out."

"The stranger wasn't unknown," Zach corrected.

"But if she knows him, he isn't a stranger," Harry reasoned.

Cass didn't want to return to the parlor at Pierce House. With two suitors, Jem was being vigilant even with Ethan present. "Let's visit Mermaid's Mirth." Cole and Jess were more lenient. She wanted to spend a few moments alone with Zach.

They strolled along Seventh Avenue where it crossed the mall and paused at the remains of the Smithsonian Institute. Known as the Castle because of its Twelfth Century architect, the building's red sandstone walls and towers were charred from a January 24 fire. Established to increase and diffuse the knowledge of men, it had housed a large library and lecture halls. The fire had destroyed the apparatus room, the picture gallery, the Regent's room, and the lecture room along with personal writings of Secretary Joseph Henry.

"It reminds me of Richmond," Ethan said. "Walls without a roof. Empty shells without occupants."

"Did you see it before the fire?" Cass asked.

"From a distance," Harry said. "We never visited inside. Now it's too late."

"Logan said they'll rebuild it," Cass said. "Not everything was destroyed. They have the Egyptian mummies on display."

"I've seen enough dead people to last a lifetime," Ethan said.

She wanted to avoid topics that caused the boys to withdraw into silence. "What about the Capitol? Have you seen the changes?"

"We marched past it," Harry said. "I have to admit, I was impressed."

"You need to go inside," she said. "Constantino Brumidi is painting the Apotheosis of Washington in the eye of the Rotunda."

"Art?" Harry shook his head. "I don't mind gadgets, but paintings seem like a waste of time."

"It may be the last time you're in Washington City," Cass said. "What do you want to see?"

"We'll visit the Capitol tomorrow," Zach suggested. "With or without Harry."

"If Miss Cassie is the guide, I'll be happy to visit." Harry smiled at her. "It's the company that counts."

Harry was sweet, but no fires ignited with his nearness. His words failed to stimulate more than a polite response. Zach could be standing in the distance, and the sight of him drove her heart to race at a frantic pace. She memorized the witty phrases he spoke and reflected on the tone, wondering if there was a deeper meaning. She had witnessed the same passion in her sisters when they looked at their husbands, but Zach never mentioned marriage or a future together.

Courtship was rigid with rules and restrictions that forbade her to take the initiative. What thoughts dwelt behind those sour apple green eyes? She dreamed of their romance, proper and demure in the beginning, but desire would win out, and they would make passionate love. Her imaginings were so real, she would wake wet and panting from the erotic experience. She needed to gain control of her longings, or someday she would tear Zach's clothes from his body and ravage him.

"Are you all right?" Zach stared at her. Ethan and Harry were studying her.

She searched for her handkerchief. "It must be the heat."

They reached Mermaid's Mirth where Morgan and Blake had hitched Romulus and Remus to the wagon. Sid was seated at another wagon with a box of tools in the back.

"What's going on?" Zach asked.

"We could use your help," Blake said. "Soldiers are dismantling the hospital tents and makeshift buildings where the wounded stayed. We're gathering the wood and canvas."

"To burn?" Ethan asked.

"No, to rebuild," Morgan said. "I received a letter from Captain Otis Baker. He was in my regiment and knows several families in Virginia who lost homes, barns, and out buildings during the war. I hope we can convince them to take the donations."

"Why wouldn't they?" Harry asked.

"They're not fond of Bluecoats," Morgan said. "You're the ones who burned them out."

"We did our burning in Georgia," Ethan said.

Morgan towered over him, a frown on his face.

"You're lucky you're related. I have friends in Georgia."

Zach stepped between them. "We want to help. What needs done?"

"Sid is taking us to the site where he's purchased a few wagons and teams," Blake said. "You can help load them."

Cass was no stranger to work. "I'd like to help."

"Your sisters are packing food, clothing, and blankets into my wagon," Blake said. "We'll come back this way and form a wagon train."

"It'll be like old times for Jess and me," Morgan said. He had *borrowed* Blake's team and wagon in the retreat from Gettysburg, taking Jess as prisoner.

"I'm driving Romulus and Remus," Blake said. Morgan was his best friend but sharing only went so far.

"Get aboard," Sid called. "We're wasting time. The scavengers will beat us to the wood."

The men climbed into the back of Sid's wagon and waved as they headed to the closed camps.

Jess carried several blankets outside.

Cass examined them. "These look new."

"Sid bought them. The army is selling its surplus supplies."

"Didn't he buy them for the hotel?"

"We don't need them," Jess said.

She was lying, but Cass didn't argue. "Do you think the Southerners will take charity?"

"Morgan said they may not accept handouts, especially from Yankees, but Confederate currency is worthless, and Sheridan's cavalry didn't leave much behind when they burned the farms and fields to starve

Lee's army."

"Then how are we going to make them accept our gifts?"

"Morgan's friend is going to take the items and distribute them. They're working on a story."

"Story?"

"Unguarded warehouse, stupid Yankees, something to save their pride."

"They fought against the government of the United States," Cass reminded her. "Men we know died in the battles. They need to be humbled."

"You admired Abraham Lincoln," Jess said. "Sometimes we have to put aside our personal feelings and do what is right for the future of everyone. If we give Southerners their dignity, the women and children won't starve this winter."

"I'm still angry about the war and Lincoln's death," Cass confessed. "It seemed so futile. I need someone to blame."

"Booth blamed Lincoln for his imagined troubles and killed him. Others are crying out for blood from the Rebel soldiers even though Booth never fought in the war. They'll say we're traitors for helping our enemies. Morgan hears the name from both sides."

Morgan had fought for Virginia. His home. He never owned slaves, and he treated the blacks at Mermaid's Mirth with respect. But none of that mattered to the few loud voices stirring hatred for an unknown gain hidden in their dark hearts. "How does he bear it?"

"He does what is right. That's why I fell in love with him. Men talk about moral integrity, but only a few live it."

Chapter Nine

By the time the men returned, the women had packed the wagon with supplies, including chickens, three piglets, and a pair of turkeys that were being fattened for Thanksgiving. Sid approached in the lead wagon and three other wagons followed, loaded with wood and canvas.

Harry washed his hands in the water trough. "You women don't have to go."

"A bunch of men coming into town will look like an army," Cole said. "A man and woman driving a team will look like a sociable visit."

"She's right," Blake said. "We want to look friendly. No talk of war. No talk of revenge."

"Then we better take these off." Zach removed his coat and kepi and gathered the others from Harry and Ethan.

Cass took them. They would be more comfortable without the wool coats. "You're going to need hats in this sun."

"I keep my old straw hats in the barn." Sid pointed. "You can borrow them."

Zach headed for the barn while Cass took the uniforms inside. She returned with a basket decorated with pink ribbons woven among the slats.

"You're bringing the magical basket," Morgan said when he saw it.

"Magical?" Cass examined her mother's basket. It had traveled to Washington City with Jem in 1861.

"Cole and I took it to Antietam, and I took it to Gettysburg," Jess said. "It never remained empty."

"A fairy named Theo filled it." Morgan winked at Jess.

Cass shook her head. "Sometimes I wonder what you're talking about."

Jess laughed. "If that basket could talk, it would speak of tales and adventures beyond imagination. It's yours now. Enjoy."

"We're ready to go." Cole held Jake's hand as she struggled with a larger basket.

"What do you have in there?" Blake took the basket. "Jackson?" He looked around. "We're taking the children?"

"Jackson will go hungry if we don't," Jess called from her wagon seat.

Morgan took the basket. "I believe that one is mine." He placed Jackson next to Jess.

"I waited three years for you to come home. From now on, we travel together." Cole helped Jake climb into their wagon. "Besides, Jake wants to help his daddy."

"My daddy!" Jake pointed at him.

Blake boarded and took the reins of Romulus and Remus. Cass waited until Blake finished kissing his wife before handing Cole a small bag. "It's for Jake." Inside was fruit and a few toys to keep him occupied on the trip.

Tootie toddled toward the front wagon.

Sid jumped to the ground. "Are you sure you want to go?"

I'm a Southerner," Tootie said. "I know how to talk to the women."

"You don't need a bumpy ride," Sid warned.

"Then don't hit any holes." Tootie softened her words with a kiss to his cheek as he helped her board.

Ethan was driving the last wagon. Zach jumped to the ground. His straw hat was battered with a hole in the crown and a broken brim, but it would keep the sun off his face. He helped Cass board.

"There's enough room for you to sit beside me." Cass moved aside, and Zach joined her.

"What about me?" Harry asked from the back.

"You can't sit on my lap," Ethan hollered.

"Keep an eye on the cows," Zach said.

Cass counted four cows tied to the back. "Where did you find them?"

"The army wants to reduce its stockyard. Sid negotiated for these."

Cass glanced in the distance at a tall solitary pillar and laughed. "Sid could buy the Washington Monument."

"Do you think they'll ever finish it?" Harry asked.

"They have to tear down everything built for the war before they can erect new structures in the city," Zach said. "Let's help them."

****

The four wagons headed out of town toward the Virginia countryside. Some Southerners had abandoned their homes and farms completely, but those who had returned faced a land desecrated by war. Anything that had benefited the Confederacy had been ransacked, looted, or burned. Out buildings that once contained animals or feed were empty. Homes were vacant shells, the wind whistling through broken windows with varmints taking cover in cold chimneys or dark corners.

Zach looked around. "How many times did we march through here?"

"Too many to count," Ethan said.

"Does it feel strange to help the enemy?" Cass asked.

"Former enemy," Zach said. "I think President Lincoln would have wanted us to care for those who have nothing. He wanted to heal the wounds, and not only those that can be seen."

Zach sounded like a man of integrity. He wasn't driven by greed or fame. He stated his principles and stood by them.

"It's going to take more than a few gifts to erase the hate we saw in their eyes," Ethan said. "I should have brought my rifle."

"The last thing we need is a weapon on a mission of peace," Zach said.

"Love your enemies and pray for those who persecute you," Harry said from behind.

"You can try to convince them with words, but if I hear gun fire, I'm taking cover," Ethan said. "Too many men are like Booth. Their hate has festered to madness."

"Then let's deliver sanity into the world," Cass said. "Let's offer them hope."

The farm they stopped at belonged to Otis Baker, a former school teacher. A Confederate captain, he had served with Morgan in General Richard Ewell's Corps. He had been part of General Jubal Early's raids in 1864 in the Shenandoah Valley and had burned his share of Northern buildings.

They unloaded supplies, wood, and canvas. The small house had served as a school and living quarters for Otis. It needed a roof and one wall replaced. The men divided the tasks and set to work.

Cass helped her sisters build a camp while Tootie supervised the children under a canopy the men had erected to create shade. She collected wood for a fire. Then she dug a shallow pit and lined the hole with rocks. She arranged the wood to allow air to circulate beneath and placed a metal tripod with a hook over the stacked limbs.

Cole was cutting vegetables, and Jess returned with two rabbits she had snared. "I haven't lost my touch." She sat on the ground cross-legged and removed her knife from her boot. "Bring me the newspaper, Cassie."

Cass spread the newspaper on the ground for Jess to work on. Jess had been the hunter in the family, but Cass had been in charge of the livestock, and that meant killing chickens or helping the butcher with a cow or pig. Animals were raised to be slaughtered, dressed, cooked, and eaten.

Efficiency was key. Jess cut around the legs and slit the fur from hind leg to hind leg. She pulled the fur from the body like turning a sock inside out. She dressed the rabbits by removing the internal organs and cutting off the head and limbs. She handed the meat to Cole to chop into pieces for the stew.

Cass wrapped the remains in the paper. "Do you want me to bury it?"

"Do you mind?" Jess removed matches in a tin holder from her pocket. "I'll start the fire."

Cass grabbed the shovel she had used earlier and walked away from the camp. The smell of blood might attract unwanted animals. She dug a hole and buried the carcasses.

When she returned to camp, Tootie was seated by the fire stirring the seared meat. Cole added a bowl of chopped vegetables and water to the pot. Jess was sitting in the shade of a wagon nursing her son. "What can I do?"

"Jake is getting up from his nap. Do you mind taking him for a walk?"

"I'd love to." Cass found Jake standing on the edge of the wagon, his gown tucked under his chin, peeing on the ground. He had wiggled out of his diaper, which was dry. "Who taught you to do that?"

"Daddy."

Men had such interesting habits. "You'll need your diaper and shoes for a walk."

"Walk?"

"We're going to explore the countryside." Cass dressed him, and they proceeded across the field. The grass was high, and she made noises to frighten away snakes and animals they might startle. A butterfly landed on a yellow flower. Jake chased after it, trying to catch the brightly-colored insect.

"You can't catch it." She pointed to wild flowers nearby. "Why don't you pick those for your mommy?"

He broke the head off at the top of the stem. Cass showed him how to break the stem near the bottom so he could hold it in his hand, and he gathered a fistful of flowers.

Cole shouted for them to come and eat. The men were at the table filling their plates.

"Come on, Jake. It's time to eat." She held out her hand, but he refused to come. He pointed toward the woods. A woman with two children stepped out of the shadows and approached the camp. "Welcome!" Cass waved them forward.

Jake was too excited to wait on their cautious approach. He ran toward the girls. "I'm Jake." After circling them twice, he ran back.

Cass led them to the camp.

Otis stood. "Good day, Leah." He turned to the others. "This is my neighbor, Leah, and her daughters, Betsy and Sara."

Leah placed a small square basket on the table. The handle was broken and tied together with twine.

"Berries!" Jake reached for one.

"No, Jake," Cole said. "Those aren't ours."

He made a sad face.

Leah offered the basket to him. "Take some, but I'm afraid there aren't many. The birds found them first." Sara clutched her mother's patched skirt, hiding behind it. Betsy held her mother's hand in a tight grip.

"We'd be happy to share what we have," Cass said. "We're helping Mr. Baker rebuild his house."

Leah looked at Otis. "Are these the friends you spoke of?"

"Yes. Come join us." He offered her a seat.

"Are you sure?"

"We have plenty." Cass helped the girls sit in the folding chairs they had brought. She filled the plates with biscuits and stew and handed one to each of their guests. "It's made with rabbit."

"We've been eating squirrel when I can catch them." Leah took a bite. "It's delicious."

"Leah's husband was killed at Spotsylvania," Otis said.

"I missed that one," Morgan said. "I was wounded at the Wilderness."

"My husband fought there, too," she said. "On the Confederate side."

"That's the side I was on." Morgan pointed to Otis. "With the captain."

"This is Major Morgan Mackinnon," Otis said. "I told you about him."

"Oh," Leah gasped and surveyed the men. "I thought you were all Union soldiers."

"Not all," Tootie said. "And I was raised in Richmond."

"They brought supplies," Otis said. "Would you like them to rebuild your house?"

"Yes," Sara shouted. "I don't like living in a chicken coop."

Harry snorted. "People don't live in chicken coops."

His remark was met by silence.

"I'm done." Zach stood and nodded toward the ladies. "Thank you for the meal." He turned to the men. "Why don't we take a wagonload and start framing her house?"

"I'll bring a second wagon," Morgan said. "And we'll take your friends. Sid and Blake can finish here and join us later."

Cass gathered a broom and rags.

"Are you going with them?" Jess asked.

"Do you need me here?"

"No, but you better take medical supplies in case someone is hurt." Jess fetched her medical bag.

Cass looked inside and withdrew a saw. "Do you expect me to perform an amputation?"

"No, and don't let anyone use it to saw wood. It dulls the blade."

Cole handed her the magic basket. "I packed it with food for the men. They'll probably work until dark. We'll have a meal ready when they call it quits."

Cass turned to Leah. "Do you want to go with me?"

She glanced at Otis boarding the first wagon. "I don't want to be underfoot. I trust Otis will know what to do."

"Any requests for your house?"

"I'd like a window. There aren't any in the place we're staying."

The chicken coop. Cass nodded and headed for the second wagon.

Zach helped her board. "You're not staying with the women?"

"I'm a musketeer." She lifted the medical bag. "Besides, I have bandages if one of you is clumsy and falls or smashes his thumb with a hammer."

Harry shoved his hand toward her. "I have a splinter."

"You should wear gloves," Zach said.

Cass bounced in her seat as they hit a rut. "I'll look at it when we reach the farm."

Otis led them along the road to the neighboring property. They traveled along an overgrown path to the former buildings. The house had been burned to the sandstone foundation. The barn was partially burned, but the trusses were intact. The only untouched building was the chicken coop. It was made of hewn logs and had gaps between the uneven boards. The door swung outward, offering no protection from curious strangers.

Feathers swirled in the air as Cass stepped inside. Boards were placed over the nesting boxes to form beds. A few towels and clothing items were draped over the roosting poles, and a wooden box rested on flat rocks arranged on the dirt floor.

"They are living in a chicken coop," Zach said. "That little girl wasn't joking."

Cass looked at the humble surroundings. "Make sure her house has windows."

Chapter Ten

Ethan and Harry erected a canvas tent and placed a table beneath it. Cass placed her basket and medical bag next to the water barrel. "Let me look at your hand, Harry."

"It's nothing."

She sorted through the medical tools for what she needed. "You said you had a splinter."

He turned over his hand. A chunk of old wood was lodged beneath the skin. She grabbed his hand to steady it and found the entry point. After teasing the sliver to the surface with a needle, she removed it with her tweezers. She washed the wound with soap and water. "Wear gloves."

"I will," Harry promised. "Thank you, Miss Cassie."

Zach stood nearby, a sparkle in his eyes. She raised her tweezers. "Do you have a splinter?"

He placed his hand on his chest. "Only in my heart."

He was teasing, or was he? She didn't want to encourage Harry, but she couldn't be rude. Besides, the splinter had to be removed to prevent infection. Zach turned the spigot on the water barrel, filled his canteen, and joined the others. She watched him go, her heart thumping against her chest. Zach was lucky he didn't have a splinter. Her hand would shake too much to remove it.

The men had built makeshift shelters, roads, and bridges during the war. They took a few measurements and began sorting boards to frame the walls.

Cass wandered into the remains of the barn. A shovel, pick, and scythe were among the tools stacked in a corner stall that had survived the fire. The curved blade on the scythe had been sharpened. She headed outside and began cutting the tall grass around the house. She was on a back swing when someone tapped her shoulder. She swung around.

"Careful with that," Zach warned as he jumped out of the way.

"You shouldn't have startled me." She wiped beads of sweat from her face. "I cleared most of the yard."

"You're going to be sore tomorrow." He placed his hands on her shoulders and rubbed. She moaned. "You need to take a break."

"Are you?"

"We have the roof on. We'll finish the walls tomorrow unless we run out of wood. We can use canvas to rig something temporary until we return."

"You're coming back?"

"We're coming back until we run out of supplies or they send us home," Zach said. "For once, I may be able to sleep without being haunted by the past two years."

They returned to camp with the empty wagons. During their absence men and women had arrived as if invitations had been sent out. A veteran missing an arm was holding a rope tied to a cow. Cole handed the boy with him a sack made from a blanket and holding supplies.

"I don't want to take what I don't need," the veteran said.

"Then share it with your friends and family," Cole said.

Cass looked at the few remaining items to be distributed. "You've been busy. Did you save anything for Leah and her girls?"

"In the wagon," Jess said. "How far along are they on her house?"

"They should finish it tomorrow."

"You have a sunburn." Cole examined her face. "I have some lotion to soothe your skin."

Cass relaxed in a canvas chair. The heat radiated from her scorched skin. She closed her eyes as Cole applied the cool cream to her face. Each stroke brought relief from the sunburn. "That feels so good."

"It's my pleasure." It was Zach's voice.

She opened her eyes. Zach knelt in front of her, rubbing the lotion onto her nose. "Where's Colleen?" Her voice squeaked.

He nodded toward the tent. "She asked me to take over so she could serve the food."

Cass grabbed the jar from his hand. "That's enough." Instead of relaxed, her heart was pounding in an accelerated beat.

His green eyes danced. He dipped his fingertips into the lotion. "I missed a spot."

Cass dodged his fingers, using the jar to block his attempt to touch her face. It was too intimate a gesture, and others were staring. His hand hit hers and knocked the container from her grasp. It crashed against a rock.

Cole rushed at them, waving a large spoon. "That was my expensive face lotion."

Zach stood. "I'll buy you a new jar."

"Gather the broken shards before someone is cut." Cole turned. "And come eat."

Cass picked up the jar. "It's only chipped."

Cole examined the marred container. "You keep it. Mr. Ravenswood will buy me a new one." She stared at him the same way their mother, Maureen Beecher, did when she gave an order that was not to be questioned.

Yes, ma'am."

She waved the spoon at him. "Don't call me ma'am. It's Miss Colleen or Mrs. Ellsworth, do you understand?"

"Yes, ma'…Mrs. Ellsworth."

They ate around the fire, husbands and wives paired off. Ethan and Harry sat with Cass. Zach kept his distance. Was he embarrassed being reprimanded by a woman? He had gathered husk leaves from the ears of boiled corn and was making small dolls. He showed them to Leah's girls. Betsy and Sara were awe-struck by his talent and clung to his side. Sara chattered about a kitty she once had for a pet. Betsy bounced her doll along the length of his outstretched leg.

"Aren't you hungry?" Ethan pointed at her untouched plate.

She gripped her ear of corn and bit into the tender kernels. What she wouldn't do to rest against Zach's muscular thighs, her arms curled around his neck. He looked up, his gaze locking onto hers and shrugged. He was unaware how his boyish charm melted her heart.

Everyone retired for bed for an early start in the morning. The couples took the wagons. Cass shared a large tent with Leah and her daughters. Zach, Ethan, and Harry slept under the stars near the fire. Zach was turned toward the opening in the tent. Could he see her? Did he think about her the same way she thought about him? Was it wrong to fantasize about making love? She glanced toward the wagons. Were her sisters coupling with their husbands? She rolled onto her back and stared at the canvas above her. How long would she have to wait?

"You and your friends are nice to help us," Leah said from the dark.

"They should finish the house tomorrow," Cass said. "I hope you don't mind sleeping in a tent."

"I love it," Betsy said from her cot. "It doesn't smell like chickens."

****

The men headed to Leah's home after breakfast. Morgan drove Cass, Jess, and Jackson in the wagon with items set aside for Leah and her home. They planned to decorate the interior while the men finished the outside.

They completed their labors at noon and returned to camp to eat. When they finished, the men dismantled the tents and packed the supplies in Blake's wagon.

"What's going on?" Leah asked.

"We're done," Zach said. "You can return to your house."

She gathered her children. "We're going home."

"Do you know how to drive a wagon?" Morgan asked.

Leah looked around. "Why would I need to drive a wagon?"

"We're leaving this one behind for you."

Leah stared at the wagon and two mules.

"That's generous of you," Otis said. "I'll show her

how to hitch the team."

Morgan slapped him on the back. "Good, because we're leaving the other wagon for you."

"That's an expensive gift," Otis said. "I can't accept it."

"We expect you to share it with your friends," Zach said.

"Don't you need it for more supplies?"

"We'll return in four wagons and leave two," Morgan said.

"How can you afford that?"

"I put aside some silver and gold from the sale of my father's store," Morgan said. "I can't think of a better use."

Otis helped Leah and the children board their wagon and drove it to her home. Blake and Morgan pulled into the yard. They had added a run-in shelter to the chicken coop for the mules. Three hens were scratching the ground for grubs, and a cow was tied to the split rail fence.

Leah saw none of it. Her eyes were fixed on the house. It was modest by most standards with one room, a stone floor, and no stove. She stepped inside and paused. A breeze blew through the two windows on opposite walls.

The cots that had been in the tent were placed in a corner, and the table and chairs were in the center. Cass and Jess had moved their belongings from the chicken coop to a spot near the window.

"Is this our house?" Sara asked.

Leah didn't answer. She couldn't. Tears flowed as she walked around her rebuilt home. Leah hugged Cass and the other women. "I didn't think there were any kind people left in the world. Thank you."

"We'll have more supplies on our next trip," Cass promised.

"You're coming back?"

She looked at Zach and the others. "Tell your friends and neighbors we'll be back."

They waved and returned to Washington City. "I wish we could have done more," Cass said.

"We made a small dent in a hostile world," Zach said. "You made a friend."

"No one should have to live in a chicken coop."

****

Orders were given for the Twenty-ninth Ohio to board a train June 9. Politicians and residents were claiming Washington City from the military. Cass and the others had done their part to take the wood, canvas, and unneeded supplies to neighboring Virginia.

Helping others had allowed the men to come to terms with their role in the war. Rebuilding what they had helped destroy healed the darkness and guilt that no one wanted to talk about. Harry, Ethan, and Zach said they were returning home with lighter hearts.

Unfortunately, the work had kept Cass and Zach too busy to spend time alone. His kiss was a distant memory as they gathered at the depot. Cass plotted a way to permit Zach a few moments alone to kiss her goodbye.

She stood by the side of the depot as the soldiers formed lines to board the box cars of the train. Those with loved ones, dropped their bags and spent a few precious moments saying farewells. Zach met her gaze. The sun was low in the sky and the semi-darkness would provide the perfect setting for a tender farewell.

She smiled and disappeared behind the depot, waiting in the shadows of the building for him to join her.

The thumping of footsteps approached. She remained perfectly still until he was close. He tapped on her shoulder, and she turned. Before she could react, he kissed her.

Only it wasn't Zach. It was Harry.

She stepped back, shocked by his bold behavior. They stared at one another. Harry made a puzzled face. "That was not what I expected."

Cass giggled and shook her head. "Colleen says you can't marry a man until you kiss him. You have to know if there's any passion." She nervously bit her bottom lip. "I'm afraid I didn't feel any."

Harry looked hurt. "Could I try again?"

"I don't think it'll change anything."

Harry leaned forward, hesitated, and kissed her on the mouth, lingering a little too long. It didn't matter. No desire flamed between them. Not even a spark.

He stepped back and stared. "I've been waiting for an opportunity to kiss you since I arrived. How could it be so…"

"Ordinary?" Cass laughed. "I'm afraid we're not meant to be husband and wife, Harry."

He placed his kepi on his head. "Have you kissed Zach?"

"Yes." When Zach kissed her, a warmth rose from her toes and fanned to the extremities of her body, tingling in all the secret places lovers shared.

"Same feeling?"

"No. When Zach kisses me, I think about spending the rest of my life with him."

Harry sighed and offered his arm. "He's a lucky

man."

Cass tucked her hand into the space by his elbow as he escorted her. "He's lucky to have you for a friend. So am I."

"You're one of the musketeers." He laughed as they neared the train. He was too easygoing to hold any grudge about her rejection. "We'll see you in Ohio."

"You'll find the right girl someday, Harry."

"I hope she's as wonderful as you." He claimed the bag he had left by the tracks.

"Where have you been?" Ethan demanded. "The train is ready to leave."

"Discovering the sad truth," Harry said.

Cass looked around the depot. "Where's Zach?"

"He bolted past me and boarded." Ethan gave her a kiss on the cheek. "I'll see you soon in Darrow Falls. We'll ride the canal boat for old times' sake."

"I'd like that, Ethan."

Harry and Ethan boarded the box car reserved for their company. No windows. No sign of Zach. Cass waited until they closed the door. Why hadn't he said goodbye?

Chapter Eleven

Zach placed his bedroll in a corner of the box car as the train pulled away from the depot. He couldn't believe he had seen Cass kissing Harry. All this time he had believed Cass had tender feelings for him alone. How could he have been so wrong? And to be betrayed by his best friend. How could he face Harry knowing he had lost the woman he loved to him?

The men claimed an empty space on the floor and spread their bedding. Ethan and Harry tried to reach him, but there were no open areas.

"We have room over here," Ethan said, claiming a spot on the other side of the car.

"I'm going to get some sleep." Zach turned his back to his friends. He couldn't talk to them. He doubted he could be civil. He stared at the dark wall. What had he done wrong?

Travel was slow with so many troop trains exiting Washington City. They passed Frederick as the sun was coming up. Zach ate his breakfast. Cass had given each of them crackers, cheese, and apples wrapped in linen to eat on their trip. Ethan and Harry joined him in his corner.

"It was nice of my cousin to give us this food." Ethan looked at the other men. "Do you think we should share?"

Zach had lost his appetite. "I'll give them mine."

Some of the men played cards to pass the time. Ethan joined in while Harry watched.

Zach sat near the opened doors that allowed fresh air and sunlight in the dark interior. As they traveled along the tracks, he searched his past actions. Nowhere along the trip did an insight burst forth to explain the awful turn of events.

Zach recognized Harpers Ferry and called to the others to take a look. They had passed this way after Gettysburg. The three of them had marched from Pennsylvania to Georgia and back again. If Cass had chosen Harry, then he would step aside. Their friendship was too important to allow a woman to tear it apart. And yet, he couldn't stop thinking about her.

His noble thoughts warred against the empty chasm widening in his heart. He loved Cass. Losing her, even to a friend, was bitter and painful. A melancholy settled on his thoughts as the sun lowered in the sky. The train pulled into the depot at Cumberland, Maryland, and the women of the town served coffee and food before the train headed on to Parkersburg, West Virginia.

They boarded the steamer *Pickett* and transferred to the *Ohio No. 3* before another night greeted them. It was a beautiful sunset, and flags were hanging from every building on the northern side of the river. People gathered near the banks and hollered, "Congratulations!" to the men, who tipped their hats in appreciation. They passed Cincinnati and docked at Louisville the following evening. The men gathered their gear and marched to Bardstown to camp.

Once the tents were pitched and campfires built, Zach had no excuse to avoid the company of his friends. Ethan and Harry sat across from him at the fire he was tending. Even though he had decided to be gracious and wish Harry the best, the words stuck in his throat.

"What are we doing in Kentucky?" Harry surveyed the row of tents. "We muster out in Cleveland."

"Did they think we wouldn't notice this wasn't Ohio?" Ethan demanded.

Harry smacked Zach on the back. "Let's find out what's going on."

"You're not going to find anyone tonight who can sort out this mess."

Harry tossed another log on the fire. Sparks shot into the sky.

Zach smacked at cinders landing on his sleeve. "What did you do that for?"

"It's nothing," Harry said. "You've been in a foul mood since we left Washington City."

"What's wrong?" Ethan laughed. "Didn't my cousin kiss you goodbye?"

"She kissed someone." Zach glared at Harry.

"Is that what this is about?" Harry laughed. "It didn't mean a thing."

It was insulting enough to witness Harry kissing the woman he loved. It was beyond forgiveness to dismiss her kiss as unimportant. Zach tackled Harry and drove him to the ground. All the rage he had been nursing on the ride erupted in a fury of fists aimed at Harry's head. They wrestled in the dirt before Ethan pulled Zach off. "Hey, what's going on here? The war is over."

Harry sat on the ground, rubbing his jaw. "You're in love with her."

Zach struggled free from Ethan's grasp. "I

wouldn't trifle with her affections or take them as lightly as you do."

"What's this about?" Ethan asked.

"He kissed Cass at the depot." Zach pulled Harry to his feet, his hands gripping his coat. "Are you going to marry her?"

"No," Harry said.

Ethan stepped beside Zach. "I should throw a few punches."

Harry stepped back and raised his hands. "Nothing happened."

"After I saw you kissing, I retreated to the train. You were strolling arm in arm and laughing." Zach kicked a stone, sending it flying against the canvas of a nearby tent. "You might as well have stabbed me in the heart."

"I should let you suffer, but I'll be a pal and put you out of your misery," Harry said. "I kissed her and nothing."

Nothing? "What do you mean?"

"When you kiss Miss Cassie, does the earth spin? Does your breath catch in your throat? Does your pulse pound in your head?"

Zach heaved a heavy sigh. "You, too?"

Harry shook his head. "Not a bit. None of that happened. We were laughing because we realized there was no passion. I'm in the same group as Ethan."

"Ouch!" Ethan scrunched his face. "At least I'm a blood relative."

What did they mean? "What are you talking about?"

Ethan put his arm around Harry's shoulders. "My darling cousin considers Harry a friend only."

Zach flexed his fists. "Your kissing looked friendly enough."

"You missed the evaluation," Harry said. "I failed the test."

He relaxed his stance. Failed what test? Was a kiss a test? "She's not in love with you?"

"No." Harry retrieved his kepi from the ground. "Do you know how she feels about you?"

Zach ran his hands through his dirty hair. "I have a feeling she hates me."

"She was upset you didn't say goodbye," Ethan said. "You should write her."

He had judged her wrongly. "What am I going to say?"

"I could offer a few choice words," Harry said.

Zach entered his tent and searched through his haversack for paper and a pencil. He'd been jealous. He'd hit Harry, his friend, because of a misunderstanding. He had ignored Cass, the woman he loved, because of an imagined betrayal. How did a man apologize without looking weak or stupid?

I look forward to seeing you, but our mustering out has been delayed. I regret not saying goodbye. I hope you can forgive me for being rude.

It wasn't an admission of guilt, but it was an apology. When he arrived in Darrow Falls, he'd explain in person.

****

Cass had help Jem and Logan pack their belongings in Washington City and unpack them in their new home in Akron. He was working for the mayor, but Akron was rural enough for them to have several acres with a barn for horses, cows, and chickens. Everyone had pitched in to help with the move from Washington City to Ohio. Sterling and Maureen met Morgan and their grandson, Jackson, who were greeted with open arms.

After the Pierce household was settled, the Ellsworth and Mackinnon families headed for Cleveland to check on Blake's property, and life at the Beecher home returned to normal.

Cass and Jules helped their mother with the garden and canning the fruit and vegetables as they ripened to maturity. They accompanied their father when he had calls. Jules had shown little interest in medicine, but if Cass married Zach, Jules would have to help with her father's medical calls. She dragged her along, hoping to teach her baby sister the basics.

Sterling had hired Matt Wheeler to do the heavier work around the farm. Matt's father owned the general store, and he brought the mail in the morning when he arrived to clean the stalls, chop wood, and make any needed repairs.

Cass was expecting letters from the boys. She hadn't received any correspondence in Washington City before leaving and nothing had been forwarded by Tootie. Matt arrived, waving a couple of letters as he joined her in the barn, where Cass was milking the cows. "These are for you, Miss Cassie."

One was from Zach and the other from Harry. "Thank you, Matt. I've been waiting for these." She tucked them in her pocket and carried the milk bucket inside. Her mother was making breakfast. Jules had already gathered eggs and was cracking several in a bowl.

She left them in the kitchen and moved to the

parlor. She read Zach's note first. It didn't resemble the long detailed letters they had shared during the war. She had expected words of affection after their months in Washington City and shared intimate moments. The short missive was apologetic without any explanation of his behavior. What was wrong with him? The letter from Harry revealed the reason.

Miss Cassie,

Zach witnessed us kissing at the depot when we left Washington City. He believed I had betrayed him. I explained how we had no deep feelings for one another besides friendship. He is writing to apologize for his behavior. I hope you forgive him.

"Forgive him!" Cass crumpled Harry's letter. She reread the few lines from Zach. "Forgive him for being rude! Idiot!"

Maureen Beecher appeared in the doorway. She wiped her hands on her apron. "What is wrong, Cassandra?"

She waved the two letters in the air. "Men are idiots!"

She wasn't shocked by her outburst. "What happened?"

She handed her Harry's crumpled letter. "Zach saw me kissing Harry at the depot and believed I was in love with him."

She examined the letter. "Why were you kissing Harry Herbruck?"

"That's not the point, Mama. He should have asked me about it instead of storming off without a word." She re-read his note. "I've been guilt-ridden, thinking I did something wrong."

Her mother returned Harry's letter. "Perhaps seeing

you kiss another man was reason enough to be upset."

Cass sat on the sofa, a sigh escaping. "It's not like I enjoyed it."

"I'm confused." Maureen sat on the sofa beside her. "If you don't enjoy kissing Harry, why did you kiss him?"

"I was hoping Zach would kiss me goodbye at the train depot," Cass said. "Only Harry surprised me and kissed me. It was the first time. Once it was obvious we had no passion, we headed back to the train."

"Then you don't know if there's any passion with Zach?"

Cass didn't answer. Her face was warm from the memory of Zach's kiss.

"When did Zach kiss you?"

She didn't question how her mother knew. "In Jem's parlor during a visit. Cole said a woman has to kiss a man to know if he's the right one."

"You listened to Colleen?" Maureen stood and paced the floor. "I can't count how many times I lectured her on proper behavior between a man and woman. She ignored all the rules of proper decorum in the parlor. Who knows what rules she broke when not chaperoned."

"But Blake married her," Cass defended. "And it was good advice. I know I love Zach." She crushed his letter in her hand. "But he's an idiot."

Maureen sat beside her and patted her knee. "If he's as passionate about you as you are about him, he was probably deeply upset by your behavior."

What did her mother mean by that? "My behavior?"

"How would you feel if Zach kissed another

woman?"

"I'd kill him!" Her body trembled with outrage. Had Zach felt the same way? Had he been too angry to talk to her? "How do I make this right?"

"Jealousy is normal when you care about someone and you're afraid they care for someone else more than you," Maureen said. "Zach was afraid he'd lost you."

Cass smoothed out Zach's letter. "I'll write him and tell him I forgive him."

Maureen read the note. "It doesn't say anything about being in love with you."

"He hasn't declared his love."

"Then you don't owe him an explanation," Maureen said. "You can kiss anyone you want."

Cass studied her mother. "I don't understand."

"Until he tells you he loves you and wants to marry you, let him stew a bit."

Cass sighed. "But that seems cruel."

"A woman needs commitment from a man. And he won't stake a claim unless he values you."

Her sisters had given her advice and now her mother. What should she do? "Why does love have to be so complicated?"

Maureen stood. "Would you prefer your father arrange a marriage?"

"No!" she shouted, shaking at the thought. "But why can't I tell Zach I want to marry him?"

"Cassandra, the young man is taking on the responsibility of caring for you. He does the asking when he is ready."

"What if I were rich?"

"Do you have a hidden treasure I am unaware of?"

"No, but it could be years before Zach could

support a wife. I don't know if I want to wait."

"There's more to marriage than passion," Maureen said. "A lot of compromise occurs when two people join lives. That requires communication and honesty to discuss how you feel or misunderstandings occur. Love can fade or grow as a result. Many marriages start out with high hopes only to end in infidelity or unhappiness."

"Are you unhappy with Papa?"

"Heavens, no."

"But you work so hard."

"So does Papa," Maureen said. "Life is hard. I was a poor canal brat when I met your father. He was a young doctor from a well-known family. It was a mismatch, but we respected each other. We still do."

"How did you encourage Papa to propose?"

"My father demanded he marry me or stop calling," Maureen said. "When he walked away, I cried for two days. On the third day, Sterling returned with a ring."

"I don't want Papa to browbeat Zach."

"It's the duty of your father to voice expectations of any young man who calls upon you. He's had quite a bit of practice, and I think he enjoys it."

Cass studied the letter. "It may be some time before Zach visits. I should write him, but how do I accept his apology without condoning his behavior?"

"Wait until you're less emotional," Maureen warned. "Then you'll know what to say."

Emotional? "Mama, I'm not flirtatious like Cole or bold like Jess. Zach isn't going to know how I feel if I don't tell him. He may take advantage of my feelings, but I can't be dishonest."

Maureen touched her cheek. "You always favored your father. Straightforward and honest. That's why I married him, but a lady should maintain a little mystery. It keeps a man from taking her for granted."

Chapter Twelve

Zach and the others passed time writing letters, playing baseball, and planning their futures. As days grew into weeks, Zach inquired about the length of their stay in Kentucky and was given no definitive answer. Because they were enlisted in the army, they weren't free to leave although a few soldiers threatened to desert. They received their regular pay in late June. Some spent it on beer, and when fights broke out, it was Zach, Harry, and Ethan who had to intervene before someone was injured, maimed, or killed. Morale sunk to an all-time low as they waited on paperwork to send them home.

Harry blamed the fortune teller. "The dark arts are nothing to fool around with. We're being punished for trying to make a deal with the devil."

"It was all in fun," Zach said. "We're stuck here because someone forgot they sent us to this god-forsaken land."

"It's god-forsaken because we fooled around with magic."

Zach ignored Harry and addressed Ethan, "Do you believe in sorcery?"

"I'm Irish. We believe in enchantments, wee folk, and hidden treasure. It makes life exciting."

"I was raised on scripture, and there's a reason witches were put to death," Harry said.

"I'm pragmatic," Zach said. "I look at a problem and search for a solution."

"Between the three of us, we ought to figure out what to do," Ethan said.

"We're enlisted men," Zach said. "We stay put until we're ordered to move."

"Why don't you read us the letter Miss Cassie sent you," Harry said.

"It's private."

Harry circled around him to block his escape. "Did she forgive you?"

"Forgive me? I wasn't the one kissing you."

Ethan pushed Zach toward Harry and laughed. "Then kiss Harry, and you'll be even."

"I didn't think I'd be here this long. I wanted to explain in person how I felt."

"When have you been at a loss for words?" Harry asked.

"Let us help," Ethan said. "Read her letter."

Zach retrieved the correspondence from his tent. They sat around the fire pit. "I'm not sure what she means in her letter." He unfolded the pages.

"It distressed me deeply when you did not say goodbye at the train station. Harry wrote that you witnessed the kiss we shared."

Zach looked up. "I appreciate you going behind my back, Harry."

"You should have written more than two lines."

"Did you read my letter?"

"We read all your letters," Ethan said. "We wouldn't want you to divulge any military secrets in your love-struck state."

"What military secrets? The war is over, and my

letters are personal."

"They certainly are," Ethan agreed.

Zach waved the letter in the air. "Then you know what this one says."

"We like the next part," Harry said. "Read it aloud."

His friends were incorrigible, but their hearts were in the right place. They wanted to help him.

"I would hope as friends, we could discuss any misunderstandings openly and honestly. When we see one another in Darrow Falls, we can determine the depth of our relationship."

Zach looked up. "What does she mean by that?"

"She wants to know whether you are a friend or more," Ethan said.

He loved her, but if witnessing Harry kissing her had left him broken, her rejection would destroy him. He kept his eyes downcast. He didn't want his friends to laugh at him, but he couldn't deny his feelings.

"She doesn't seem to be aware of the *depth* of your emotion," Ethan said.

"You have to tell her," Harry urged.

"I could write her a letter."

"No!" both men echoed.

"You have to tell her in person," Ethan said. "Declare your love."

Declare his love without a job or means to support her? "Shouldn't I wait until I know how she feels first?"

"That is the burden of being a man," Ethan said. "We declare our love first. The lady reacts. Sometimes favorably and sometimes not."

"Then she can kiss you," Harry added.

"Better hope she doesn't think of you as a cousin,

too." Ethan slapped Harry's kepi on his head. "Like this poor soldier."

****

It was July 13 before the Twenty-ninth Ohio received the necessary papers to muster the regiment out of the army. They prepared for the trip to Cleveland to receive an official stamp on the paperwork.

Before heading north, the men turned in their tent halves and Enfield muskets. Some soldiers bought their rifles for six dollars. Zach didn't want any reminder of the war. He was a man of peace now. The sound of drums woke them from sleeping under the stars, and the regiment boarded a paddle wheeler, the *Melnotte*, to Cincinnati and transferred to a train to Cleveland.

When they lined up, Zach counted two-hundred and thirty-five men mustering out. Regiments were recruited with a thousand men, but the Twenty-ninth had always run short. Wounds, illness, and death had taken their toll on enlistment, but the band of soldiers had bonded like lifelong brothers. Zach recorded each man's name and address in a book he had used for recording the wounded and dead.

"We'll keep in touch, fellas," Zach said. "We kept each other's backs during the war. If you ever need anything, don't hesitate to ask."

They marched for review, listened to a speech, and ate breakfast before reporting to Camp Cleveland where their papers were signed and each man received his final pay before heading home.

When the soldiers reached Darrow Falls, the townsfolk had gathered at the depot to welcome them. It was similar to the time they had furlough in January of 1864, but the crowd was bigger, and the stay would be permanent.

Family and neighbors escorted them to the center of Darrow Falls where River Road intersected with Main Street to form the town square. The mayor made a speech in front of the Town Hall. The bells rang in the tower of the Community Congregational Church on the opposite end of the square. In between, people gathered on the grass where tables and benches had been arranged for a picnic.

Harry was surrounded by his parents, brothers, and sister. Ethan's parents and brother joined him. Zach stood by himself. He'd corresponded with Cass throughout their separation but had not revealed his deepest feelings. Their letters had been friendly but lacked the quality of lovers separated by distance, longing to be reunited. He wanted to declare his love in person. He had rehearsed several speeches, but none seemed adequate.

He would have only a few days to express his devotion and plan their future before returning to Ravenswood. Three days before leaving Kentucky, Seymour had written that his grandfather had died. The delay in mustering out had been costly. He had looked forward to spending time with Elijah Ravenswood. He was planning to help him with the sale of the horses. Now he would return to an empty house without any guidance or help to carry on as owner. How long would it take to learn to manage a large horse farm?

Before leaving Darrow Falls, he needed to convince Cass not to abandon him in his absence. He searched the crowd for her, but she wasn't present.

The soldiers were served first, and Zach sat near Harry, Ethan, and their families.

"It's more fun coming home in July than January," Harry said between bites of thick steak prepared for the soldiers.

Harry's brother, Art, stole a biscuit from his plate. His left arm was in a brace. He had lost a section of bone in his forearm, and the brace allowed him to position his arm in order to use his hand. "What took you so long to muster out?"

"The paperwork didn't meet army standards," Ethan said. "When Billy Sherman inspected the troops, most of the men refused to line up."

Art frowned. "What about you?"

"We're sergeants," Harry said. "We convinced enough of the men to make a decent showing for the general."

Zach looked around. Still no sign of Cass. "Looks like the whole town is here to welcome us home."

Ethan voiced his thoughts. "Where are the Beechers?"

"Doctor Beecher is delivering a baby. Miss Cassie and Miss Jules are taking care of the mother." Art lifted a cup to his lips but didn't sip. "Lots of callers on Sunday afternoon with only two Beecher girls unmarried."

Was he warning him not to hesitate? He'd been worried about Harry and had forgotten about all the other men in the area. No wonder the letters from Cass had seemed aloof. He'd lost her.

"They might attend the dance tonight," Art said.

"Dance?"

"In the church." Art nodded toward the Congregational Church to the north. "They had a dance July 4 and kept the decorations in place for your

129

homecoming."

A dance. He would never have an opportunity to be alone with Cass even if she granted a dance. The older women of town carefully chaperoned social events. Young gentlemen and ladies were required to participate in group dances where partners changed with each set.

Someone tapped him on the shoulder. "Hello, soldier."

He turned at the familiar voice. Cass wore a wide-brimmed straw bonnet that shaded her delicate features from the afternoon sun. She wore a yellow gingham dress with blue flowers splashed across the checkered material. Her parasol was trimmed in a matching ribbon. She was as light as a breeze on a summer day. The sight of her took his breath away, and he couldn't speak.

"You remember my father, Dr. Sterling Beecher."

Zach stood and shook hands.

"And my mother and sister, Jules." Maureen Beecher had wavy ginger hair worn in a chignon. A few lines near her eyes were the only sign she was the grandmother of five with more on the way. Where Cass was cool and steady, Jules was a bundle of nervous energy. She surveyed the crowd, honed in on a group of young women, and hurried off.

"Have you eaten?" Zach asked.

"No, we were delayed."

"Art said you were helping deliver a baby."

"A boy, but he was stubborn about making an appearance," Cass said.

Maureen lifted a basket. "I'll find a shady tree to sit under. I hope you can join us."

"Of course." Zach offered his arm to Cass and escorted her to the tent where food had been placed for the guests. "You look lovely."

Although he had eaten, Zach filled a second plate and recommended several dishes to Cass. They joined Maureen who had spread blankets on the ground for them to sit on.

Sterling found a bench and placed it nearby. "Shall we see if there is anything left?" He offered his arm to Maureen.

Zach wasn't alone with Cass long enough to form his first question. Harry and Ethan took seats on the blanket. Their plates were filled with desserts.

"I was beginning to think you boys were never returning home," Cass said. "What took so long?"

"Clerical error," Ethan said. "We wanted to get off the train in Akron, but they insisted we travel to Cleveland to show us off."

"At least the farewell speech was short," Harry said.

"The line to be paid was long but worth it," Ethan added.

Every man from the Twenty-ninth was carrying regular pay and bonuses. Zach had his money hidden in a shirt pocket.

"What are your plans?" Cass asked.

"Nothing," Harry said. "Absolutely nothing."

"I had plenty of nothing waiting to muster out," Ethan said. "I think I'll help Grandpa and Paddy on the *Irish Rose*. At least until something better comes along."

Harry bit into a strawberry tart. "Aren't you going to need help at Ravenswood?"

Zach nodded. "I'll send word once I'm settled."

Cass turned. "Did you write your grandfather about Harry working for you?"

"No." Zach withdrew a letter from his coat. "Seymour wrote that my grandfather died."

She gasped, and the pain of death was etched on her delicate features. She reached out and touched his sleeve. "I'm sorry."

"I should have been with him." Zach stared at the simple message Seymour had sent.

Elijah Ravenswood died during his sleep on July 7.

The date was significant. The trial for those involved in Lincoln's assassination had begun May 10 and lasted seven weeks. The jury deliberated for three days, and on the morning of July 7 co-conspirators Mary Surratt, Lewis Powell, George Atzerodt, and David Herold were hanged. Dr. Samuel Mudd, Michael O'Laughlen, Ned Spangler, and Samuel Arnold were sentenced to prison.

The final chapter of Lincoln's assassination had ended, but the closure produced little peace. A man who had the potential to heal the country was dead. And no amount of justice could restore his life. Others would have to carry on his unfinished work. Zach turned his attention to the letter.

When will you visit?

Visit. Did Seymour think he wouldn't claim Ravenswood as his home? Pax had been the heir. Zach had been a spare. But after Pax died, his grandfather had taken him under his tutelage, sharing the history of Ravenswood and the dreams he hoped Zach would fulfill.

"I was looking forward to seeing him again." He

crumpled the letter. "This war robbed me of so many things. I lost my brother and now the last of my family."

Cass looked at him with misty eyes, and he regretted his outburst. "When do you return to Ravenswood?"

Zach had replied to Seymour's news that his discharge had been delayed, but any questions could be answered by his lawyer, Tyler Montgomery.

Seymour had always handled the financial and legal matters for Elijah, but last January while on furlough, Zach had contacted Tyler about representing him while he served out the remainder of his enlistment. As far as he knew, Seymour had been unaware of the arrangement until now. Tyler had written that he had visited Ravenswood and later met with Elijah about a new will. "I need to meet with your brother-in-law, Tyler. Is he here?"

Cass surveyed the crowd and turned to her parents when they returned. "Are Tyler and Cory coming?"

"Olivia has the chicken pox."

"Didn't the boys have that several weeks ago?"

"They generously shared it with Olivia," Sterling said.

"I'll take you to Glen Knolls tomorrow," Cass said. "Unless you need to return to Ravenswood immediately."

"I have the rest of my life to manage Ravenswood," Zach said. Seymour would discover his visit would be permanent.

"If you're visiting Glen Knolls, I have a mixture of oats with chamomile and lavender oils for a bath to help with the itching and keep Olivia from scratching,"

Sterling said.

Maureen turned to Zach. "Where are you staying?"

"I left my bag at the depot. I hear Mrs. Stone's inn is nice."

"You'll stay with us," Maureen said. "We have plenty of room."

"I don't need anything fancy. I slept under the stars last night."

"We all did," Harry said. "They collected our tent halves so we had no choice."

"At least it didn't rain," Ethan said.

"I want to thank you boys…I mean young men for your service." Sterling extended his hand to each of them. "If you need any medical care or need to talk, your visit is free."

"Thank you, sir," they echoed.

Cass looked at the setting sun. "Tonight ought to be beautiful for the dance."

"I'd like to escort you if the role isn't taken," Zach said.

"I'd be honored."

Chapter Thirteen

Cass had planned to keep Zach guessing about her feelings until he declared his own. But news of his grandfather's death had softened her heart, and she had agreed to accompany him to the dance. The ladies retired to the Town Hall to change into their ball gowns. The sandstone building was two stories high with double doors that opened to a small foyer and the main room beyond. A narrow staircase led to the second floor. The offices on the upper level had been opened for the ladies to transform from day dresses to formal wear.

Cass and Jules helped each other dress. Their grandmother had made the gowns for the Independence Day dance, but no one would fault them for wearing the dresses again.

Jules wore a dress of red and white stripes with a belt of blue. She wore her hair high on her head with a cascade of strawberry curls. Jules examined the low-cut bodice of her gown. "When am I going to have a bosom?"

Cass laughed at her sister's worry. "None of the Beecher sisters has ever lacked a bosom. By next year you'll fill out."

Cass leaned close to Jules to study their reflections in the mirror. Cass with her dark hair and hazel eyes was a sharp contrast to the strawberry blond curls and blue eyes Jules had inherited. Jules was pretty like a doll while Cass had a more classic beauty. Her dark brows and lashes emphasized her eyes. She rubbed some oil on her lips. She wanted Zach to kiss her followed by words of love. Their letters had been painfully formal, unable to express the gnawing desire to be together. Events had worked against them. First, Lincoln's assassination, then the long wait to be mustered from the army, and now his grandfather's death. Would they ever have a normal courtship?

"Why did you agree to allow Zach to escort you?" Jules asked. "You said you were mad at him for not saying goodbye."

"I've had plenty of time to think matters over," Cass said. "Being angry at a man only delays the conversation you need to air how you feel."

"Didn't you write him how you felt?"

"I have to see him in person. I have to see his reaction to my words. I couldn't explain the reason I kissed Harry in a letter. How do I explain Harry means nothing to me? He's Zach's best friend. That's the worst betrayal."

"You didn't kiss him."

"I sort of did."

"What?"

"I wanted to make sure," Cass said. "The first kiss was so boring. No kiss could be that bad, but I was wrong. That's when we laughed about any chance for a romance. We could never be more than friends."

"Did Zach see you laughing?"

Cass didn't know. She had hurt Zach and needed to make amends.

"You better not tell him about kissing the men who

have called on you."

"I kissed two men and don't you dare say a word," Cass threatened. "I was only confirming my theory."

"When did you become a scientist?"

"Remember how Cole taught us you didn't know if there was any passion without a kiss?"

"On the *Irish Rose* in '62."

"They all failed. Why do you think I sent them packing? The only man who has sparked a blaze in my heart is Zach Ravenswood."

"Do you think I'm too young to kiss men?"

"Yes," Cass said.

"I'm fifteen going on sixteen."

"You're the baby of the family, and you've only been wearing long skirts since last fall," Cass said. "You're lucky our sisters are too busy advising me about love. Wait until you're the target of their wisdom. I hardly had a minute alone with Zach in Washington City."

"All the poetry reading and tea sipping seems silly," Jules said. "But I like the gifts."

"Courting isn't about gifts. You're shopping for a husband."

"I don't want to marry," Jules said. "With everyone gone, I have the entire house to myself."

Was Jules serious? "You don't want a husband?"

"Big brutes," Jules said. "A handyman is as good, and Matt does whatever I ask."

"You'll change your mind when the right man comes along and you fall in love."

"What if he crosses my path but I don't know it," Jules said. "I may have met him and didn't notice."

Her logic was making Cass dizzy. "That's not how

it works. You have to meet. You share a look, maybe a touch of the hands, even a kiss." She clapped her hands. "Magic. And you know he's the one you want to spend the rest of your life with."

Jules threw her day dress and other items into the dress box. "Zach?"

Cass closed the lid and tied a string around her dress box. "He has to propose first."

"Do you think he'll do it tonight?"

Cass tugged on her gloves. "I hope not. I'm still mad enough to say no."

"I think it's romantic he was jealous." Jules cradled her box beneath her arm.

"How do you know he was jealous?"

"I was in the kitchen when you talked to Mama. I think he's stewed enough."

Cass led the way to the first floor. "Did I say you were more inexperienced than me?"

"I like Zach. He's funny. Doesn't he make you laugh?"

"Sometimes unintentionally." Zach's lopsided grin made his eyes sparkle with a hint of mischief. After Lincoln's death he had found ways to lift her spirits with a flower, a joke, or book of poetry. Gifts that had come from the heart. "You gather the gifts from your suitors, Jules. I plan to keep mine."

Maureen was talking with Zach as they waited outside. She took their dress boxes. "I'll put these in the buggy."

Zach offered his arm to Cass. He looked around at the empty square and offered his other arm to Jules.

"Thank you," Cass whispered. Jules hadn't secured an escort. She'd learn, but Zach's act of chivalry softened her heart, and Cass tightened her grip on his arm, snuggling close.

They joined the line of men and women waiting outside the double doors to the church to enter. The men in uniform were given priority at the front of the line. Harry offered his arm to Jules, and they formed a foursome for the promenade around the room as the musicians played "When Johnny Comes Marching Home."

The march was followed by a social mixer. The men stood in a circle, and the women faced them on the outside. Each pair completed a series of dance steps before changing partners and repeating the steps.

When the band played a waltz, Cass looked for Zach. He tapped her on her bare shoulder with his gloved hand. "May I have this dance?"

She curtseyed and accepted. Camp life had bleached his hair blond, and his sour apple green eyes appeared lighter against the tan on his face. "Are you glad the war is over?"

"Yes, but the ending wasn't how I imagined it. Lincoln assassinated. My grandfather dead. These sergeant stripes gave me command over other men during the war, but I feel ill-equipped to run Ravenswood."

"I have confidence in you, Zach. I believe in you."

"Then I would do you a disservice to doubt my abilities," Zach said. "I never considered Ravenswood my home, but now that it is, I want to make it a place I can be proud of."

"A home isn't a building, Zach. It's the people who live there."

"Then I don't want to live alone." The music

stopped, and he grabbed her hand. "Come."

Cass followed him toward the refreshment table, but he didn't stop. He pulled her to the foyer, down the stairs, and through the church doors. He gripped her hand and hurried along the wooden sidewalk in front of the church.

He was heading toward Mill Street. "Where are we going?"

"Ethan and Harry have been interrupting us all night."

"They're our friends."

"For a few minutes, I would like to have you to myself." He pushed open an iron-wrought gate and entered the cemetery next to the church. Silver rays of moonlight penetrated through the foliage, casting long shadows behind the grave markers. An owl hooted.

Cass glanced around. "I don't like this place, especially at night."

He pulled her against his chest. "I'll protect you."

The wind rustled the branches and stirred year-old dried leaves into a swirl that pattered against the stone markers. "Against imaginary threats?"

He stuck the fingers of his glove into his mouth and tugged his hand free before he gently stroked her cheek. His touch sent shivers down her spine. "My imagination ran wild when I saw you with Harry. I had lost you to my best friend. I convinced myself to do the noble thing and step aside."

"You stepped too early." The idiot.

"I understand that now. Harry explained that the kiss meant nothing."

"Nothing?" Cass stomped her foot. "Harry shouldn't have said anything. A gentleman doesn't spread gossip about a lady."

"We had an altercation that forced the dialogue."

"You hit Harry?"

"He wasn't hurt." Zach shrugged. "Harry has a hard head."

"There's been too much violence in the world. I want you to promise not to resort to your fists to solve a problem. There has to be a better way."

"I'll try." Zach studied her. "I couldn't write the words to express my feelings in a letter, and all evening I've hesitated to speak with this rift between us."

"Why didn't you say something? Why didn't you confront us at the depot?" Cass said. "This waiting has been like a knife in my heart, wondering if we could repair the damage."

"I was jealous and angry." Zach pulled her closer. "I had feared I'd lost you. I never felt so alone."

"You were never alone." He had his friends. "All for one and one for all, remember?"

He laughed, dancing in a circle with his arms around her. "I should have known you wouldn't consider any other man but me."

Cass pulled away. "And why wouldn't I consider other men? Do you think you're the pick of the litter? Or do you think I can't do any better? You think I'm not worthy of marriage after allowing a few kisses."

"That's not what I meant." Zach ran his hand through his hair. "You're the most beautiful woman in the world. I can't believe you would speak to me after I was so rude. I know you had to be polite when I was wounded, but when you kissed me, I concluded you had to be in love with me as much as I love you."

What? "You love me?"

A smile formed on his lips. "Since that winter in your parents' parlor when I met you, I haven't been able to forget you. I looked forward to the letters you wrote. I spent hours agonizing over each word I penned to paper. I couldn't be a proper suitor with a broken leg, and then all the horrors of Lincoln's death and the aftermath kept me from declaring my love. But I hoped for a future together. I can't imagine my life without you."

She closed her eyes waiting for his kiss. When none came, she opened her eyes. "This is where you kiss me."

A frown creased his brow. "I'm worried. A kiss dismissed Harry as a suitor. What if you don't feel anything for me?"

Had her feelings changed for him? Her heart was racing as he held her in his arms. "I'll be brutally honest. If I think of you only as a brother, I'll let you know."

"That's what I'm afraid of." Zach hesitated.

Cass put her hand on the back of his neck and pulled him close. He kissed her, playing a game of discovery on her vibrating lips. A warm glow began in her belly and spread outward to her fingertips. Her knees buckled, and she molded against him, fearing she would faint. Her passion for Zach was true, and she responded to his kisses in a matching rhythm of desire.

When he pulled away, his breath was ragged. "Did you feel that?"

"You're not my brother, cousin, or friend. I love you, Zach." She glanced around. "But we're kissing in a cemetery."

"I don't think they'll mind."

A twig broke. Cass jumped, pressing her body against Zach's. "What was that?"

His arm encircled her, but they remained silent, listening for any more noises. A dog howled in the distance. Someone or something ran a stick along the fence, the clickety-click echoing in the shadows. A soft moan carried on the wind but was muffled by a swirl of dead leaves blowing among the grave markers.

"Zach!" Cass balled her fists into the fabric of his coat and buried her face in his chest.

"All right fellas. You can come out now," Zach hollered.

Cass peeked, listening for any response.

Harry and Ethan stepped from behind a tree. "How did you know it was us?"

"You should wear a hat, Ethan. Your hair glows in the moonlight."

"Like the romantic moonlight you're sharing with my cousin." Ethan rested against a headstone. "Only Zach would court a lady in a cemetery."

"We wanted to be alone."

"I think we should leave," Harry said. "A cemetery is no place to be at night."

"Ed will protect you from the other ghosts and goblins," Ethan said.

"Don't speak ill of the dead, especially my brother."

"Jake is buried here, too," Ethan said.

Harry glanced over his shoulder. "Do you think they watch over us?"

"Someone helped us survive the war." Zach helped Cass weave their way through the stones marking the graves.

Ethan paused at the gate and saluted. "Thank you, gentlemen."

A gust of wind swirled around the stones and blew against their clothing.

"I'm getting out of here." Harry rushed toward the church.

"I'll protect you." Zach put his arm around Cass and ushered her back to the dance.

Cass wasn't afraid. Zach loved her. He had made his declaration. But it was a fragile bond. Responsibilities at Ravenswood would take him away. She needed to find a way to be with him.

They returned to the celebration in time for a final dance and a prayer by the Reverend Davis for peace and prosperity that ended the festivities.

Chapter Fourteen

Zach woke with a start. He had been camping in tents or in the open air for so long, it was strange to have a ceiling overhead and a soft bed beneath. He dressed in his uniform. He planned to buy civilian clothes at the Wheeler Dry Goods store in town.

The guest room was above Dr. Beecher's office and as he entered the adjoining room, the doctor's door was ajar. He needed to speak with him and knocked on the doorframe.

"Come in."

Sterling was seated in a black leather chair behind an oak desk. Several leather-bound books were stacked in the corner. One was marked *Births and deaths.*

"Sit, Sergeant Ravenswood."

"It's Zach now." He had never asked permission of a father to court a daughter. Should he have presented a gift?

Sterling studied him. "Is this a medical call?"

"No, sir. My leg is completely healed."

"Did you have any trouble sleeping?"

Zach ran his fingers through his long hair. "A little. I'm not used to sleeping indoors."

"I've talked with soldiers who have returned from the war, and each one has different physical, emotional, and mental challenges. The sound of thunder reminds them of cannons or a cornfield becomes a battle site,"

Sterling said. "We can't undo the experience, but we can learn to control how we react to the reminders of war."

"I was affected more by witnessing Lincoln's assassination than any battle," Zach said. "I have dreams about it."

"You relive the night?"

"I dream about saving him," Zach said. "I know Booth is waiting for the audience to laugh so he can fire his shot. I leap on the stage and climb to the balcony in time to place myself between Lincoln and Booth. I take the shot for the president. He lives, but I die."

"A heroic gesture, but there was nothing you could have done, Zach, even if your leg wasn't broken. Logan and I talked about it at length. Booth had enough knowledge to succeed, and others were ignorant to the danger. Even Major Rathbone, who was in the box with the president, failed to stop the fatal shot."

"I wish I could have done more."

"Men are protectors," Sterling said. "When we can't save someone dear to us, we can feel helpless. It takes time to accept our limitations."

"While I waited in camp to be discharged, I thought about Lincolns' speeches," Zach said. *"With malice toward none, with charity for all, with firmness in the right as God gives us to see the right, let us strive on to finish the work we are in, to bind up the nation's wounds, to care for him who shall have borne the battle and for his widow and his orphan, to do all which may achieve and cherish a just and lasting peace among ourselves and with all nations."*

"His words are a fitting way to remember him," Sterling said. "Cassandra said your grandfather recently died. I'm sorry. Is there anything I can do?"

"I'm visiting Tyler Montgomery this morning. He wrote my grandfather's will."

"And I was going to send along some medicine for Olivia." He retrieved several bottles from his cabinet and placed them on his desk. "Is there something more?"

Zach took a deep breath. "I'd like permission to court your daughter."

Sterling's eyebrows shot up as he sat. "I am a man with six daughters, and I find myself surrounded by young men who have married them. My daughters have made wise choices, and I trust Cassandra will do the same, but I have a few questions."

"Yes, sir."

"Why do you want to call on my daughter?"

"I love her."

"Have you spoken to her about your feelings?"

"Last night, sir."

"And what are her feelings?"

"Our desires are mutual, sir."

"What are your plans? How will you support her?"

"My grandfather left me Ravenswood, but I need to learn to run the farm. Raising horses takes work, but I plan to offer Ethan and Harry jobs."

"Do you trust your friends to work for you?"

"I trust them with my life. I can't think of anyone else I would trust more."

Sterling looked at the papers on his desk. "What does Cassandra think about your plans?"

"I talked about Ravenswood, but I wasn't the owner then. It will take a couple of years for me to learn the business."

"You plan to wait several years before marrying my daughter?"

"That's why it's important to have your approval."

Sterling leaned back in his chair. "Have you discussed this with Cassandra?"

"No, sir. As men, we should come to terms first."

"If I owned my daughter, you would be expected to ask permission, but I've never owned any of my daughters. They chose their husbands as much as the men chose them. I appreciate you talking with me, but it will be Cassandra's decision as to whether she marries you. And I wouldn't count on her waiting too long."

"I want Ravenswood to be ready before we wed."

He leaned forward. "Let me explain something about the Beecher women, son. They are not princesses waiting for a knight to carry them off to a beautiful castle. Without considering the consequences, I have trained my daughters to help me with my patients. They have taken those skills to the battlefield and to the hospitals. Did I want to pamper and protect them? Yes. But it is not in their character to be spoiled with idle adoration. If Ravenswood needs to be rebuilt, you should ask my daughter to lend a hand."

"I was planning to invite Ethan and Harry for the annual sale of the horses at Ravenswood. Are you saying I should invite Cassandra as well?"

"No." Sterling looked flustered. "I would have to consider the appropriateness of such a trip."

Cass poked her head in the doorway. "What trip?"

"I was asking your father if you could join Ethan and Harry when they visit Ravenswood."

"That would be wonderful!" She ran around the

148

desk and hugged her father.

"I did not approve any trip," Sterling stated. "All I approved was Mr. Ravenswood's request to court you."

"Court me?" Cass placed her hands on her hips. "Did you reach an agreement, or do I have a say in the matter?"

"We have an understanding," Zach said.

"Wonderful." Cass poked Zach's arm. "Perhaps you can barter a fair price for me like you do your horses."

"He offered two geldings and a carriage," Sterling said. "I think it's a fair price."

Zach raised his hands. "I did not."

"Oh, Papa!" Cass put her arms around Sterling's neck. "You are a horrible tease. Besides, I'm worth more than two geldings."

He patted her hand. "Mr. Ravenswood has not been enlightened by the writings of Elizabeth Cady Stanton as I have. My wife and daughters are suffragettes. You would do well to become acquainted with their teachings."

"A bunch of words without action," Cass said. "No one can agree on anything but the right to vote, and we don't have that. For each step forward, we take two steps backward. I don't think we'll ever be equal to men."

"Equal?" A warning look from Sterling changed his words. "Men are the inferior ones. We call for war when women, who give life, pray for peace. We solve problems with violence, but women reason with common sense and cooperation. We left a path of destruction, but it will take women like you to rebuild the beauty of this world for our children and grandchildren."

Cass ran to Zack and embraced him. "Isn't he wonderful?"

Sterling stood. "What you lack in experience, son, you succeed in poetry."

"Lincoln inspired me." Zach looked at Cass.

"*It is the eternal struggle between these two principles—right and wrong—throughout the world. They are the two principles that have stood face to face from the beginning of time and will ever continue to struggle. The one is the common right of humanity, and the other the divine right of kings,*" Zach said.

"The struggle between tyrants and slaves," Cass explained.

"*You toil and work and earn bread, and I will eat it,*" he added.

Cass rested her hand against Zach's chest. "Then let the slaves toil and eat their own bread," she said. "And the tyrants can starve."

****

Zach hitched the black gelding to the buggy while Cass gathered the medical supplies her father had prepared for Olivia's chicken pox. He placed the box in the back and helped Cass board. "I'll take the reins."

Cass relinquished control of the horse. "Blackie is old so be gentle."

"I'm sure there are several horses that could replace Blackie at Ravenswood. Do you think your father will let you visit?"

"You've already done the hard part."

"What is that?"

"You put the idea in his head. I'll cultivate it to fruition."

He drove into town and then north on Main Street to Glen Knolls, the home of Tyler and Cory Montgomery.

Tyler had bought the home five years ago. The yellow house had faux pillars and a portico above the entrance, typical for homes in the area.

Zach stopped the carriage in the back yard near the barn. Two boys were chasing chickens in the yard.

"Aunt Cassie!"

Sterling Montgomery had been named after his maternal grandfather, but he resembled his father with dark hair and pale blue eyes. His companion was Jefferson Vandal who had hair the color of wheat and dark brown eyes.

The boys had been born in 1861, the first year of the war. Jefferson's mother, Regina, had died two years ago along with her infant daughter and were buried on their farm, the Silver Pheasant, in Vandalia, West Virginia.

Tyler had been raised in Vandalia. Regina had entrusted him to find her husband, Edward Vandal, but the man had disappeared like many of his fellow Confederate soldiers.

Cass had shared the story with Zach. "Does Jefferson remember his father?"

"I don't see how," Cass said. "He was too young. Cory and Tyler explained how his father fought in the war and nobody knows what happened."

"So many men were buried where they fell," Zach said.

The boys stopped chasing the chickens and joined Zach and Cass. "Who is this, Aunt Cassie?"

"I've forgotten my manners," Cass said with a

slight smile. "This is Sergeant Zach Ravenswood." She turned to Zach. "This is Mister Sterling Montgomery and Mister Jefferson Vandal, two fine gentlemen of Summit County."

"It's a pleasure to meet you." Zach extended his hand.

"Where's your gun?" Jefferson asked.

"Don't you know? The war is over."

Cass steered the conversation away from war. "Are you enjoying the summer, boys?"

"We sho' are," Jefferson said. "I caught a fish."

"Papa took us to the fishin' pond," Sterling added. "He put the worms on for us."

Jefferson made a face. "Yuck."

Tyler headed toward them but was attacked by the boys with stories of their day. He was a big man who had worked as a blacksmith when he was home summers from boarding school, adding muscle that disguised the fact he had attended Harvard and was a lawyer.

Cory followed, smoothing loose strands into a chignon at the base of her neck. The eldest of the Beecher sisters, Cory had dark hair like Cass but with red highlights. She had been the leader of the siblings, but after her marriage, each sister had left home to seek an adventure and a husband.

Was Washington City her adventure, or was there something more in her future? Cass asked Zach to remove the box she had packed. "Papa mixed some bath mixtures to ease the itching for Olivia. How is she doing?"

"I had to put mittens on her so she doesn't scratch. I don't want her to have scars like these two rascals."

Cory ran her fingers through Sterling's dark curls and Jefferson's straight locks.

"I only scratched a little," Sterling said.

Cass examined the boys. "I don't see any scars."

"None on the face," Cory said.

"Boys can't be too pretty," Tyler said.

"They can earn their scars when they're grown men," Cory said.

"Do you have any battle scars?" Jefferson asked Zach.

"Afraid not," Zach said. "The first thing I learned was to duck. But I broke my leg when a sharpshooter took out…"

"I picked up your mail." Cass scowled at Zach. "No talk of killing. They're four years old," she whispered before retrieving letters from atop the box of medicine.

"Sorry." He carried the box.

Tyler frowned and tore open a letter. "It's an old friend I wrote to about Edward Vandal. He was home the winter of '62, but no one has seen or heard from him since. I sent a letter to Vandalia. I figured if he was alive, he'd return home, but no news from the Dunking Witch."

Cory gasped. "The Dunking Witch? I thought you sold it."

"I did. I wrote the new owner." Tyler escorted Cory to the house as the others followed. "I figured he would inform me if Edward showed up in town."

The Dunking Witch was more than a saloon. As family, Cass was privy to Tyler's past. His late mother, Olivia, had owned the Dunking Witch when it had been a whorehouse. Edward Vandal had discovered the secret and shared it with everyone in town. There was no love lost between the two men, and yet Regina Vandal had chosen Tyler to be guardian to Jefferson before she died.

The two boys marched across the yard, arm in arm. No one would guess their fathers had hated each other.

"You should stop looking," Cory said. "Jefferson is part of the family now."

"I'm fond of the boy," Tyler said. "But as a lawyer, I need to do my due diligence. I wouldn't want Edward to accuse me of kidnapping his son."

"That's preposterous," Cory said. "Esther brought him to us."

"Esther was his slave," Tyler said. "I'll keep trying to find him until I've exhausted all my leads."

"And if he's dead?"

"Then we'll adopt Jefferson." Tyler held the door as everyone entered the kitchen at the back of the house.

"And if he's not dead?" Cory whispered.

"Then Edward will need to prove he's a decent father, or I'll fight him in court for custody," Tyler said. "Reggie entrusted me with her son's care. I won't turn him over to a man I don't trust to care for him properly."

Tyler had beat Edward in court once. He could do it again, if necessary.

The sick room was off the kitchen. Olivia, named for her grandmother, was sleeping in the single bed. She had mittens on her hands and a quilt covering her small body. The poor child had to be hot. It was July.

"Quiet, boys," Cory warned as they sat at the kitchen table. She served them biscuits and raw vegetables from the garden.

"No need. She's awake." Tyler stood in the doorway of the sick room. "How are you feeling, Liv?"

Olivia chattered in a ramble of words, some real and some only a two-year-old understood.

Cory examined a muslin sack tied with twine in the medical box Zach had placed on the table. "What am I supposed to do with this?"

"Papa said to put it in her bath. It'll soothe her skin." Cass looked for a bucket. "I'll fetch the water."

Chapter Fifteen

Once the boys had eaten and been dismissed outside, Tyler led Zach into the adjoining dining room. "Let's talk in my office."

"Yes, sir."

"You don't have to address me as sir." Tyler led the way across the hallway that ran from the front of the house to the rear to encourage the flow of any breeze. He opened the door to his office. A large desk was the centerpiece with a shelf filled with books behind him and a side table near the window. He pointed to a leather seat, and Zach sat. "I didn't serve in the war, Zach. I had my reasons, but I admire you for doing your duty."

"I wanted to follow Pax's example. I had no family. My grandfather barely acknowledged me. Seymour was to be administer of the estate until I turned twenty-five."

"I visited your grandfather on your behalf after your furlough in 1864. He contacted me shortly after," Tyler said. "Do you know why?"

"He wrote he had changed his will," Zach said. "Fighting in the war convinced him I was mature enough to run Ravenswood on my own. I don't plan to disappoint him."

"He spoke proudly of you," Tyler said.

"We made amends. I was happy for that. When he

wrote about training me to run Ravenswood, I looked forward to returning to help him. His death came as a shock. I feel a bit overwhelmed now."

Tyler handed him an envelope. "This is a copy of the will. It makes you sole owner of Ravenswood. He provided for the employees and Seymour."

"Has Seymour seen the will?"

"I wrote him a letter and confirmed the court executed the will after your grandfather had died," Tyler said. "I was expecting Seymour to contact me."

"Did he know about the will?"

"I made no secret of the reasons for my visits last year. But he may not have known the contents," Tyler said. "I don't know what was in the previous will. Elijah burned it."

"Why?"

"So there would be no confusion as to his wishes."

"I'm his only heir. I don't see how there could be any confusion." Seymour had been mentioned in the will. "What did Seymour receive?"

"It guarantees Seymour boarding and an income as long as he remains employed at Ravenswood. You can't fire him. You are required to pay him unless he quits of his own volition."

"He's an accountant. He could find work anywhere."

"Perhaps he will." Tyler rubbed the side of his nose. "Did Elijah treat Seymour differently from the other employees?"

"My grandfather sent Seymour to school and college." Zach interlocked his fingers. "My mother mentioned a mistress, and Seymour could have been the result. She didn't like him and refused to live under the same roof. We stayed at the cabin by the lake."

"Families can be complicated," Tyler said. "My mother led a colorful life. I had to come to terms with her choices, but it helped to know she was doing what she thought was best for her family. Your grandfather provided Seymour with an education and a position at Ravenswood."

"Do you think Seymour was expecting more?" Zach asked. "He could be disappointed by the will."

"Ravenswood was your grandfather's property to dispose of as he wished. It doesn't matter what Seymour expected or wanted. When do you leave for Ravenswood?"

"Tomorrow. I'm not sure what to expect."

"It's your home, Zach. No one can take it away from you."

****

Zach stared out of the window of the stagecoach. Although a train route passed near Ravenswood, it traveled north and south and didn't intersect with the train route through Darrow Falls. He had taken the stage to make the western journey. Farms were nestled among gently rolling hills and clusters of virgin forests.

He had come home for Paxton's funeral in August of 1862. Zach had returned to Western Reserve College after his brother's death but didn't remain. With Harry and Ethan, he had enlisted.

On a wintery night in 1864, he had met Cassandra Beecher as she entertained the three young men in her parents' parlor. She had agreed to write him. His broken leg had given him the opportunity to spend time with her and share their first kiss. She had stood with him at the stage depot in downtown Darrow Falls. He had kissed her goodbye, and the memory hadn't faded. She had promised to visit with Ethan and Harry for the sale. He was eager to show off Ravenswood.

Zach didn't bother to notify Seymour about his arrival. He had expected to be home in May or early June, and it was the end of July. The delay meant he had missed the only opportunity to say goodbye to his grandfather. Would Ravenswood feel like home? Only with Cass and his friends.

After claiming his travel bag from the roof of the coach, Zach entered the general store at what was once the center of Ravenswood Town. The Town Hall, store, a church, and a boarding house were the only remnants remaining. The railroad had been built five miles west, creating a new downtown and leaving the old one a ghost town.

After a hot, dusty ride on the coach, the cool darkness of the store offered relief from the drenching humidity. He smacked his kepi against his thigh to knock the dust off. Marcus Wheeler had finished the alterations to the length of his trousers and sleeves of his coat, but he wore his uniform, too proud to hide it. The floorboards creaked beneath his steps, and the store owner turned.

Zach had known Fred Kettler as a boy. He was mayor, county clerk, and store owner. He had been present at all the sales of his grandfather's horses, notarizing the transactions and recording them at the county courthouse. Fred had lost most of his hair with a fringe of gray remaining beneath a bald cap. He wore a long apron and was sweeping the floor. "How are you doing, Mr. Kettler?"

He studied him. "I know those eyes. You must be

Zachary Ravenswood." He extended his hand. "You've come home."

"It's been a long time."

"Your grandfather followed Paxton in the Seventh Ohio and you in the Twenty-ninth Ohio. You fought in your share of battles."

"Some I would like to forget."

"From what I read, you have no reason to be ashamed. Your grandfather fought valiantly against death until you returned, but his heart wasn't strong enough."

"My regiment's mustering was delayed." He tampered his anger. "Seymour wrote me, but he didn't share many details." He trusted the storekeeper and freely shared his feelings. "I wish I could have seen him one more time."

"I visited the day before he died. He was out of his mind at the end. Talking about horses and the sale."

"He was waiting until I returned for the sale."

"That's what I thought." Fred handed him a flier stored in the cubbyhole where he sorted mail. "Seymour had these printed a week after your grandfather died. Said he needed to pay the bills. He asked me to mail a stack of invitations with the flier inside. I kept a few announcements to hand out to the locals."

The flier announced the sale of the horses at Ravenswood on July 29.

"It's a week from Saturday. He must have known you would be arriving and planned accordingly," Fred said.

"Of course." Fred was fishing. Seymour had planned the sale without him, but Zach wasn't ready to accuse him of anything until he heard his side of the story. He studied the flier. "Do you have an envelope and a pen? I want to invite some friends to the sale."

Fred provided the supplies. Zach wrote on the back of the flier, folded it, and placed it in the envelope. He wrote an address on the front and handed it to Fred. "Could you post this?"

"The eastbound coach won't come through until tomorrow."

"That will be soon enough."

Zach took a second flier, folded it, and tucked it in his uniform coat pocket. Seymour hadn't asked his permission to sell the horses. If his mustering had been delayed a little longer, he might have missed the sale completely. What was Seymour planning to do? Sell Ravenswood out from under him?

Zach relaxed. Two years of fighting in a war had made him wary of enemies behind every tree and building. He was a civilian and needed to trust others. To a point. He removed a pair of leather boots from the shelf and tried them on. "I'll take these." He added a wide-brimmed hat and handed Fred a ten-dollar bill.

He examined it in the light.

"What's wrong with it?"

"We had some counterfeit bills spent here last month. County sheriff said they were old Confederate bills bleached and then printed to look like Union money." He snapped the bill. "This one is real."

Fred gave him his change and handed him a stick of hard candy. "For old time's sake."

Zach put the boots and hat inside his valise.

"You're not going to wear your new hat?"

"I wanted to return home a soldier," Zach said.

Seymour had always frightened him as a boy. He wanted the old crow to see him in uniform. He couldn't order Seymour to leave Ravenswood, but a little intimidation would show him who was boss.

Without a ride, Zach had to walk the final distance to Ravenswood. It was a couple of miles, but years of marching had conditioned him for any distance. The light was low, casting long shadows in his path when he passed the stone pillars marking the entrance to the eight-hundred acres of property.

He had drawn Cass a map of Ravenswood and recalled the details as he walked along the tree-lined road. The main house would come into view soon. The carriage barn, shed, and broodmare barn were built in the rear. Grandfather liked to be close to the mares and foals born in the spring.

From his second floor bedroom window, he could view some of the run-in sheds and fenced off grazing pastures that separated the horses by age and training. Other pastures were used to grow grass mixed with alfalfa and clover that would be mowed, dried, and stored for feed. In the northeast corner was a lake with a log cabin where he had grown up. Guests stayed there if they weren't invited to the main house. Horse trainers and workers had barracks to live in.

The four stone chimneys and top of the towers of Ravens Roost appeared above the tree tops, and he quickened his pace. The roof was dragon scale slate, and the walls were cut stone from the quarry by the lake. The round turrets graced the front corners and were mirrored in the rear. Three rows of seven arched windows were framed between the towers except on the main floor where a large arched doorway replaced the center window.

Seven dormers broke the smooth line of the roof and their pointed peaks matched the high caps of each tower.

The drive passed in front of the massive oak doors and around to the back. Zach paused in front of the entrance. Twin stone staircases with ornate iron railings formed an arc to the keystone decorations surrounding the entrance. The half circle framed by the steps had been a rose garden, the pride of his grandfather, but weeds were overgrown in the briars. A shutter was missing from one window, and another hung at an angle, ready to fall.

He had expected Ravenswood to have aged but not been neglected. The front pasture, home to normally a dozen horses, was empty, and the grass had grown high. What had happened?

Zach didn't bother knocking. It was his home. The entranceway opened into a large hall that ran from the front toward the back of the house. Through an archway was a parlor for entertaining guests. It opened to a stone terrace overlooking the grounds. To the left was a dining hall and kitchen toward the rear. The library was to the right with an adjoining study. All the bedrooms were on the second and third floors. Servants lived on the fourth floor. Double staircases, one on each side of the hall rose to the second floor landing where the master bedroom doors could be seen. Elijah Ravenswood's former room.

Zach slid his hand along the dusty railing that curved along the inside of the staircase. He and Pax had raced with their bellies against the smooth surface, crash landing on the stone floor no matter how many times Seymour yelled at them.

He paused when he reached the landing and stared at the closed doors of his grandfather's room. He wanted to enter and find him inside, resting in his large four poster bed or seated at his rolltop desk. But he was gone. Zach turned right and carried his belongings to his room, the last one facing the back of the house.

The draperies were drawn, and a mustiness prevailed in the closed room. He pushed the fabric along a metal rod and opened the window. The bed, dresser, washstand, and storage box were coated with dust. No preparations had been made for his return. The coverlet was one his mother had made and transferred with his belongings from the cabin after his parents had died of influenza. Pax and Zach had preferred boarding school to visits to Ravens Roost. They had spent weekends with the Herbruck brothers and Donovan cousins before the war changed all their lives.

He dumped his valise on the bed. It sagged under the weight. The ropes needed tightening. He found the bed key in the frame and tightened the ropes beneath the cornhusk-filled mattress. When he was done, he put his clothes in the dresser. He used a washcloth hanging on the handle of the washstand to remove the dust from the wood surfaces. Zach arranged his personal items on top of the dresser. He stared at the photograph of Cass he had purchased in Washington City when they had visited Matthew Brady's studio at 625 Pennsylvania Avenue. "I hope your father allows you to visit. I miss you."

He surveyed the room. It was habitable. The pitcher needed filled so he could bathe. He opened the door and peered into the hallway. Where were the servants? Ravenswood employed a cook, two maids, and gardener not to mention the foreman and stable hands for the horses.

He hadn't expected a throng welcoming him at the door, but finding Ravenswood deserted was unnerving.

Voices drifted through the open window. He looked outside. Two men talked by the door to the stables. He recognized Seymour with his thin frame and hunched shoulders. The other man wore a wide-brimmed hat that shaded his face. His straight brown hair hung about his shoulders. He had a familiar stance. He was military.

Chapter Sixteen

Zach hurried downstairs. When he reached the foyer and turned the corner, Seymour loomed before him and only his quick reflexes prevented them from colliding.

Seymour's dark eyebrows rose in alarm. "Zachary." The immaculately dressed man wore all black with a crisp white shirt beneath the coat and vest. He was in his fifties, and his dark hair had begun to gray. He had been a fixture at Ravenswood all his life, but Zach had never paid much attention to the family accountant. Were the rumors true? It didn't matter. He was master of Ravenswood. "I believe it's Mister Ravenswood now that my grandfather has died."

Seymour bristled at the correction. "From your last letter, we didn't know when to expect you, sir."

"As soon as I received my discharge papers, I hurried home. I was distressed to learn my grandfather had died. If I had known he was ill, I would have sought permission to come home sooner."

"Elijah Ravenswood expected to recover," Seymour said. "I was unaware your regiment had traveled to Kentucky until I reviewed your grandfather's correspondence. I sent you word. Did you not receive my latest missive?"

He was shifting the blame. "I did. I regret my delay."

"He died peacefully."

Seymour's words didn't comfort him. He should have been home to say goodbye. Zach looked around at the dust-covered furniture and worn carpets. "What's happened to Ravenswood?"

"Many of the staff have died or left over the years, and your grandfather didn't replace them. The remaining workers have had trouble maintaining the estate. The house and grounds fell into disrepair."

"Now that I'm home, that will change. I intend to begin repairs immediately."

"I wouldn't be too hasty," Seymour warned in a silky voice. "Ravenswood depends heavily upon the annual sale of its horses. Your grandfather delayed the date, waiting for you to return. Then he became ill, and funds have nearly been depleted."

The sale advertised in the flyer in his coat pocket? Instinct, honed by years of eluding the enemy, warned him to avoid showing his hand. He changed the subject. "Who's taking care of the horses?"

"I hired a new foreman and his men last month. They're experienced horsemen."

"What happened to the old foreman and his workers?"

"Old age," Seymour said. "Your grandfather shouldn't have kept them on as long as he did. You'll find the trainers and handlers are competent and hard workers."

"I hope so. Ravenswood depends upon healthy, well-trained stock. I plan to hire a veterinarian and more staff." He looked around the room. "The house feels like a mausoleum. Is anyone left?"

"A cook, but as I said, Ravenswood has little cash

until the horses are sold. I recommend a sale as soon as possible."

Seymour had already arranged one. "I will consider it," Zach said. "It was a long trip, and I'm tired and hungry."

"I'll have the cook prepare a meal."

Zach returned to his room and removed his uniform. It had served its purpose. Seymour had shown him respect, but he doubted it was sincere. He dressed in the civilian clothes he had purchased. He stroked the familiar wool uniform discarded on the bed. That part of his life was over, and another was beginning, albeit not the one he had imagined. He folded the jacket and trousers for storage.

He opened a trunk, expecting it to be empty, and found the clothes he had sent home from Western Reserve College after he had enlisted with Harry and Ethan. He removed them. They had belonged to a skinny youth. The jacket was too narrow and the pants too small. In the bottom were several books from his childhood, a copy of Washington Irving's *Rip Van Winkle* and *The Legend of Sleepy Hollow*. He placed them on the nightstand next to the bed. Books were meant to be read. When Cass visited, she could take them back home for Sterling and Jefferson.

The lamp was low on oil and the wick needed trimmed. He retrieved his military notebook from the dresser top and opened it to a blank page. He listed *lamp oil*. One thing at a time. He dropped the clothing into the chest along with his field glasses, mess kit, and other military items he had kept as souvenirs. He should have purchased his Enfield musket. No, Cass had warned against violence. They had experienced too much in their young lives. He would deal with Seymour with tact and the maturity of a grown man.

Zach passed Pax's room, paused, and opened the door. Like his room, a layer of dust covered the furniture. Another quilt his mother had made covered the bed. He lifted the lid to a matching footlocker. Inside were clothes Pax had worn in civilian life. His school books were stacked to one side with a package on top. It had been opened but left intact. Inside was Pax's army haversack with his personal belongings. He sorted through the razor, mirror, knife, and a few coins. He found an opened letter and read it.

I regret to inform you that your grandson, Paxton Ravenswood, was mortally wounded at Cedar Mountain. He was transported to Washington City where we made his last days as comfortable as possible. He spoke fondly of you and his brother, Zachary. The Seventh Ohio lost one of its best. My sisters and I offer our condolences.

It was signed by Jennifer Pierce, Colleen, and Jessica Beecher, care of Mermaid's Mirth in Washington City. Soldiers talked of fate, Harry preached God's plan, but Zach believed in idealism tempered by realism. He was going to take advantage of whatever circumstances had caused Paxton to cross paths with the Beecher sisters and introduced Cassandra into his life. Ravens Roost would only be a building until she joined him as his wife.

He returned the letter and closed the lid to the storage box. His grandfather's bedroom was next along the back of the house and in the center facing the double staircase. He turned the knob.

The smell of a strong cleaning solution assaulted

and burned his nostrils. The bed had been stripped of bedding and both the feather and cornhusk-filled mattresses. He opened a drawer. The dresser was empty. All of Elijah's personal belongings and his favorite hat were gone. Nothing remained. No memories.

Zach slammed the door and hurried downstairs. There had to be a reason for the ravishment, but an answer eluded him. He entered the dining room.

The familiar surroundings soothed him. The polished table with matching oak chairs, the long sideboard, and the two chandeliers were the same. Light filtered through the stained-glass windows above the tall sectioned windows. A castle, knight, beast, and fair damsel were illustrated in the different panels of colored glass and leading. The last panel was a blooming rose. It symbolized prosperity at Ravenswood. But the roses in front were being strangled by the weeds.

The dining room table was set for two. "Do I have a guest?" Zach asked Seymour when he entered.

"I was planning to join you." Seymour took the seat at the head of the table. "We could discuss your plans."

Zach had earned his stripes by taking command. "I'd feel more comfortable if you weren't sitting in my chair."

Anger flashed across the older man's face, but Seymour rose and took the seat on the side. "Your position as master of the house will take some adjustment."

Zach took the seat Seymour had vacated. Paxton would have sat here if he hadn't died. Second sons were ill-prepared to inherit. But Seymour would discover the frightened youth he bullied in the past had grown into a man. He had fought and killed to stay alive. In Georgia, he had gone on reconnaissance missions to discover the enemy's position, a weakness, and victory. He had less than two weeks before the sale to uncover Seymour's plans.

An elderly woman with white hair and wearing a black dress and white apron pushed a cart into the room with a large bowl on top. She looked back and forth between the two men. "Why is a guest sitting in your chair?" Her loud voice echoed off the wooden beams decorating the ceiling.

"This is Mister Ravenswood," Seymour shouted. "This is Mrs. Graves," he explained in a normal voice.

A familiar face, but one that had aged and gone deaf. "I hope you remember my favorite dish."

"Favorite fish?" She looked confused. "I didn't fix fish tonight."

"Dish!" Seymour shouted.

"It's all right, Mrs. Graves. Whatever you cooked, I'm sure it's delicious."

She studied his face. "Young man, do I know you?"

"I'm Zach."

Her face brightened. "Pax. I remember you. You were such a smart young man. Nothing like your brother. He was always getting into trouble."

Seymour snickered. "She's old and senile and has nowhere to go." He pointed to the bowl on the cart. "The soup is growing cold, Mrs. Graves!"

With a shaky hand, she ladled soup into their bowls and set a board with sliced bread on the table.

"What are you serving, Mrs. Graves?" When she didn't answer, he pointed at the bowl. "What is it?"

"Squash soup."

Squash? He tentatively tasted the orange liquid. The seasoned soup was surprisingly delicious. Mrs. Graves was a good cook. Her deafness could be overlooked.

During the war years, an evening supper had replaced the noon-time dinner as the main meal. Mrs. Graves served roasted rabbit that fell off the bone, fried potatoes, and green beans. Dessert consisted of pound cake topped with strawberries.

His appetite satisfied, Zach turned to Seymour. "My grandfather's room was empty. What happened to his personal belongings?"

"They're in a trunk on the fourth floor," Seymour said. "When he died, we cleaned and removed all his belongings in the room. Do you plan to stay in it?"

"Not immediately," Zach said. "I plan to be here a long time, so I'm in no hurry to make changes. And with limited funds, I'll need to prioritize what is done first."

"I'm here to assist in any way."

He leaned toward Seymour. "I'd like to see the books and determine how much Ravenswood is in debt."

Seymour's normally bland expression registered a worried reaction for a moment. "I'll see to it."

"Tomorrow is soon enough." Zach strode to the library. Elijah hadn't updated his collection with any current authors. When Cass visited, he'd ask her to recommend some purchases. She had read to him while he was convalescing. Her rich, expressive voice had turned any story into an adventure.

He selected several books on horses. They were dusty. Seymour had never shown an interest in the animals, only their value on paper. Without his grandfather's expertise, Zach would have to learn how to run the farm on his own.

He sensed someone in the room and turned. Seymour stood in the doorway. "Did you find what you were looking for?"

"A few books to read."

Seymour sneered. "It's a pity you didn't finish your schooling."

"The battlefield taught me to survive," Zach said. "You don't learn that at a college." He passed Seymour and headed upstairs.

****

The next day Zach wandered through the rooms to regain a familiarity with what was now his home. It was missing something. Or he was lonely. His friends couldn't arrive soon enough, especially one dark-haired lady. If necessary, he'd use his military pay to make repairs to Ravenswood. He didn't want Cass to be disappointed with her future home.

He entered the kitchen and found Mrs. Graves stirring eggs in a skillet on the stove. Biscuits were steaming on a round baking sheet on the table. The tops were golden brown. He grabbed one. It was hot, and he passed it from hand to hand.

"You'll ruin your breakfast, Mister Ravenswood."

He spoke loud and clear. "I have to compensate for two years of starving in the army." He bit into the hot flaky layers. "This ought to do it."

She smiled. "You have your mother's eyes."

"Do you remember my mother?"

"She was a beautiful woman and devoted to your father. Pity they died. Ravenswood could have been a happy place. So much death."

The old woman was alone in the kitchen. "Where is the rest of the staff, Mrs. Graves?"

"I'm it," she said. "Seymour fired the staff after Elijah Ravenswood died. He kept me on to cook, and once a week, a woman comes to do the laundry. Seymour said Ravenswood was in debt, and he had to cut expenses. But that didn't stop him from hiring handlers for the horses or keeping on the nurse."

"Nurse?"

"Sister Lucia took care of your grandfather." Mrs. Graves served scrambled eggs, crisp bacon, applesauce, and hot coffee. He had his choice of jams or butter for the biscuits.

No other plate had been set at the table. "Do you know where Seymour is?"

"He never rises this early." She poured more coffee into his cup.

Zach was used to military time. "I don't miss the sound of the drums waking me, but you won't catch me in bed once the sun is up."

Mrs. Graves took his dishes when he was done. "Do you know where my grandfather's belongings are? Seymour said they were on the fourth floor."

"Come." Mrs. Graves led the way along the servants' staircase to the fourth floor landing. The hallway was narrower and the rooms smaller than the second and third floor guest rooms. She opened a door and lit a lantern. She pointed to a small chest. "Seymour had me pack his belongings after the will was read."

The new will? Zach met her gaze. "Who read the will?"

"Mr. Kettler. He handles all the legal matters for the county."

He could imagine Seymour's reaction. "Is that when he fired the staff?"

"Yes, sir. Then he tore Elijah Ravenswood's room apart looking for a different will."

Seymour wasn't happy with his position. Zach carried the box of his grandfather's belongings to his room. Elijah's old hat was on top. He had worn the same style of fedora all his life. The beaded band had been made by a native woman. When a hat had become too battered, the beaded band was removed and sewn onto a new hat.

Zach compared the hat he had bought from Fred Kettler. It was the same style. He removed the band from his grandfather's hat and placed it on his. He'd carry on his grandfather's tradition.

Zach headed to the stables where the broodmares were kept. Most of the foals would be a couple months old and fully bonded with their mothers. They were his horses now. He wanted to become acquainted with them so he could identify them, and they wouldn't be skittish around humans.

He walked through the empty barn. A man was cleaning a stall. He filled a wheelbarrow with the wet straw and pushed it up a ramp created with a plank and dumped his load in the back of a wagon. The manure piles were kept away from the house. Once dried and decomposed, they were spread on the fields to grow hay and alfalfa.

The cleaned stalls were banked with straw, and the

water buckets were full. They were ready for the mares and foals to return and escape from the hottest part of the day. At least the horses weren't being neglected.

He passed through the opposite end of the barn and surveyed the mares and foals in the pasture. The young ones stayed close to their mothers, but in a couple of months they would bond with the other foals and be weaned before winter.

Chapter Seventeen

A lean man with a patch over his left eye stood by the gate that led from the pasture to the barn. His jacket was a bleached Union cavalry coat. He hadn't replaced the military buttons.

"I'm Zach Ravenswood." He extended his hand.

"Bryce Dawson." He removed a glove. The grip was firm, his palm calloused. His other hand rested on the handle of a revolver in a holster on his hip.

"Did you serve in the war, Bryce?"

"Cavalry rider."

"Which side?"

Bryce grinned. "Does it matter? I know horses."

Zach leaned against the fence rail in a casual pose. "What do you think about this year's foals?"

"Good potential. Ought to fetch a good price when you sell them."

"I won't be selling them for several years." Zach tugged on the brim of his hat. "Better get them out of this sun."

"I'm waiting for the lead mare to come closer," Bryce said. "I always like to take her in first."

"Phantom." Zach remembered the gray mare with a black mane and tail. "She's been around since I was a boy." He held out his hand for the halter and lead rope. "Do you mind if I lead her in?"

"You were in the Union cavalry?"

"Infantry."

Bryce snickered. "No one who owns a horse chooses to walk in a war."

Confederates provided their own horses. "I enlisted against my grandfather's wishes so no horse, but I remember how to care for them."

Bryce handed over the equipment.

Zach waited for Phantom to spot him and approached from the side to avoid the blind spot in front. He talked to her in a low, calm voice and held out his hand to allow her to sniff his scent. He took a position on the left side near her head and stroked her neck. He slipped the halter noseband in place and moved the crown behind her ears. He buckled the halter and led the mare to the gate. Her foal followed.

Bryce opened the gate. "She likes the second stall on the right. Don't forget the piss bucket."

Zach put her in the stall with her foal and looked for a bucket. He placed it under the mare in time to catch her urine. It kept the straw cleaner longer.

He carried the bucket outside the stall and locked the door.

Bryce escorted another mare inside with her foal tagging along.

When they were done, Bryce and Zach fed the mares and added water to the buckets. The man who had mucked the stalls boarded the wagon with a load of manure and wet straw. Bryce told the driver to wait and extended his hand to Zach. "I have to head to the barn by the lake. Lot of work on a place this size."

Zach shook his hand. "I appreciate your help."

"You're not a bad guy for a Yank."

"You're not a bad guy for a Reb."

"Seymour didn't ask the major what side we were on when he hired us," Bryce said. "Should we pack?"

Zach shook his head. "The war is over, but who's the major?"

"Vance Edwards," Bryce said. "He's been our commanding officer the past two years."

"I'd like to meet Vance. Ask him to join me for supper."

"I'm sure he'd like to meet you."

****

Zach spent the afternoon in the study reviewing the ledgers in which Seymour had recorded the income and expenses for Ravenswood. He could find nothing wrong in his accounting. Money had run short with the sale delayed, and Seymour had cut as many expenses as possible.

He closed the book and stared at the portrait of Elijah Ravenswood on the wall to his right.

The portrait had been painted shortly after Elijah's marriage to the fair Rachel Young of Philadelphia during happier times. Years later, Rachel had taken their son, Clayton, to her hometown amid rumors of Elijah's infidelity. She never returned to Ravenswood, but Clayton visited when he was older and arrived with his bride, Allison. His parents. They had moved to the cabin by the lake when Zach was a baby.

In the portrait Elijah had dark hair and whiskey-colored eyes, a far cry from the white haired frail man he had last seen. Zach bore little family resemblance. Clayton had resembled his fair mother, and Zach had inherited his father's blond hair and mother's sour apple green eyes.

Seymour burst through the door. He was

immaculately dressed, but his eyes were bloodshot and dark circles emphasized his deep-set eyes. "What are you doing in my study?"

Zach didn't move. With Seymour in front of him, he could study any resemblance to Elijah's portrait. He could see none. His grandfather possessed a strong square jaw and piercing eyes. Seymour had a weak chin and avoided eye contact. He couldn't confront Seymour about his illegitimacy without opening wounds of guilt and shame. The topic was better ignored. His remark was a different matter. When had Seymour claimed Elijah's study as his own? "Isn't there a room next door where you did your work?"

Seymour shoved his hands into his coat pockets. "I moved my belongings in here when Elijah took ill."

Zach lifted the ledger. "I've been reviewing the accounts. He opened the heavy leather-bound book and flipped to the last marked page. "I see you kept the entries current."

"It was my job to oversee the financial well-being of Ravenswood."

"I appreciate your diligence in my absence," Zach said. "I'd like a list of the domestic staff and any grooms you dismissed. I might want to rehire them."

"If you reviewed the numbers, the debt at Ravenswood won't allow any hiring." Seymour pointed to the bottom desk drawer. "May I?"

He removed a metal box and opened it. All the bills, receipts, and invoices were sorted by month. He placed a stack on the desk top. "These are the outstanding bills I haven't been able to pay."

Zach examined the invoices. Seymour had been telling the truth when he said the funds from last year had been depleted. The farm depended upon the annual sale of the mature horses to pay for feed, equipment, household necessities, and taxes. "Do you think we could attract enough buyers this late in the summer to sell the trained horses?"

Although he kept his head lowered, Zach could see a sly grin appear on Seymour's face.

"It's the only way to pay the debts, sir."

He paused, waiting for Seymour to admit to the sale. "I'll need to send out an advertisement."

"Allow me, sir," Seymour volunteered. "I have old ones I can use as a reference for the wording."

"I'll want to see the flier before you send it out," Zach called as Seymour left the room. He had given him an opportunity to confess, but instead Seymour had denied any plans.

He needed to clear his head. Zach saddled one of the geldings in the carriage house and rode to the family burial plot on the high ground near a grove of trees. The grave of his great-grandfather, Gabriel, was in the center with a large stone. On his left were markers for his two wives and on the right was the fresh grave of his grandfather, Elijah Ravenswood and an empty grave beside him. Rachel had been buried in Philadelphia. Zach's parents and brother Paxton were in another row with space for wives and children. He knelt by Pax's grave. "I made it home, Pax. I wish you had, too."

From the gravesite he could see the cabin by the lake. Memories of his parents and brother filled those walls. That was home. He surveyed the farm's fenced pastures, the run-in sheds, storage sheds, and training rings. Horses were separated by age. Yearlings were taught verbal commands and accustomed to a saddle blanket and long reins. The two and three-year olds were introduced to equipment and the weight of a rider. The four and five-year olds were saddled or hitched to a vehicle and taught to maneuver.

Training a horse properly involved hands-on work. Ethan and Harry would find plenty of work at Ravenswood, but to pay them he would need a profitable sale. Pay. There had been no entries for wages to Vance Edwards or his men. What arrangement had Seymour made with his hires?

****

Zach entered the dining room where Seymour was talking to the man he had recognized as military. The major. Vance removed his hat to reveal straight brown hair and a high forehead. A scar was visible near his hairline. His droopy mustache and goatee covered most of his face. His brown eyes were lined and tired. He extended his hand as Seymour introduced them. "This is Vance Edwards, Ravenswood's foreman."

"Bryce mentioned you," Zach said. "I'm glad you could join us."

Mrs. Graves served the food while Zach talked with Vance. Seymour concentrated on his meal, but slight reactions betrayed his interest in their conversation.

"Are you from the area, Vance?"

"No, I'm from Virginia."

"I toured the Virginia countryside during the war," Zach said. "What part are you from?"

"The western part."

Vance was cautious, but Zach remained friendly, hoping to learn more. "I was only as far west as Harper's Ferry. I served in the Twenty-ninth Ohio

Veteran Volunteer Infantry."

"I was in the cavalry."

"Who was your commanding officer?"

"John Mosby."

Zach didn't reply. Mosby's Raiders had formed shortly before Gettysburg. The Twenty-ninth Ohio had skirmished against them after the Confederate retreat. It didn't take the accomplished Southern riders long to gain a reputation for lightning strikes. Its small bands on horseback attacked and withdrew before a response by Union forces could be organized. The raiders disappeared into the countryside like ghosts on a foggy night.

"I'm afraid I was fighting in Tennessee and Georgia during your attacks in the Shenandoah Valley." He noted the .44 caliber Colt army revolver worn in Vance's belt holster. Mosby's raiders preferred revolvers to rifles. They were deadly shots as well as expert horsemen. His foreman was a dangerous man.

"If your reputation is true, my horses are in good hands," Zach said. "How many of the men working at Ravenswood are under your command?"

"Three."

Was he telling the truth? It didn't matter. Four trained soldiers was an army next to the old men who had worked for his grandfather and had remained. Would Ethan and Harry be walking into trouble or would they help to even the odds?

Mrs. Graves served chicken halves. "Will Sister Lucia be joining you?"

"No," Seymour said, "but she'll need a plate delivered to her room."

"I was looking forward to meeting Sister Lucia,"

Zach said. "I wanted to thank her for taking care of my grandfather."

"She isn't feeling well," Seymour said. "I'm allowing her to stay on until she's strong enough for the trip to the convent."

"I'm sorry to hear she isn't well. Of course she's welcomed to stay as long as necessary." Zach sliced into the tender meat. "Have you finished that flier we talked about? I'd like to start on repairs at Ravenswood, but I'll need funds. When do you think we can have the auction?"

"Vance thinks we can send the word out and have plenty of buyers by July 29."

"That soon?" It was the date on the flier Zach had seen at Fred Kettler's store. He turned to Vance. "How many horses do you think I'll be able to sell?"

"Two dozen," Seymour blurted before Vance could answer. His gaze was directed at the major, sharing a silent message.

"Are they all trained for saddle and harness?"

"They're all in fine shape and ready to be put to work," Vance said. "You should have a profitable sale."

"Do you figure a hundred fifty dollars each?"

"More," Vance said. "The demand for horses is high because of the conflict between the states."

"You mean the bloody war," Zach said. "It made me cry to see the horses crippled and slaughtered on the battlefields. The only thing more of a waste were the corpses of men left to rot in the sun while we marched to our next confrontation."

"Who did you serve under, Zach?"

"Who didn't I serve under? Hooker, Meade, Sherman."

"Sherman?"

"He took us for a march through Georgia." A flash of hatred sparked in Vance's eyes. "We fought on opposite sides, Vance. But we fought." He glanced at Seymour. "I respect *you*." The implication hung in the air.

"You were on the winning side," Vance said. "I bet you have more to show for your labors and sacrifices than the worthless paper money we were given."

"My Union wages will help pay the bills until the auction," Zach said. "And pay your salary if you and your men don't want to work for a Yankee."

"Your money is better than any I've seen these past years. Seymour promised our pay and a bonus after the sale."

He had an answer to the absence of wages in the ledger. Vance trusted Seymour more than he did.

Seymour surveyed the others. "The sale of the horses could net more than three thousand dollars."

"You'll be a rich man, Zach," Vance said. "I envy you. I have land but nothing to grow on it. I could take my pay in horses instead and start my own farm."

Zach stabbed the bird on his plate. "Take my advice, Vance, and raise chickens instead." He looked at Seymour. "From what I can decipher from the books, the sale of the horses barely pays the bills from one year to the next, isn't that right, Seymour?"

"Ravenswood is an expensive place to maintain, but your grandfather always paid his debts."

Zach took a bite and looked from one man to the other. "I plan to do the same."

Chapter Eighteen

The next day Zach joined Vance at the pasture holding the older horses that would be auctioned. He had brought a list of each horse with its description to match with the actual inventory. If Vance was interested in horses, he could be holding a few back from the sale to claim as his own.

Vance ordered Bryce to lead one horse forward at a time for Zach to examine and evaluate. It would have been nice to have Harry's expertise to help him, but he knew what flaws to look for that might lower the price.

Bryce escorted a tan mare with a brown mane into the training ring. "Here's a beauty, Major."

Zach examined her joints and conformation. Bryce led her around to detect any lameness or health problems. Zach rubbed her muzzle. "She's a gentle girl. What's her name?"

"Peaches."

Zach wrote a five next to Peaches' name with five being the highest for ranking the horses.

"Put her with the best ones," Vance said.

"Yes, Major." Bryce led the mare to a separate fenced area.

"The war is over. Why do your men still address you as major?"

"Habit," he said. "What rank were you, Zach?"

"I was a sergeant when I mustered out. I quit

college to join. My grandfather wasn't happy with my decision, but he eventually accepted it."

"My father's death prevented me from going to college, although I had little interest in books or studying. A degree wouldn't have helped to run the farm. I learned that through trial and error."

"That's how I plan to learn how to run Ravenswood," Zach said. "It would have been easier if my grandfather had lived long enough to pass on his knowledge."

"The future is unpredictable," Vance said. "I was going to be a gentleman of leisure. Then the war came. It took my wife and son." His brow furrowed and a sadness entered his voice. "The war took everything."

"Not quite," Zach said. "We survived."

"You're too young to have been married and lost the love of your life."

"But I am in love." Zach's voice betrayed his excitement. "I'm hoping she visits soon."

Vance showed a rare smile. "I look forward to meeting her."

They worked on evaluating the horses through Friday, but Zach was unable to gleam any more information out of Vance about any subterfuge plans Seymour might have designed. The evaluations appeared above board so why had Seymour lied about the original flier? It was time to confront him.

Zach found Seymour in the study seated at his grandfather's desk. He stood. "I was looking for the inventory for the sale."

"Vance has it. We finished rating the horses today. He made a list for the sale." Zach looked around the room, giving Seymour a chance to vacate the desk so he could claim it. Seymour finally took the hint and stood. Zach claimed his seat. "He made a copy for me. Would you like one as well?"

"No need. I trust Vance to prepare everything for the sale."

"It's remarkable how quickly you arranged the auction."

"I've done it in years past," Seymour said. "Elijah picked a date, and I would make the necessary contacts."

"But it took months to prepare." Zach withdrew a sales announcement from the top desk drawer and placed it on the desk. "The printers did a good job with the flier. Have all of them been sent out?"

"Yes, yesterday."

"Yesterday?" Zach asked. "Don't you mean a week ago?" He withdrew the one Fred had given him from his coat pocket and spread it next to the other. They were identical except for a notation on the new one that Zachary Ravenswood would conduct the sale. "Why the lie, Seymour?"

His face reddened, and he snatched Zach's flier and examined it. He returned the paper to the desk. "I was desperate, sir. The money was running out after your grandfather's death, and you had not sent word when you would be mustered out. As you can see for yourself, Ravenswood needed funds. As the family accountant, I arranged a sale and hoped you would return in time to supervise, which you did."

It was all plausible, but Zach's instincts cried otherwise. "I'm glad you took the initiative, Seymour. I hope that in the future you don't feel it necessary to lie to me."

He bowed his head. "Of course, sir. I am deeply ashamed of my behavior. I hope you will overlook it."

The contrition appeared natural to Seymour, like a part in a play, but was it sincere? He had seen plenty of soldiers give lip service to the officers only to insult them behind their backs. "Don't let it happen again." Zach placed both fliers in the drawer, but noted Seymour's clenched fists before he spun on his heels and departed.

Elijah had provided for Seymour, but he had never acknowledged him as his son. It was a secret that everyone knew but never spoke of. Most bastard children didn't inherit. The church said they were soulless and wouldn't allow them to be buried on hallowed ground. It was pulpit blackmail to discourage fornication and encourage marriage if a child resulted from a premarital union. Had Elijah included Seymour in his original will? Zach had always treated Seymour as an employee in his grandfather's home. Did he expect anything different?

Zach locked the door and stared at the portrait of his grandfather. Behind it was hidden a wall safe. During his furlough, Elijah had shared the combination, and he had memorized the numbers. He removed the contents and examined the papers. Zach sorted through the titles for the horses, separating those for the sale. He pulled the paperwork for the best horses and set them aside for his friends.

When he was done, instead of returning the papers to the safe, he slid his hand along the smooth bottom and pressed near the back. A spring latch opened to a secret compartment his grandfather had shown him. He placed the titles and his inventory list inside. They represented the wealth of Ravenswood.

Seymour knew the combination to the safe, but Elijah had assured him he did not know about the secret compartment. Even if he did, the papers were useless. Only Zach had the authority to sell his horses. He closed the secret compartment and placed the remaining papers and his grandfather's copy of the will in the safe's normal walls. The will would remind Seymour of his place at Ravenswood.

****

Zach was awakened by voices echoing from below in the study. How long had he been asleep? He threw the covers off and stood. The ropes were tight enough to barely creak with the shift in weight, but he hesitated. The voices continued. He moved to the window and brushed back the draperies. It was dark. Who would be in the study at night?

A woman's voice sharpened his hearing. It wasn't Mrs. Graves.

He pulled on trousers and a shirt and crept to the end of the hall. A tapestry covered the opening to a servants' staircase. It matched the one Mrs. Graves had used to reach the fourth floor, but with no other servants, this one wasn't used. A thick layer of dust covered the railings and steps. Zach descended to the first floor. Instead of proceeding to the central hallway, he turned a decorative flower on a sconce on the wall, which released the lock on a hidden panel. The door opened into the library. Pax had shown him the shortcut when they were boys. He brushed away the cobwebs and entered the darkened library.

The secret passage was one of the amusements his great-grandfather had created in the house. This one was for midnight reading excursions. The twin on the opposite side of the house provided a passage to the dining hall and whatever food could be found in the adjacent kitchen.

Zach crossed the empty library to the opposite wall. A swinging bookcase opened. A twin would gain him entry into the study, but he didn't want to reveal himself and listened to the voices, now clear and angry.

"What are you going to do?" the female demanded.

"Quiet, Lucia."

The nun?

"You said the boy wouldn't be a problem."

"He returned earlier than expected." Seymour cursed. "The boy has grown into a man. He wants to be lord of the manor."

"You should have destroyed the new will."

"Zachary has a lawyer. A good one. He didn't waste any time having the papers filed in court. Even if I could have found a copy of the old will, it wouldn't have done any good."

"But you're the rightful heir of Ravenswood," Lucia said. "Firstborn son of Elijah Ravenswood. Didn't he believe in free love?"

"My mother did and paid the consequences when Elijah married another so he could sire a legitimate heir."

"But you said you were going to inherit Ravenswood."

"I spent years turning Elijah against Clayton. After his summer visits, I would point out his endless flaws. When he married Allison, Elijah wanted Clayton to live here and raise his children at Ravenswood. I couldn't have that. I stole things from their room, made noises in the hall, and left a dead bird on their bed. Nothing scared them until Pax fell down the stairs. The tumble left him unharmed, but Allison was hysterical. I swore I didn't touch the boy, but Allison insisted upon moving to the cabin by the lake. I used their absence to manipulate the old man against them. Elijah had agreed to give me the house and half the property. If Zachary had followed his brother's fate, I would have had it all."

"So why did he change his will?" Lucia asked. "You're more equipped to run Ravenswood than any boy."

"When Zachary returned home for furlough in his uniform and tales of war, Elijah couldn't stop bragging about him. The old man set his dreams and hopes on his legitimate heir, and I was no longer needed. But I didn't think he would change the will. Tyler Montgomery said he was Zachary's lawyer and visited last summer. I thought it was about his military pay. It was a shock when Kettler read the new will that left me nothing."

"Nothing?"

"Oh, I have my position as Ravenswood's accountant," Seymour snarled. "Room and board and a pittance allowance while I serve the boy!"

A loud bang shook the dust from the books above him and showered down on his head. Zach pinched his nose to stop a sneeze. He didn't dare move or breathe. Seymour moved away, his footsteps pacing across the floor.

"He sent me to school, gave me a position in his household, filled me with dreams of running Ravenswood as my own," Seymour said. "Then he took it all away."

"Calm down, Seymour. The sale is going on as

planned."

"Exactly as planned."

The door opened, and footsteps echoed on the main staircase. Zach replayed the words in his head. Zach didn't recall the tricks Seymour had claimed to play on his family. But his parents had protected him and Pax by moving to the cabin by the lake. How far would Seymour have gone to gain control of Ravenswood? How far was he willing to go now?

Zach closed the bookcase and retreated to his room. Seymour considered him an ignorant boy, but his years as a soldier had trained him to survive. He would discover his enemy's weakness and exploit it.

If Seymour thought he could wrestle Ravenswood from his grasp, he was badly mistaken. He was the rightful owner. His grandfather had guaranteed Seymour a job, but he didn't specify what work. He might enjoy mucking stalls.

He wrote a letter to Tyler and reread the last paragraph.

I hope my gut feeling is wrong, but I have concerns after returning to Ravenswood. Seymour is upset about the new will. Does he have any claim on Ravenswood or its profits? Could you prepare a will leaving my property to Cassandra Beecher, Ethan Donovan, and Harry Herbruck if anything happens to me?

Zachary Ravenswood

The next day Zach looked for a horse to ride to town and found one saddled and tied to the barn with the mares and foals. Vance was writing in a ledger. When Zach approached, he shoved the book into his coat pocket.

"Are you making a list of the foals?"

Vance withdrew the ledger. "I was matching the foals to the mare."

Zach extended his hand. Vance handed him the ledger. Each mare was listed with a description and name. The foal was listed beneath with a description of coat color and any markings. "I'd like a copy when you're done."

"Of course." Vance moved to the next stall. "Did your grandfather sell broodmares?"

"Only those who stopped conceiving." Zach flipped through the book. "You have all the horses listed in here."

"I use it to track training and exercising."

He paused on a page. "These are the five-star horses. I'd like my friends to look at these."

"Your friends?" Vance looked toward the house.

"They haven't arrived yet," Zach said. "I expect them soon though."

"Does Seymour know about the visitors?"

"No." Zach closed the book and handed it to Vance. "Why would I have to inform the accountant about my guests?"

"I forgot you were in charge," Vance said. "Are your friends planning to buy a horse?"

"Several," Zach said. "And one of them is a veterinarian. He knows a five-star horse so don't think you'll fool him."

Vance stroked the side of his nose, which had been broken in the past. "I wouldn't think of doing anything deceptive."

Zach liked the fellow veteran, but trust needed to be earned. "Do you need the horse outside? I have a letter to post."

"I'm going into town. I'd be happy to take it."

Zach had plenty to do around Ravenswood. He handed Vance the letter.

His hand shook. "Tyler Montgomery."

"He's my lawyer. Do you know him?"

The hot anger passed from Vance's expression. "I hear he's a good one."

"He specializes in helping veterans."

Vance tucked the letter in his deep coat pocket. "I'll keep that in mind if I ever need help."

****

That night Zach was awakened by a noise. Was is Seymour and Sister Lucia? Tonight he would confront them and discover their plot. The room was lighter than normal. He pulled on his trousers and opened the draperies. Could it be morning already? A shattering of broken light burst into the sky. He had seen similar hungry flames after torching buildings across Georgia to destroy anything providing food and provisions for the enemy. Was it a memory? He opened his window. The wind carried the acrid smoke to his nostrils. The flames were real, scorching his tired brain with the truth. The crackling of timbers being devoured echoed across the night. The broodmare barn was on fire.

He stepped into his boots and dashed downstairs and out of the house. Spirals of dense smoke filled the sky above shooting flames. The building was fully engulfed, the ravished trusses fighting to support a collapsing roof. The heat on his flesh forced him to stop. Where were the workers to put the fire out? A figure stood in the light from the flames. Seymour. A smile creased his excited face. A smile?

Seymour pointed toward the barn and cried out,

"Save the mares!"

Zach stepped toward the inferno, but the heat stopped his advance. A sharp pain radiated on the back of his head, and he fell into darkness.

Chapter Nineteen

Cass glanced at the clock on the mantel. The three young men calling on her and Jules had been entertaining them with stories for two hours. Who would think being courted was so exhausting? Her mother had encouraged her to socialize in case the romance with Zach didn't result in matrimony. Cass didn't encourage the young men, but Jules enjoyed the attention and flirted and flattered the callers with ease.

No matter what her parents thought, she had given her heart to Zach. His invitation to visit Ravenswood had arrived soon after his departure. She was eager to make the trip, but her father needed convincing. He had said he would think about it. She had been on her best behavior, doing extra chores, and helping with any medical calls.

"Let's have a song." Jules clapped her hands, and Cass sat at the piano. The sheet music to Stephen Foster's "Beautiful Dreamer" was open and ready to play. It was her sister's favorite. Jules had a beautiful voice, and the three young men in the room were mesmerized by the lilting notes. The song also was a signal to their parents they were done entertaining and should make an appearance to bid the visitors farewell.

As Cass finished playing the last note, Sterling dutifully appeared in the parlor. He talked with each man, shook hands, and Jules distributed their hats. She claimed a vase of flowers. "I think I'll put these on the kitchen table so Mama can enjoy them."

"She'll like that," Cass said.

Harry remained behind. Cass had enlisted him to convince her father she should be allowed to travel to Ravenswood. "I won't be calling next Sunday," Harry said.

That was her cue. "Are you and Ethan going to Ravenswood?"

Harry fumbled with his top hat. "We plan to leave Tuesday."

Sterling frowned. "But the sale isn't until Saturday."

"It'll take a day to reach Ravenswood, and we want to look around before the sale," Harry said. "Zach said we would have first choice of the horses."

"We need a replacement for Blackie," Cass reminded her father.

"I'm sure Ethan and Harry can select a horse for us."

"But Zach invited me." Cass removed the flier from her skirt pocket. "We discussed the trip to Ravenswood last week, and you said you would consider it."

"I have. Three young men and a single lady is not a good combination."

"Ethan is my cousin, and Harry is my friend." She paced across the floor. "The four of us visited the sites in Washington City and helped rebuild the homes and barns in Virginia together. We're practically family."

"Your mother and I discussed it. A day trip would have been acceptable, but Ethan and Harry plan to spend several days at Ravenswood. That's a long time to spend in the company of a young man. Especially without adults present."

"Adults? Papa, you insult my friends," Cass said. "They spent years fighting in a war. If they don't qualify as men, then I don't know who does. I only spent a few months in Washington City, but I was there for the worst of the wounded. Double amputees. Men who were blind. Others horribly burned. And worst of all, I witnessed the murder of our president. Child? I could never be a child again, Papa. I know you mean well, but Zach, Harry, and Ethan would rather die than let any harm come to me."

Sterling sighed. "It should have become easier after letting the older girls go, but with only you and Juliet left, I'm more cautious than ever to part your company."

"I won't be gone forever, Papa," Cass said. "All my sisters have gone on adventures. You can't begrudge me this little one. What could happen on a farm?"

"It's safer than a battlefield," he agreed.

She was wearing him down. "What sort of horse would you like?"

"I'd feel better if buying a horse was the only reason you were going."

Cass danced around him. "Then I'm going?"

"To buy a horse." He entered his office and returned with a lockbox. "How much will you need?"

"A hundred and fifty dollars," Cass said. "I have some money if the horse is more."

"Perhaps I should allow you to marry Zachary first." He handed her the bills. "It would save me money."

She hugged him. "Thank you, Papa. And I promise to be on my best behavior."

"It's not your behavior I'm worried about." He looked at Harry. "Contact Ethan and tell him I wish to talk to him before you leave Tuesday. I'll have a word with you, now." He waited for Harry to enter his office. Sterling Beecher rarely lost his temper, but with six daughters, he had mastered intimidation when it came to young men. Poor Harry looked like a condemned man.

****

Harry Herbruck slapped the reins on the rump of the gelding pulling the double seat buggy that belonged to his parents. Cass sat beside him, and Ethan sat in the back with a basket of food beside him.

"Anything left?" Cass asked as Ethan searched the contents.

He handed her an apple. "This basket has seen some wear and tear."

"That basket has been on journeys with all my sisters except Jules."

"I remember it at Gettysburg with Jess." Ethan closed the lid. "Not much left. I hope we reach Ravenswood in time for the evening meal."

She turned forward and searched the empty road. "We must be getting close. Mr. Kettler said this was the road to Ravenswood, and it was only a couple of miles."

"I didn't think the trip from Darrow Falls would take so long," Harry said. "I hope this old buggy makes the trip home."

"Home?" Ethan leaned forward. "We have to reach Ravenswood first. I wonder if it's as grand as Zach bragged."

"If it is, I wouldn't mind offering my veterinarian services for the right price," Harry said.

"Working with horses can't be too different than driving mules," Ethan said.

Harry laughed. "You could always shovel manure."

Ethan slapped Harry with his hat.

Cass waited for their spat to end. "Don't you like working on the canal with Grandpa?"

"It's fun for a boy, but I need a serious job," Ethan said. "Besides, he's talking about retiring the *Irish Rose*."

"Jules and I barely had a chance to learn the ropes," Cass said.

"You're better on a horse than a boat," Ethan said. "Paddy still brags about you riding to fetch your Pa after Blake was shot."

"That's before I had to ride side saddle," Cass said. "Who created the rule women should ride perched on the side of a horse instead of astride? A crinoline makes even buggy riding a challenge." Cass adjusted her position. "I'll be grateful to sit on something that doesn't bounce with every hole and rut."

"If you're going to be one of *The Three Musketeers*, young d'Artagnan, you will need to learn to rough it."

Cass enjoyed Ethan's teasing. Most men treated her too seriously. "I love that story, but why do all the heroes have to be men?"

"You should write a story where the woman is the hero," Ethan said.

Harry frowned. "Don't women like being

rescued?"

Cass laughed. "Like Jess enjoyed being saved from Morgan?"

"And Blake was worried about her," Ethan said. "His best friend was the one in danger."

"Miss Jessie could always take care of herself, but Miss Cassie…"

"Are you saying I'm helpless?" Cass crossed her arms and stared at Harry. "I can take care of myself if not outnumbered."

Ethan leaned against the back of his seat. "I made a promise to my uncle to be a vigilant chaperone. Don't get any ideas, Harry, or we may not remain friends."

"I'm not the one you have to worry about," Harry said. "Besides, Dr. Beecher made me promise to treat Miss Cassie like my sister."

"That leaves Zach. Do you want us to have a talk with him about marrying you?"

Cass swirled in her seat and poked her finger in Ethan's direction. "Don't you dare! If Zach doesn't want to marry me, then that's his choice. I'm not begging." She settled in her seat. "Besides, my father expects me to purchase a horse not a husband. Zach promised me first pick."

"How many horses is Zach selling?" Ethan asked.

Cass unfolded the flier he had sent. "It doesn't say." She turned it over and read the note he had written.

"Please come to the sale with Ethan and Harry. I may need your help.

Zach"

"I expect to be paid for my help."

"Don't be a mercenary, Harry." Ethan chuckled.

"Don't you have any of your pay from the army left?"

"Ma took most of it."

"Why did you let her do that?"

"She's my ma." He patted his breast pocket. "She gave me enough for two horses."

"I don't see any sign of a horse let alone a farm," Ethan said. "Maybe Zach was ribbing us about being rich."

"Look there." Cass pointed at the split rail fence. Someone had cut the hay, and it was piled to dry. "Signs of civilization."

When Harry reached the top of a hill, he let out a whistle. "That's not a house. That's a castle."

"Zach was telling the truth about the grand house his great-grandfather built," Ethan said.

Ravens Roost loomed in front of them. The road was straight the remaining distance, allowing a visitor to view the symmetrical stone structure as it grew larger into view. Four turrets framed the corners of the medieval structure in the rolling hills of Ohio. "It's beautiful."

"Don't look too close," Harry said as they neared.

The lawn was overgrown, and weeds grew among the roses in front of the entrance. Several shutters were hanging loose or on the ground. Why would Zach neglect his beloved home?

Harry stopped the carriage in front of the steps leading to the doors, and Ethan helped Cass reach the ground. "What happened to the place?"

"We won't find out standing here." Cass climbed the stone steps and raised the iron ring on the double oak doors. She banged the knocker against the metal plate. The noise echoed inside.

Ethan's eyebrows bunched, and he frowned. "Sounds empty."

Cass rapped the knocker again, louder this time.

Ethan put his ear to the door. "I hear footsteps." He stepped back.

One of the massive doors creaked open. Framed in the doorway was an elderly woman dressed in black with a long white apron. Her white hair was topped with a black cap. "May I help you?" she shouted in a loud brittle voice.

"We're here to see Zach Ravenswood," Ethan said. "He's a friend of ours."

"Who?"

"Zach Ravenswood," Ethan repeated louder.

She wiped her hands on her apron. "Is Mister Ravenswood expecting you?"

"Yes," Cass said. "He wrote and invited us to visit." She showed her the note on the flier.

She shook her head and released a long sigh. "When did poor Mister Ravenswood write?"

"A week ago."

"Wait here." The woman closed the door without inviting them inside.

Cass turned to her companions. "That was rude."

"What's going on?" Ethan asked. "And why did she say *poor* Mister Ravenswood?"

The woman took her time returning. She barely opened the door. "Mister Ravenswood is ill and isn't receiving guests."

"But we traveled all this way," Cass said. "Isn't there going to be a sale?"

"A gale?" The old woman looked at the sky and pointed at a dark cloud. "It looks like rain."

"We were asking about the horse sale!" Ethan shouted.

"The sale is on Saturday. You should return then." She pushed the door closed. The clank of a bolt locking the entrance echoed from inside.

"Well, I never." Cass stared at the wooden barrier, willing it to open. "We're here to see Zach! If he's ill, I can help!" Her shouts were unanswered.

"Come on." Ethan pulled her away and helped her into the buggy.

She turned. A curtain moved. Someone was watching them.

Harry took the reins and glanced at the sky. "She was right about a storm. We better hurry to the village. We can try again tomorrow."

Ethan relaxed against the back seat. "Any of you buying that fairytale the old witch was telling?"

"No, but what can we do?" Harry asked. "We've been thrown out of the castle."

"Old witch," Cass repeated Ethan's description.

Harry slowed the horse. "Are you all right, Miss Cassie? You look pale."

"Don't you remember the fortune teller's prediction? I think Zach is in trouble, and he needs our help."

Ethan leaned forward. "How do you propose we sneak past the crazy doorkeeper?"

Cass grabbed the side as the buggy hit a rut and nearly threw her out. "Stop the carriage once we're past the hill." She turned to Harry. "You said the buggy was old. Do you mind if we break a wheel?"

"Break a wheel? How will we return home?"

Ethan held his hand out as raindrops fell. He

grinned. "A broken buggy and rain. They can't turn us away."

Harry stopped the buggy. "Better unhitch the horse first." Cass examined the spokes on the wheels of the buggy. "Any of these look like they could break apart?"

"This one is splintered." Ethan kicked the spoke until it broke. A few more kicks and the wheel was damaged enough to prevent travel.

Harry led the horse around. "They might make one of us ride the horse."

"Not in this rainstorm." Cass packed her gloves, reticule, and other loose belongings into her empty basket.

Harry and Ethan grabbed their bags, and they headed back to the house.

By the time they reached the door, the heavens had opened. The deluge thoroughly soaked them, and they shivered on the threshold. "No one could turn us away looking like this," Ethan said.

Cass rapped the knocker and waited for the woman to come. Her teeth chattered when she gave her explanation. "The wheel broke on the buggy."

"We would appreciate some shelter," Ethan added when the woman looked as if she wouldn't invite them inside.

"You can't drag the horse in."

"Where's the barn?" Harry shouted.

She pointed at the drive. "Behind the house."

Harry handed Ethan his bag and led the horse along the drive.

Ethan and Cass stepped into the foyer. Their wet clothes dripped on the stone floor. Their miserable appearance contrasted against the grandeur of the interior. The ceiling was two-stories high in the entranceway and framed by the double staircase leading to the second-floor landing. Dark wooden beams contrasted against the white plaster in a Tudor style of architect. A massive chandelier sparkled above them. "It's beautiful." Cass emphasized her compliment with a sneeze.

"My cousin needs to change into some dry clothes," Ethan said.

"I must inform Seymour of your return." The old woman left them dripping and shivering.

"She could have offered a towel." Ethan wrung out his coat, leaving a puddle on the floor.

Chapter Twenty

The old woman returned with a man dressed in black. The professionally tailored suit failed to hide the stoop in his shoulders, and the only thing paler than his skin was the starched paper collar on his shirt. His piercing eyes were surrounded by deep squint lines and showed no warmth. A salt and pepper mix colored what remained of his thinning hair. "I'm Seymour Woods."

"Pleasure to meet you." Cass extended her cold, wet hand.

He grunted, unwilling to touch it. "Mrs. Graves tells me you are seeking lodging. The village has a boarding house. Farther west are two inns near the railroad."

"We were invited to Ravens Roost by Zachary Ravenswood." Cass shivered. "He's our friend."

"He isn't receiving visitors."

Ethan stepped forward. He was taller than Seymour and had at least thirty pounds of muscle compared to the older man's frail frame. "I'm Ethan Donovan and this is my cousin, Cassandra Beecher. We traveled here with our friend, Harry Herbruck. Harry and I served with Zach in the Twenty-ninth Ohio. We were turned away by your housekeeper." Ethan turned toward Mrs. Graves. "As you can see, we were caught in the rain after a wheel on our buggy broke."

"We won't be turned away again," Cass said.

"You're an impertinent young woman," Seymour said.

"Only when faced with rudeness." She squared her shoulders. "Zach is a dear friend. What seems to be the nature of his illness?"

A sinister smile crept onto Seymour's face. "Zachary was horribly disfigured in a fire."

Cass covered her mouth. It couldn't be true. "How?"

"One of the barns caught on fire," he said. "Zachary rushed in to save the horses. He's lucky to be alive."

"Has a doctor seen him?"

"Of course. Now he's under the care of Sister Lucia."

A nun? "Is she experienced? Did she help soldiers during the war?"

A dark eyebrow rose on Seymour's face. "She provided comfort to many soldiers during the war."

Cass wasn't convinced. "I would like to see Zach."

"Sister Lucia is his nurse," Seymour said. "It will be her decision whether he is well enough to receive any visitors. It's important Zachary remain calm."

"We wouldn't want to make matters worse." Cass steadied her voice. "We'll follow orders." To a point.

Seymour turned to the old woman. "Mrs. Graves, fetch some towels for our hapless travelers."

The woman looked around the room. "Fowls?"

"Towels, you batty old woman."

Mrs. Graves nodded and climbed the stairs to the second floor.

"Zach invited us." Cass showed him the flier.

He snatched it from her hand. "When did you

receive this?"

"Recently." He looked disturbed. What was wrong with the flier?

Harry opened the front door and stepped inside. "Are we staying?"

"We're staying," Cass said before Seymour could argue.

Mrs. Graves returned and distributed the towels.

"It seems we have guests." Seymour tapped Mrs. Graves on the shoulder. "Prepare a couple of rooms."

"Brooms?"

"Rooms, you daft woman. Rooms for our *guests*!"

She looked confused. "I'm the cook, not the maid."

Seymour's voice raised to a high pitch and his face reddened. "You won't be either if you don't do what I say."

"All these strangers in the house." She shook her head. "Where shall I put them?"

"Near Zachary if they can endure his screams." The briefest smile appeared on Seymour's thin lips. He had enjoyed shocking them.

Mrs. Graves climbed the staircase at a tortoise pace while they waited below.

Cass refused to be intimidated by Seymour who was studying his unwelcomed guests. "When was the fire?"

"Saturday night. We lost the barn with the broodmares and foals."

We? "Zach must have been devastated."

"He braved the flames to save them, but the structure was compromised," Seymour said. "That's how he was burned."

Cass rubbed her hair with the towel. "Poor Zach."

Seymour stared at her, his eyes lingering on the wet, clinging fabric of her gown. "You're the woman in the photograph Zachary keeps on his dresser. How long have you known him?"

Cass draped the towel over her shoulders and breasts. "Zach and I corresponded for the past year. We spent time together in Washington City after he broke his leg."

"He broke his leg?"

Cass swiped a drip falling from her forehead. "It seems you know little about *Zachary*."

He snorted. "I'm not his grandfather. We did not correspond."

"Is that why it took so long to notify him about his grandfather's death?"

"I sent word as soon as possible. It wasn't my fault he couldn't return home for the funeral. Fate can't be avoided."

"I don't believe that," Cass said. "Oedipus Rex would never have killed his father or married his mother if his parents had ignored the seer's prediction. Their fear caused the future they had hoped to avoid."

Seymour was surprised by her statement. "You know the classics?"

"My father enjoys them. So does Zach."

His eyes narrowed. "How did their fear fulfill the seer's words?"

"They tried to get rid of Oedipus thinking it would prevent the prediction, but because his mother and father were strangers when he met them, he fulfilled the prophecy," she said. "Ignorance can cause us to stumble, but knowledge aids us in making the right decisions in life."

Seymour's stern visage cracked into a hostile sneer. "Then I'm lucky I make my own fate."

Cass met his hostile gaze. "So do I."

"I'll see what is keeping Mrs. Graves." He ascended the steps while they remained in the foyer.

"Who's Oedipus Rex?" Ethan asked. "I never met him."

Cass shivered. "A dead Greek."

"Cousin, that's insane."

"This place is insane," Harry said. "Didn't Zach mention a ghost haunting Ravenswood? I don't know who's scarier, Seymour or Mrs. Graves."

The elderly servant stood at the top of the stairs. "Your rooms are ready." Her message echoed past the foyer and into the open hall beyond.

They gathered their belongings and climbed the marble steps. Cass cringed at her reflection in a large mirror on the wall. She looked like a drowned cat. A crack of thunder echoed outside the stone walls, and a flash of lightning lit the sectioned windows flanking the door. The summer rainstorm had transformed into a violent downpour that turned the sunshine into darkness.

Mrs. Graves waved a candle at the top of the landing. "This way, children."

Harry scowled. "Is she blind, too?"

Cass ran her finger along a layer of dust on the bottom of a portrait frame hanging on the wall. Mrs. Graves had stated she was the cook. What had happened to the maid? Cobwebs had formed between the balusters on the staircase. How long had cleaning been neglected?

"Ethan looked around. "What has Zach gotten us

into?"

"Whatever it is, Zach needs our help more than we imagined." Cass paused on the landing and looked around. Ravenswood had been grand at one time, but carpets were worn and floors needed polished. She turned toward the master bedroom, centered between the twin staircases.

"That room belonged to the late Elijah Ravenswood," Mrs. Graves said.

"Where is Zach's room?"

"Down the hall." Mrs. Graves led the way. "He is staying in the room he occupied as a boy."

"Did you know Zach as a boy?"

"Yes. My husband and I worked here for forty years. He died two years ago, but Elijah said I had a job as long as I wanted." She made a sour face. "Seymour is of a different mind. He fired all the other servants, but I wouldn't go." She stopped at the first room on the right and opened the door. "You two gentlemen can share this room." She lit a candle resting on a table near the door.

"Share?" Ethan asked. "Who's in the room across the hall?"

"That was Paxton's room. Zachary's brother. It's been closed since his death. So much sorrow these last few years and now the young master. A curse hangs over the house of Ravenswood." She nodded toward the room at the end of the hall. "Mister Ravenswood is in the room on the end. The young lady can stay in the room across from his."

"Thank you." Cass grabbed her bag from Harry, who had carried it. "I need to change into dry clothes."

Mrs. Graves opened the door for her and lit a

candle by the bed. "I hope you'll be comfortable in here."

Cass dropped her bag on the bed. A scream echoed from the nearby room. "Zach!" She ran across the hallway and opened the door. Seymour blocked her entry.

"Sister Lucia is giving Zachary his treatment. You cannot interrupt."

"Treatment?" Cass looked at Harry and Ethan who had rushed into the hallway. "I want to see him."

"I know you won't heed my warning, but it would be better to remember him the way he was," Seymour warned. "Burn victims are badly scarred."

Cass pursed her lips. "I'm not the type of woman to faint."

"She isn't," Ethan confirmed.

"Let me see if Sister Lucia will allow a visitor." Seymour closed the door.

Cass turned to the two men. "I'm getting tired of people slamming doors in my face."

A crash of thunder shook the house. Harry jumped and looked around. "It might be better to wait to see him."

"Harry, I've seen you stare into the face of charging Rebs during a battle. Why are you afraid of a little thunder and lightning?"

"It sounds too much like cannon fire," Harry said. "Death always follows."

Ethan put his arm around him. "Not this time."

"You're braver than me," Harry said. "I don't know if I could face seeing Zach in pain. Remember when he broke his leg? It was bent in the middle, and his foot was turned the wrong way." Harry closed his eyes and looked nauseated.

"Have you forgotten our pledge? All for one and one for all," Ethan reminded them.

"Instead of Cardinal Richelieu and Milady, we have Seymour and Sister Lucia," Cass said.

Harry squared his shoulders when the door opened. Seymour blocked the entrance. "You don't want to see him."

"Stand aside," Ethan ordered.

Seymour moved back. "I warned you."

They entered the darkened room.

"We keep the curtains drawn for his comfort." Seymour pulled aside the draperies. A glimmer of light penetrated the thick rain clouds casting objects in shadows. A flash of lightning illuminated the room for a moment followed by a crash of thunder.

A single candle cast an eerie glow on a female figure standing by the bed. She was dressed in the white robe and wimple of a nun. She wore white gloves on her hands. It was difficult to determine her age with only her face exposed, but her almond-shaped eyes and full lips gave her an exotic look as the flame flickered.

Cass stepped into the dim light and stared at the man on the bed. How could this be Zach? His face, arms, and chest were bandaged. A blanket covered the rest of his body. Ropes were wrapped around his wrist and attached to the bed post behind him, holding his arms stretched over his head. "Why is he tied like that?"

"It's to prevent him from harming himself," Sister Lucia said. "If he was free, he would tear at his skin."

Cass reached for his bandaged arm.

"Don't touch him!" Sister Lucia raised her glove-covered hands. "The bandages are medicated for the burns."

Sister Lucia's shout startled her, and Cass jerked her arm away from the nun and brushed her bare forearm against the oily bandages.

Zach screamed. "I'm on fire! Help, I'm burning up." He struggled against the ropes and thrashed his legs and hips side to side to break free.

"Zach, Zach," Cass called. "It's me. Harry and Ethan are here. We've come to help."

He opened his sour apple green eyes wide with pain and fear. Swollen lips exposed between the bandages covering his face moved in hoarse words. "I'm going mad." He screamed. "My flesh is on fire. Stop it!" He fought the restraints.

"Do something," Cass pleaded.

Sister Lucia took a spoonful of powder from a glass bottle and mixed it with honey in a bowl. She placed a spoonful of the mixture on his lips. "Take this."

"What are you giving him?"

"Opium and honey. It eases the pain." The nun offered him the remainder of the mixture and a drink of water.

Zach relaxed as the opium dulled his senses.

Ethan touched her shoulder. "We better let him rest."

Unable to speak without bursting into tears, Cass nodded. She followed the boys out of the room.

Mrs. Graves had waited outside. "Poor Mister Ravenswood."

Seymour joined them in the hall. "Now you understand why I didn't want you to see him."

"He needs us more than ever," Cass said. "I'm a nurse. I can help."

"Sister Lucia will ask for your help if she needs it," he said. "Treatments for burns can be painful, and you are too emotionally attached to Zachary to care for his injuries."

Cass straightened her shoulders. "Do I look hysterical?"

Instead of answering, Seymour turned to Mrs. Graves. "Supper will be at six o'clock. Have the table set for five."

Mrs. Graves looked around. "A hive?"

"Five." Seymour showed her the fingers of his hand. "Sister Lucia will be joining us."

"She always takes her meals in her room," Mrs. Graves announced.

"Not tonight." He waited until Mrs. Graves left. "Sister Lucia has been spending her evenings in prayer. Things have been stressful with Elijah Ravenswood's death and Zachary's unfortunate condition."

"Then she should welcome my help," Cass said.

Seymour's stern visage revealed no emotions. "I hope you won't be tempted to visit your friend without Sister Lucia or my supervision." He strode away, his coattails flapping behind him like a bat in flight.

Ethan raised an eyebrow and stared at Cass. "His orders fell on deaf ears, and I don't mean Mrs. Graves'."

"He wants us gone, which is why we're staying." Cass headed for her room.

"What can you do for Zach?" Harry asked.

Cass paused. "I have some herbs and poultices for burns. They would be better than dosing him with opium."

"Some wounded men became addicted to that stuff," Harry said. "Do you think Zach is?"

"Not yet, but if a patient is on it long enough, they can't stop using it," Cass said. "Hospitals had to guard the supplies of opium, laudanum, and morphine to prevent patients from breaking in and stealing it."

Ethan touched her cheek. "Are you sure you're all right, Cousin?"

Tears were hot, brimming on her lower lashes, but she hadn't cried in front of anyone. She would if she didn't leave them. She nodded, turned, and disappeared into her room.

Chapter Twenty-One

Alone, Cass leaned against the closed door and allowed hot tears to burn wet trails on her cold cheeks. "Zach, poor Zach." She went to her bag and removed a small photo album and flipped through pages of her family until she reached the one of Zach taken at Matthew Brady's studio. She traced the outline of his uniform and studied his handsome face. She didn't need Madame Cherie to tell her what to do. She was determined to help Zach through this dark time in his life. And no matter how badly he was scarred and deformed, she would stand by him. She loved him.

She lifted her bell-shaped sleeve and examined her arm where it had brushed against Zach's bandaged arm. What sort of burn medicine couldn't be touched? She removed the wide belt holding the thin summer bodice in place and untied the matching skirt. Both were soaked. She wrung the excessive water out over a tin tub and spread them across the dressing screen hiding the washstand and chamber pot.

She removed her shoes and stockings. The bottom of her crinoline and petticoat were damp. She had a spare petticoat, but she would have to wear the bell-shaped crinoline underneath her formal gown for supper.

After pouring water from the pitcher into a bowl, she washed her tear-streaked face. She would need to

219

be strong for Zach.

She removed her best dress from her travel bag. The green silk she had worn to Ford's Theater was wrinkled, but she didn't have time to heat an iron. She had chosen the gown for Zach's enjoyment in spite of the tragedy of Lincoln's assassination associated with it. She had hoped for an opportunity for Zach to hold her in his arms for a dance. Now, that might never happen. What wicked force kept preventing her and Zach from pursuing their romance and ultimate happiness?

She put the gown over a chair and chose another. It wasn't as nice, but the lavender gown with white trim would be appropriate for the evening. Dry stockings and a pair of dress slippers took away the chill in the air. She undid her braids, brushed the long dark tresses, and arranged her hair in a chignon at the base of her neck. The loose style would allow her thick hair to dry. She unpacked the remaining items in her bag and opened the window to dispel the staleness hanging in the air. When was the last time the room had been occupied?

She removed a lacy shawl from her bag and draped it around her shoulders and tucked it across her bosom. She didn't like the way Seymour had stared at her wet dress clinging to her body.

Someone knocked. She opened the door. Ethan and Harry had changed into their Sunday best. Whether in their uniforms, work clothes, or formal wear, she had no reason to be ashamed of their company. "You look handsome."

Both men offered their arms. She paused by Zach's door.

"He's quiet," Ethan said. "Let him sleep for now."

She nodded in agreement. She would tend to Zach when Seymour and Sister Lucia were otherwise occupied. They descended the staircase.

The grand dining hall had been designed for entertaining a large number of guests. A long mahogany table reflected the chandelier's lights in its polished surface. Seymour sat at the head of the table with Sister Lucia seated to his right. Cass was placed to his left with Harry next to her and Ethan next to the nun.

Mrs. Graves placed a bottle of vinegar and oil on the table after placing bowls of fresh garden greens in front of each guest. She placed a large basket of freshly baked bread in front of Seymour. A sweet aroma rose with the steam. Sister Lucia grabbed a thick slice. She reached for a crock with her knife and harvested a dab of creamy butter.

Harry lifted his clasped hands. "I hope you don't mind if I say grace?"

She placed her knife coated with butter and the bread slice on her plate. "Of course not." She bowed her head.

Harry prayed, and they ate.

Supper consisted of thick beef slices au jus, potatoes, and raw celery and carrots. Cass picked at her food, her thoughts on Zach upstairs.

The storm continued outside with flashes of lightning outlining the intricate leaded glass in the top panels of the tall windows. The patterns burst into colorful images. A knight on a charging horse decorated the window opposite her. "That's beautiful."

"Gabriel Ravenswood was obsessed with the

medieval period," Seymour remarked.

"Gabriel?" Harry asked.

"Zachary's great-grandfather. He built Ravens Roost complete with drafts and strange noises. I hope the storm doesn't keep you awake."

"I like storms," Cass said.

"I don't," Harry interrupted. "Sounds too much like a battle."

"If you have any nightmares, you're sleeping on the floor," Ethan said. "I don't need you thrashing about next to me. I still have bruises from sharing a tent."

"I enjoy when the storm ends, and the sunshine breaks through the clouds," Cass said. "Especially if there's a rainbow. It's symbolic of the promise that good triumphs over evil."

"You are young or you wouldn't believe in such foolish idealism," Sister Lucia said.

"That's an odd remark from a nun."

The woman stared across the table. "I have seen much in life to make me doubt man, but I have never lost faith in God."

"A lot of nuns took care of the wounded during the war," Ethan said. "Did you?"

"I was given the gift of medicine." Sister Lucia met the gaze of Seymour. "I took care of the men who requested my skills."

Ethan reached for the last slice of bread. "Zach was lucky you were here when he was burned."

"Indeed. Men with such severe burns often die from them."

Cass inhaled. She couldn't read the nun's expression. Was her remark meant to prepare her if

Zach's conditioned worsened or a boast of her skill?

"If the weather clears, I'll have my hired man repair your buggy, and you can be on your way," Seymour said.

"We would prefer to stay at Ravens Roost," Cass said, not inviting argument. "Zach promised we could have our choice of horses before the buyers bid."

"You plan on purchasing a horse?"

"Three or four horses," Ethan corrected. "You haven't canceled the sale because of the fire, have you?"

"No. The sale is Saturday."

"Did you lose any horses besides the mares and foals?" Cass asked.

"No, but losing the mares is a huge loss," Seymour said. "Without the foals, the future of Ravenswood is in jeopardy."

"Then Zach should welcome our money," Ethan said. "And I guarantee he won't mind his friends staying to help him recover."

"Physically and financially," Cass added.

Seymour clenched his jaw but didn't argue. "I'll have one of my men show you the horses when the weather clears."

Supper ended efficiently, and Mrs. Graves provided lit candles against the darkness the storm had brought. Seymour and Sister Lucia led the way upstairs but turned left at the landing.

Cass bid them goodnight. They disappeared down the dark hall, a single candle disappearing into one room and then the last light going into an adjoining room. She turned to Ethan and Harry. "Did anyone think it odd Sister Lucia didn't say grace?"

Harry led the way to their rooms. "She was ready to bite into her bread."

"There's a lot of different orders for nuns," Ethan said, "but all of them pray."

"She doesn't wear a cross or carry a rosary, either," Harry added. "Plenty of nuns took care of the wounded, and they always had their hardware handy to pray over a dying soldier."

"I could smell perfume, and it wasn't lilac like you wear," Ethan said to Cass. "And it looked like powder on her face."

"Maybe she's hiding scars," Harry said.

"She's hiding something." Cass stopped at their door. "Then we agree to help Zach."

"Of course." Ethan looked at Harry. "But what are we going to do?"

"We've already taken the first step," she said. "We're staying here until we have some answers."

****

Zach couldn't remember when he had been awake or how long he had been asleep. The days and nights had blended into a timeless struggle against the torturous pain. As soon as his head cleared, the torment would begin. The urge to scratch and dig at whatever was burning on his skin would build beyond endurance. He struggled against the ropes preventing his hands to find release, and he would scream for help. Voices, questions, and the mixture of bitter powder with sweet honey eased his anguish and allowed him to drift into a cloudy twilight. He had dreamed of Cass. She had floated before him in a halo of light, reaching for him, calling his name, but it had been an illusion.

Cass wasn't here. She was safe at home, away from

the dangers of Ravenswood. Someone had hit him over the head. Or had it been a timber from the burning barn? His memories had melded into a confusing jumble of events. He was burned. His skin was aflame with blazing pain. He tugged against the ropes. The itching was driving him mad. He cried out as the irritation increased to an unbearable level.

The door opened, and two people entered. Seymour placed a candle on the small table beside the bed. Next to him was a nun. Sister Lucia. He had seen her before. She gave him medicine to stop his pain. "Help me!" Zach thrashed about. "My arms are on fire. I'm burning!"

He rolled toward Seymour.

"Don't let him touch you!" Sister Lucia shrieked.

Seymour jerked away.

"I soaked the bandages thoroughly. You don't want to come in contact with them." Sister Lucia grabbed a bottle and spoon. He relaxed in anticipation of the medicine that would take him away from the torture.

Seymour stopped her. "Not until he tells me what I need to know."

"He should be lucid enough to answer your questions."

"Are you in pain, Zachary?"

Why was he asking such a foolish question? The unreachable prickling was maddening. Zach struggled against the ropes, but he couldn't reach the bandages to scratch away the incessant itching. "Help me."

"Sister Lucia will give you the opium, Zachary, if you answer my questions."

"What do you want to know?"

Seymour's shadow blocked the light. "Tell me

where you've hidden the titles to the horses."

The titles? He had asked the question before. He had answered honestly. "They're in the safe."

"I looked. They're not in the safe." Seymour was angry.

"Yes, they are."

"I can't make the pain go away if you lie to me, you stubborn boy. Where have you hidden the papers?"

"In the safe! In the safe!" Why didn't Seymour believe him?

"He'll wake the others," Sister Lucia warned.

"Tell me the truth, or she won't give you the medicine."

Zach fought the ropes, banging his hands on the headboard. "Give it to me, or I'll die!"

"He's awakened someone," Sister Lucia said.

Seymour moved toward the door. "Give him the opium."

A woman's voice at the door sounded like Cass. But that was impossible. Lucia blocked the view. "You need to tell him where the papers are if you know what is best for you."

She waved the spoon before him. He opened his mouth and begged for the medicine. She gave him a glass of water to wash it down. He closed his eyes and let the dullness take control of his body and mind as he sunk into dark painless oblivion.

****

The sun was shining in the morning. Cass washed her face and brushed her hair to rid it of any tangles. She braided three sections on each side of her head and pinned them into buns in a style favored by her German grandmother.

She chose a lightweight day dress and began the arduous task of dressing. Lacing a corset without the aid of one of her sisters wasn't impossible, but it required pulling the laces behind her until the form-fitting frame was snug. Without the proper undergarments, the sheer fabric of her summer gown would be immodest. She secured the corset cover and slipped the yellow flowered gown over her petticoat and arranged the wide straps over her shoulders and across the bodice. A black belt hooked in front to secure the straps.

She slipped on her boots. The ground would be wet, and she planned to explore Ravenswood and view a few horses. But first she would check on Zach. She had been awakened by his screams and opened the door to gain entry, but Seymour had blocked her path. After listening for them to leave, she had entered the bedroom, but Zach was asleep. She had returned to her bed and a fitful sleep.

Zach's room was well lit with the morning sun streaming through the open curtains. His personal belongings were placed on the dresser and included her framed photograph next to a stack of letters she had written to him while he was marching through Georgia and the Carolinas. Seymour had mentioned her as the woman in the photograph.

She examined her letters. Had Seymour read them? They were private. Her words of life in Ohio must have seemed dull compared to the battles Zach encountered as he marched across the South. But he had saved her correspondence, their battered edges testimony to their value.

"The papers are in the safe," he muttered. "Give

me some medicine for the pain." He snorted and fell asleep.

"You poor baby. Her arm brushed against the oily bandages, but she didn't jerk away. Whatever the medicine, it couldn't harm her.

His hair was bleached from the sun and fell over the bandages covering his face. She brushed the long locks back. The silky strands slid through her fingers.

The bandages on his face were dry. Why weren't they medicated? His eyelids were intact, and his long lashes contrasted against a strip of cloth across his nose and cheeks. How badly was he scarred? He had been extremely handsome with his penetrating green eyes and soft, tender smile. Could she hide her repulsion if the fire horribly disfigured him?

The door opened, and Mrs. Graves backed into the room with a tray in her hands. She turned and gasped. "Oh, it's you, Miss Beecher. I was afraid it was Sister Lucia."

Cass took the tray from her hands. "Why were you afraid I was Sister Lucia?"

"She doesn't like me feeding Mister Ravenswood."

"He has to eat to maintain his strength."

"Not according to Sister Lucia. She said he needs to purge his system of poisons."

"Aren't you afraid you'll be fired if they find out you've been feeding him?"

"Seymour and Sister Lucia are like bats. They're awake all night and sleep during the day."

"They were in his room last night. Seymour blocked me from entering."

"They keep him drugged," Mrs. Graves said. "He's most lucid in the morning if I can rouse him." She uncovered scrambled eggs and biscuits. "The smell of food usually does it."

"He always had a healthy appetite."

She placed the tray on the table by the bed. "Your two friends didn't leave much on the plate."

"They've already eaten?"

Mrs. Graves pointed toward the window. "They're outside poking around the burnt remains of the barn."

Cass studied the old woman. "What do you know about the fire?"

"I was asleep on the fourth floor in the front," Mrs. Graves said. "I didn't know about the fire until morning. By then Sister Lucia was caring for Mister Ravenswood."

"Did you see Zach's burns?"

"No, Miss Beecher, but Sister Lucia said they were bad. She had him bandaged by the time I was let in the room. I feed him and take care of his toilette."

"He doesn't seem to be waking." Cass placed her hand on his chest. It rose steadily. "I wonder how much opium she gave him."

"Is it a bad thing?"

"Yes," Cass said. "He'll crave more and more."

"Why don't you join your friends? I'll feed him when he wakes."

"Don't tell him we're here if he doesn't remember," Cass said. "I don't want him to order us away."

"I understand. He doesn't realize how much he needs you and your friends."

"It's good to know he has one more." The food on the tray made her stomach growl. "Any more biscuits downstairs?"

"In the kitchen. I saved you a couple."

Cass paused by the door. "Mrs. Graves, aren't you deaf?"

"I am in this ear." She pointed to her left ear. "I hear fine out of the other."

Cass laughed. "I take it you're not fond of Seymour."

"That one was always sour and spoiled. Elijah Ravenswood sent him to school and gave him a job, but he was never grateful. Always wanted more for nothing. Always giving Elijah advice."

"What advice?"

"To send the boys away to school, away from Ravenswood even though Clayton and Allison hired a tutor."

Seymour may have thought he was clever to send Pax and Zach to Western Reserve Preparatory School and College, but Zach would not have gone to war and won his grandfather's approval otherwise. It was similar to *Oedipus Rex*. Seymour's plans had reaped the opposite effect.

"Zach said he lived in a cabin by the lake. Does anyone live there now?"

"The buyers stay there for the sale." She snorted. "They leave mud everywhere. Allison wouldn't approve. She made it a real home." Mrs. Graves waved her arm. "Allison attempted to make this place a home, but Seymour blocked her attempts. Ravens Roost was a showplace to impress guests."

"It does that."

"You eat and join your friends," Mrs. Graves said. "I'll take care of Mister Ravenswood."

Chapter Twenty-Two

Cass hurried downstairs and ate a quick breakfast. She tied her bonnet and opened the glass paneled doors at the back of the main room. A carriage building was to the left at the end of the drive. To the right was the blackened remains of the stable. She headed toward the ruins. Most of the building was gone with a section of two walls and a few rafters on the far side standing to form a shadow of the former structure. "This is awful."

Ethan and Harry kicked around the rain-soaked ashes, ignoring her.

"Why are you walking in that mess?"

Harry kicked at a clump of dirty ash. "We're searching for something."

She placed her hands on her hips. "I hope it's not the remains of the horses."

Ethan and Harry exchanged funny looks.

She stepped closer but remained outside the ashes. "What did you find?"

"It's what we didn't find," Harry said. "No horseshoes."

Horseshoes? "What do you mean?"

"We walked through the ashes and found nothing." Harry wiped his boots on the damp grass. "No bones, no animal fat, no horseshoes. There were no horses in the barn when it burned."

"But Seymour said all the mares and foals

231

perished."

"He lied."

"Then why burn the barn?"

Ethan cleaned his boots. "You tell us, Cousin."

What did it mean? "If the horses weren't killed in the fire, where are they?"

Ethan put his hat on. "How big did Zach say this place is?"

"Eight hundred acres." She reached into her pocket. "Zach drew me a map."

Harry studied the basic drawing. "Plenty of places to hide something."

"We want to buy horses," Ethan said. "Why don't we look at the merchandise?"

Cass looked around. "Do you plan to walk?"

"We've been walking everywhere for years, but if you need a buggy, we could find one," Harry said.

"Don't worry about me." She lifted the front of her skirt to escape the mud and led the way along the well-worn road leading away from the barn's remains.

They had walked half a mile along the road when a wagon approached and blocked their path. A man with a patch over one eye stared at them. "Who are you?"

"We're guests of Zach Ravenswood," Ethan announced.

"Where can we find the horses that are for sale?" Cass asked.

The man removed his hat. His black hair reached his coat collar, and his beard covered the lower half of his face. "Are you looking to buy a horse, miss?"

Her sisters had been shining examples of how to charm information out of a man. Cass smiled, and her voice took on a silky texture. "I'm Miss Cassandra

Beecher, and this is my cousin Ethan Donovan and my friend, Harry Herbruck. Zach promised we could have first pick of the horses for sale. I hope there's a pretty mare available."

"Not as pretty as you, miss." He leaned forward. "I'm Bryce Dawson. I'd be happy to give you a ride. Let me turn the wagon around, and I'll come back for you."

"That would be so kind," Cass said.

He nodded and urged the team forward.

Harry and Ethan stared at her as if she had grown horns. "What? Don't you want his help?"

"How did you do that?" Harry asked.

"It's called charm. You two should cultivate some if you plan to find out what Seymour is plotting."

Ethan shook his head. "I don't think Seymour would tell the hired help his plan."

"Then the horses will tell us something."

"Cousin." Ethan laughed. "Horses don't talk."

"Neither do horseshoes, but the absence of them speaks volumes about the barn fire."

Harry's eyes widened. "What do you think is going on here?"

"I don't know, but until we do, don't make any decisions about a horse," Cass said. "We don't want to give Seymour an excuse to send us packing."

Bryce returned with the wagon and helped Cass climb to the bench seat. "I hope you don't mind riding in the wagon."

"I'm a farm girl," Cass said. "I won't bruise."

"We don't mind walking, but we won't refuse a ride when it's offered," Harry said as he and Ethan climbed in the back.

Bryce slapped the reins against the horses' rumps. "You Yanks serve with Zach Ravenswood?"

"We were in the Twenty-ninth Ohio Veteran Volunteer Infantry with him," Ethan said. "Where did you serve?"

"Mosby's rangers."

"You're a Reb?" Harry looked at the others, his brow knit in worry. "Does Zach know that?"

"Major Edwards isn't ashamed of his past," Bryce said. "The major is our commanding officer."

"Don't you mean was?" Cass asked.

"He's the foreman. That leaves him in command."

"How many Rebs are working here?" Ethan asked.

"Four counting the major."

"We're outnumbered," Harry said.

"Four Rebs against three Yanks." Ethan laughed. "I'd say we're even, especially with Zach ill."

Bryce spat a stream of tobacco juice on the ground. "That's not how I see it."

Ethan leaned against the wall of the wagon and crossed his arms. "You forget, you lost the war."

"*We* didn't surrender."

Harry moved closer to the front. "What do you mean?"

"Mosby fought independently of Bobby Lee and Joe Johnston. Those generals may have surrendered, but we didn't."

"Doesn't matter," Ethan said. "You still lost."

Cass signaled the boys to hush. They didn't need to create enemies. "I'm sure you're glad the war is over, and we can be friends."

"I don't mind being friends with such a lovely lady as yourself." He scowled at Ethan and Harry.

"Aren't you charming?" Cass turned her back on Ethan and Harry. "I worry some men have lost their manners from fighting in the war."

They reached a rise overlooking a wide valley with a lake.

"What's that?" Cass nearly shouted.

"It's a lake."

"Turn your head, Harry." Cass pointed to a huge wooden structure nestled in the trees on the far side of the lake. "That can't be the cabin where Zach grew up. It's nearly as big as Ravens Roost." The sprawling house was made of logs and stone. The lower level was all boulders with a raised walkway supported by logs surrounding the entire structure and forming a terrace for the second floor. The roof was supported by whole logs that protruded to the edge of the awning to protect anyone standing on the terrace. Twin dormers created rooms for the third floor. If the view from the surrounding porch wasn't enough, huge windows provided plenty of natural light.

"I wouldn't know about that, miss," Bryce said. "We call it the guest house."

"It's beautiful. Is anyone staying there?"

"The major, me, and the buyers arriving for the sale."

"How many buyers do you expect on Saturday?" Cass asked.

"Eight for sure. Could be a dozen or more." He nodded toward the cabin. "A few have arrived early like you."

"I'm glad Zach gave us first choice," Cass said. "All those bidders will increase competition."

Bryce headed toward a barn and fenced pasture

where horses were grazing. "Those are the five and six-year-olds," Bryce said. "They'll go first."

"First? What other horses are for sale?"

Bryce stroked his beard. "Some of the poor-quality ones. The major said it's better to sell the runts and cripples so you don't have to feed them."

"I hope they aren't slaughtered."

"That's the buyer's decision, Miss Beecher."

"Call me Miss Cassie."

Bryce halted the team near the fenced paddock. More than a dozen horses grazed in the sunshine.

"We'll have to take them in once the sun is higher," Bryce said. "Look them over. You're going to have a hard time finding any flaws. The major hand-picked these for the sale."

Bryce helped Cass to the ground and followed the men to the fencing. Harry climbed through the rails and began examining the horses.

"The gate is over here." Bryce showed her the entrance while Ethan joined Harry.

"I don't know where to begin," Cass said.

Bryce pointed to a tan mare with a brown mane. "You might like Peaches. She has a sweet disposition."

"What about that one?" She pointed to a black horse with four white stockings. The gelding reminded her of Blackie.

"That's Black Knight with a K. He's a hard worker but needs a firm hand."

"I'm looking for a buggy horse for my father. He's a doctor."

"A sawbones from the army?"

"No, he didn't serve, but my sisters and I volunteered as nurses."

Bryce scratched at his beard. "That's hard work to do for free."

"I lost family and friends in the war. It was the least I could do." Cass stepped inside the enclosure. She extended her hand to Bryce. "Thank you for your help. It may take time to decide. Feel free to do your work while I look."

"Are you sure I can't help?"

"Have you ever shopped with a woman, Bryce?"

"No, Miss Cassie."

"Then be grateful I'm giving you an excuse. It's unlikely I'll make a decision today." She joined Harry and Ethan who were examining Peaches.

"Do you have to be friendly with a Reb?" Ethan asked.

"Yeah, he's the enemy," Harry added.

"The war is over."

"Didn't you hear him?" Harry said. "He never surrendered."

"We need answers," Cass said. "Why remove horses from a barn, burn it down, and claim the mares and foals perished. What do you gain?"

"You could sell them, especially if they didn't belong to you," Ethan said.

"You think that's Seymour's plan?"

"Greed is always a good motive," Harry said.

"Bryce said the five and six-year-old horses would be sold *first*. Then he added that part about inferior stock. Would you sell sick horses in an auction?"

"No," Harry said. "It would ruin your reputation for quality. Zach said foals were examined for potential problems and eliminated in the first year. No sense in spending money on feed and training if the horse was crippled or unhealthy."

"Then what other stock would be sold?"

"With a shortage of horses from the war, he could sell anything with four legs and a few with three," Harry said.

"Zach wouldn't agree to that."

"But there's nothing to prevent Seymour from selling them with Zach laid up."

Cass couldn't believe someone would deliberately hurt Zach. "You don't believe the fire was an accident?"

"I can't believe Zach would run into a burning barn," Ethan said. "We set plenty of fires during the war. Enough to know how fast old wood is eaten by the flames."

"Don't forget the missing horseshoes," Harry said. "Someone moved the mares and foals before the fire."

"Zach's accident was intentional," Ethan agreed. "They wanted him out of the way."

"But why burn him?" Cass fought tears. "What sort of monster is Seymour?"

Ethan looked at Bryce and two other men by the barn. "One without loyalty. There are plenty of Union soldiers who need jobs. Why hire Rebs?"

Harry stared at the strangers. "Those fellows look like more of Mosby's raiders."

Cass followed their gaze. "How can you tell?"

"The way they stand, the guns on their hips, the look in their eyes," Ethan said. "They're relaxed, pretending to be disinterested, but they're watching us closely."

"We need to tread lightly," Cass warned. "Focus on the horses, but keep your ears open for any clues to their plot."

"What plot?" Harry's voice rose an octave.

"Why do they want Zach out of the way for his own sale?"

Harry looked at Ethan. "I think the *Three Musketeers* has gone to her head."

"For that to happen, there would have to be a missing necklace and a kingdom at stake."

Cass smiled. "Not too different from missing horses and Ravenswood at stake."

Harry looked over the back of Peaches. "We should never have made her one of the musketeers."

"Too late now," Cass said. "One for all and all for one."

They took their time, but as the sun rose, the horses needed to escape the heat and were taken into the barn. Cass needed to use an outhouse or find a chamber pot. The towers of Ravens Roost could be seen in the distance, a fortress commanding respect, but it was too far away for her immediate needs. She walked toward the cabin by the lake. The setting was serene with a gentle breeze pushing colorful wood ducks across the water and rustling the leaves on the trees separating the cabin from the barns.

The interior of the cabin was cool, a sharp contrast to the humid heat of July. Cass removed her bonnet and brushed back the damp strands of her hair. The main room had a floor to ceiling stone fireplace with comfortable sofas and chairs facing each other, welcoming conversation. A large table was in the adjoining room. She climbed the winding staircase to the second floor and opened a door. The bedroom had twin beds. Both were tousled. Someone had spent the night in the room. She found a chamber pot, placed her crinoline over it, and squatted. A wooden horse was hidden in a corner. This had been Pax and Zach's room as boys.

She stepped into the hallway and entered the neighboring room. It had a large bed and dresser. Two trunks were on the floor. One had a broken handle. Someone was staying in this room as well. The outdoor sunlight made the rooms bright, but the overhanging logs provided shade and kept the interior cool from the heat of the day. The bedroom had a door that opened onto the balcony. A small table and pair of chairs created an intimate spot to share a meal. Unlike Ravens Roost, this was a home.

She was descending the steps when Bryce entered. "What are you doing in here?"

"I borrowed a chamber pot." He looked shocked. "Ladies can't go behind a tree."

He escorted her outside. "Are you ready to return to the main house?"

"Yes, but we'll want to return tomorrow," Cass said. "I warned you about shopping with a woman."

"Did you narrow your choices?"

"I'd like to try the reins and drive a buggy hitched to a few of them."

"I'll bring Peaches by for a ride tomorrow."

Cass took his hand when he helped her into the wagon. "How do you know I want to buy her?"

"You kept returning to her side."

He'd been watching closely. "She is a beauty but bring Black Knight. I think my father would prefer the gelding."

Chapter Twenty-Three

As they approached Ravens Roost, the sunlight made the huge house less formidable. The stone had strength, and the lines echoed the castles of England. Gabriel Ravenswood had built this house to last for generations, passed from father to son. It belonged to Zach. But had Ravenswood become a prison instead of a home?

Ethan helped her from the wagon. Her wide sleeves slid up. "You had too much sun. Your skin is red."

Cass rubbed her fingertips over the red rash along her forearm. Had she irritated her skin looking at the horses? "I have some lotion in my room."

Seymour was standing by the tall windows watching them from the parlor. He held the door as they entered. "Did you choose your horses?"

"I'm afraid we'll need more time," Ethan said. "I hope you don't mind if we stay longer."

"If you don't make a decision before Saturday, I can't guarantee a sale. Any horse will go to the highest bidder."

Was Seymour giving them a friendly warning or a threat? "We won't take until Saturday to decide, but we don't want to rush into an important decision. My father wouldn't want me to waste his money on a nag."

"We don't sell nags at Ravenswood."

Seymour had confirmed her speculation. Whatever

horses were being sold *second,* were not cripples and misfits. Cass hurried upstairs and changed the bodice of her day dress for something more formal for supper. She opened her medical bag and found the chipped jar with the lotion Cole had given her for sunburns and rubbed it on her skin. Her fingertips discovered raised bumps. What had she touched? Poisonous plants like foxglove, laurel, buttercups, and others were removed from horse pastures.

She returned the jar to her bag and crossed the hall. Lucia was in the room, brushing something on Zach's bandages.

The nun put the brush on a tray and faced her. "You should have knocked."

Zach struggled against the ropes, trying to break the bindings. He was in anguish. "What have you done to him?"

Lucia grabbed the tray from the bedside table. "I was treating his bandages for the burns."

Cass lifted a pestle among the items she carried. Crushed leaves and a residue remained in the mortar. She sniffed a strong woody scent and coughed.

Lucia grabbed the pestle from her. "Don't touch the bandages and don't untie him, or he'll harm himself."

After she left, Cass examined the bandages, which were wet with whatever had been in the mortar. What plant had she crushed and applied? And why was the odor familiar?

She sat with Zach, talking to him, but he was in a different world, babbling about battles, then horses, and a few words about her. She had no way to rescue him from his torment.

Ethan entered. "Time for supper."

"I'm not coming," Cass said.

Ethan stepped closer. "Isn't he any better?"

A sob escaped. "No."

Ethan put his arm around her shoulders. "How long does it take for burns to heal?"

"It depends on how deep the damage. It could be months."

"I promised your father we would return home Sunday," Ethan said.

"If Zach isn't better by then, my father will need to come here." She wanted someone she trusted to take care of Zach.

"Join us," Ethan pleaded. "You're much better at gleaming information than Harry and me."

"But I'm sitting with Zach afterward." She arranged his blanket. The bandages on his chest weren't oily. She touched the bandages on his face. They were dry as well. Why had she only applied the plant mixture to his arms and shoulders? She ran her fingers along the bandages and held out her hand to Ethan. "What does this smell like?"

"A plant."

"You're no help."

Ethan opened the door. "How could he have survived the war to succumb to something like this?"

"He's going to recover," Cass said.

"Cousin, you've seen burn victims. What about the scars?"

"Did you see Morgan's scar?"

"Hard to miss. But that was from a bullet."

"But we never saw him before the injury. We accept his scar as part of his appearance. And with time

I will accept all the changes in Zach no matter what he looks like."

****

Cass stifled a scream. The itch had begun as a small annoyance. A few scratches and the irritation had subsided for a moment. Then it had returned with a vengeance. No matter how hard she dug into her flesh, fire and pain ignited along the path. It was unbearable. She tossed the covers off the bed and jumped to the floor. She struck a match and lit a candle.

An angry red rash was the source of her torment. In her desperation for relief, she had scratched blood to the surface. The only thing she had touched were the horses. Had one of them rolled around in poison ivy? She would have recognized the three-leaf plant growing on a post or tree and avoided it, but the oil lingered on hair and clothing. Oil. The mortar Sister Lucia had used contained fragments of leaves. Oily leaves. Could Sister Lucia have coated Zach's bandages with poison ivy? But why?

On the first night of arriving her arm had rubbed against Zach's medicated bandages. Sister Lucia had been alarmed and warned her to be careful.

Symptoms for poison ivy could show in a day and could last for several weeks. She removed her medical bag from the bottom dresser drawer where she had stored it. Cass removed a bottle of jewelweed tincture and a bar of lye soap. She scrubbed her arm with the harsh soap to remove the poisonous fluids and applied the tincture to soothe the burning itch.

The clock tolled two o'clock. It would be safe to visit Zach and test her theory. Cass put on her robe and slippers. After gathering her medical supplies, she eased open the door and peered out into the dark hallway. It was empty. She quietly closed her door and froze. Was that a moan? It was in the distance and muted. Was Ravenswood haunted? She hurried across the hall and turned the nob on Zach's door.

The room was dark. She moved the draperies in front of the window to allow moonlight to illuminate the room. Zach was restless. He tugged on the ropes binding his arms to the bed posts. He rubbed his body against the mattress, seeking relief from the torture. If a small patch on her arm had nearly driven her mad with scratching, what was Zach going through?

Cass avoided the oily bandages and stroked Zach's hair back from his face. The silky strands flowed through her fingertips. Why weren't the ends singed if he'd been burned? She searched for the matches to light a candle.

"Who's there?" Zach demanded.

She abandoned her task. "It's me, Cassandra."

He struggled against the ropes. "You can't be. You're a ghost."

A ghost? "Zach, I'm not a ghost. I'm real."

"Cassandra." His voice cracked. "If you're real, go away." He turned his face away from her. "You can't help me."

She touched his bandaged cheek, but he jerked away. "You invited me for a visit. You're not being a good host."

"I was burned in a fire," he whispered between dry, cracked lips. "They said I'm horribly disfigured. I'm no longer human."

They had filled his tortured mind with lies. "You insult me with your words," Cass said. "Even if you were disfigured, I wouldn't abandon you."

"I'm hideous," he said. "I don't want to ruin your life. Go away. Forget me. Pretend we never met."

She had dealt with men in anguish before and needed to calm him before he woke someone. "Hush. I've seen men without legs or arms. I've seen their eyes blasted by powder. You won't frighten me, Zach Ravenswood."

"I won't be a burden to you. You're too beautiful to waste your time on me."

"Am I too vain, too self-centered not to care for you? What about our vow, one for all and all for one?"

"A childish game." Zach thrashed on the bed. "I'm losing my mind. I need my medicine. I can't stand the pain without it."

Footsteps echoed in the hallway. Someone was coming. "Be quiet," Cass urged. She grabbed her bag and went to the window. She pulled the drapes closed, hiding behind the thick fabric.

The door opened. A light penetrated the darkness. Cass pressed against the glass panes of the window, hoping she wouldn't be discovered.

"Is he lucid?" It was Seymour.

"By now his skin should be on fire. He has to be in agony," Sister Lucia said. "He'll beg for the opium."

"Not until he tells me what I want to know," Seymour said. "Wake up, boy."

"Cassandra?" Zach murmured.

"It's Seymour, not that lovely creature you dream of."

"She's an innocent," Lucia said. "She'd cry if you touched her."

"You could tutor her to become one of the Sisters

of Mercy." His voice had a sinister tone.

"I don't think she wants to be a nun." Lucia cackled. "Only a few of us are chosen."

Seymour made a snorting noise. "When did you hear the calling?"

"I was fourteen," Lucia said. "I gave my body on the altar over and over again."

Was Lucia talking about dedicating her body and soul to God? Seymour groaned. The same sound as the ghost earlier.

"I need to feel the lash of repentance." His voice was breathless and another moan escaped with a grunt. What were they doing? She fought the urge to peek.

"Then let's get this over with so I can punish you." Lucia's voice turned harsh. "I can't give you the medicine until you tell us the truth." She was speaking to Zach.

"Where are the papers for the horses, boy?"

"In the safe." Zach's voice was desperate.

"I've searched the safe." Seymour's heavy footsteps echoed across the floor as he paced.

"Seymour, could they be somewhere else?" Lucia asked in a quiet voice.

"I tore apart Elijah's room. Nothing. He always gives the same answer. Where are the papers?" Seymour shouted.

"Don't touch him!" Lucia shrieked. "Why do you need the papers? Can't you sell the horses without them?"

"Fred Kettler knows Zachary is the rightful owner," Seymour said. "He'll insist upon signed titles and so will the reputable buyers."

"What if the boy won't sign?"

"You said by Saturday he would crave the drug so much, he'd sign anything."

"If he had something to sign," Lucia shrieked. "You said the papers were in the safe. Zachary says they're in the safe. But no papers. I wouldn't have to play nurse if he had run into the barn."

"He was about to when Vance Edwards hit him over the head."

"He could still die." Her voice was cheerful, hopeful.

"An accidental death from a fire would have been plausible, but another attempt would be suspicious. I can't claim Ravenswood if I'm accused of murder."

"All that stands between you and Ravenswood is the boy."

"And his friends. At one time I wanted all of this. I had Elijah convinced Ravenswood was my destiny," Seymour said. "I tied myself to that old man all my life, hoping for his crumbs of affection. I did whatever he wanted, and he repays me with a boot kick. He gave everything to the boy! Now I want my share."

"Who wants an old house? Once you have the money, I'm going to show you a grand time in New York City."

"At the Sisters of Mercy convent?"

"Convent?" Lucia laughed. "The Sisters of Mercy Brothel was infamous for pleasure. I haven't begun to show you all the ways penitence can be rewarding."

"Let's forget the boy tonight."

"Should I give him the opium?"

"No. Let him suffer. It will loosen his tongue. I want those papers, and I want them signed by Saturday."

Cass remained motionless behind the draperies. What had she overheard? Harry had been right. Lucia wasn't a nun. She had partnered with Seymour to ruin Zach.

"The medicine. Give it to me."

Zach's cries moved her to action. Cass opened the curtains and hushed him. She listened at the door, slowly opened it, and peered outside. A ghost-like figure floated in the distance in the hallway. It took time for her eyes to adjust. It was Lucia in her nun habit, or was it a nightgown? She disappeared into Seymour's room with him. What did they do in his bedroom? She shuddered.

Cass took a blanket from the end of the bed, rolled it, and placed it at the bottom of the door to block any light before striking a match and lighting the candle on the nightstand. Lucia had left the bottle of opium and the jar of honey.

Zach stared at the glass bottle, drool dribbling from his lip. "I need it, please."

They wanted Zach to become addicted. "Don't think about it." Cass put the drug in her medicine bag.

Zach struggled against the ropes, his eyes haunted with pain. "How can you deny me?"

"I'm here to help you." She removed the supplies she would need to treat his inflamed skin. "I need to remove your bandages."

He shook his head. "I'm hideous. I don't want you to see me."

Cass lifted a pitcher from the washstand and poured water into a tin basin. She placed it on the table by the bed and arranged the lye soap, scrubbing brush, and soothing lotions she had in her bag. "Tell me about the fire. Was it Saturday night?"

"Early Sunday. I was awakened by the crackling of wood on fire. When I opened the curtains, I could see a bright light in the sky. The barn for the broodmares was engulfed with flames. I ran outside," Zach said. "I tried to save the horses. Then darkness."

"Darkness?"

"A beam must have fallen on my head." He jerked from her. "Don't touch me."

"I want to feel the back of your head." She ran her fingers along his skull until she found what she was looking for. "You have a bump on the crown. The swelling has gone down, but it's probably tender." She pressed against it. "Feel that?"

"Ouch. Something hit me."

"It wasn't a burning beam." The major had knocked Zach unconscious, but why? She tugged on his silky hair. "Why isn't your hair singed? You weren't burned, Zach."

"Of course I was burned." Zach struggled against the ropes. "My skin is on fire."

"Let's find out."

"No." He pulled away, but the ropes prevented any escape.

"Don't be afraid."

"I'm a soldier." Zach relaxed. His pride wouldn't allow him to show fear. "You have to promise if I'm hideous, you'll leave Ravenswood."

Her answer was immediate. "I promise."

Zach tugged on the restraints. "Do you have a knife to cut the ropes?"

Cass examined the taught ropes tied to the thick post framing the bed. Her older sisters and cousins had taught her how to tie knots aboard her grandfather's boat, the *Irish Rose*. She undid the bindings and released Zach's arms.

Zach scratched at his bandaged arm.

"Don't scratch."

He groaned as relief came. "You don't know how it feels."

Yes, she did. "A little scratching."

Zach sat with the covers draped over his lower half. He rubbed his bandaged right hand against the wrappings on his left arm. The motion increased to a frantic pace until he suddenly stopped. He gasped. "That feels better."

Cass retrieved cloth gloves from her bag and slipped them on. She began with Zach's face, cutting the knot on the top bandage and unrolling it. As she removed the wrappings, she rolled them into a bundle for easy disposal. These bandages hadn't been soaked like the ones on his arms and chest, and his face was spared from blisters, but the red rash could be mistaken for a slight burn. Clear-filled blisters rose in different sizes on his neck and jaw.

"I look hideous," Zach said. "I can see it in your eyes."

He looked repulsive but not from any burns. His skin was cool to the touch. It was poison ivy. Lucia had soaked the bandages on his arms and hands with the oil from the plant. They would be worse when she unwrapped them. She needed to distract him.

"Tell me what happened. You must have known Seymour was plotting something. You sent me the flier asking for help."

"When I arrived in the old village, Fred Kettler

showed me the advertisement for the sale I hadn't authorized. It made me suspicious, and I confronted Seymour with the flier. But I agreed to the sale, so why do this to me? Why burn the barn and kill all the mares and foals?"

"Harry and Ethan don't think the mares and foals are dead."

"The boys are here?"

"You don't think I visited alone?"

"Sweetheart, I don't think you're here. My head is so foggy, I could wake in the morning and claim you were a dream." He blinked his eyes. "Why don't they think the horses are dead?"

"Harry and Ethan searched the ashes. They didn't find any horseshoes."

"Horseshoes?"

"No horseshoes, no mares."

"Then where are they?"

"We haven't found them, yet," Cass said. "We'll look around tomorrow." She shook her head. "I mean today."

"What day is it?"

"Thursday."

"Thursday? Are you sure? How could I lose so much time?"

"Lucia had you full of opium. I'm surprised you can remember your name."

"Am I an addict?"

"I don't think you've been taking it long enough, but no more. Understand?"

"How do I keep her from forcing it down my throat?"

"I'll think of something." Her gloves were damp

from the oil. Cass wrapped the bandages and her gloves in a towel. She would have to carefully dispose of the poisonous wrappings. Cass dropped a wash cloth into the water and scrubbed it against the bar of soap. Now the hard part would begin.

Chapter Twenty-Four

Zach examined his arms in the candlelight. The skin was raw and scarlet with blisters spotting his angry flesh. It looked like burns, but there was no radiating heat or peeling of damaged skin. The incessant itching wouldn't abate. He scratched the hostile skin to stop the torment, but the relief was temporary, doubling in intensity. The flesh remained intact. "These aren't burns."

Cass shoved the sleeve of her robe upward to reveal her arm. "My arm burned and itched after I rubbed against your bandages, and I wasn't near a fire. I think Lucia soaked your bandages with poison ivy."

Poison ivy? "It can't be something that simple."

"Simple? If she had put it near your eyes, you could have gone blind. They're torturing you to find out where you've hid the papers for the horses."

"The question in my dreams is real? Seymour kept asking me over and over where the titles were. I explained they were in the safe."

"Then why can't he find them?"

Seymour didn't know about the secret compartment. If he shared the secret with Cass, they might force her to tell them. He changed the subject. "How could a nun cover me with poison ivy?"

"She's not a nun," Cass said. "Harry and Ethan noticed she doesn't pray or wear a cross or rosary. Do you know anything about the Sisters of Mercy?"

He shook his head.

"Lucia said something about a brothel in New York."

When the Twenty-ninth Ohio had been ordered to New York City to stop possible riots in 1863, other soldiers told stories of a famous brothel filled with drugs, orgies, and perverted acts. The name had sounded like a church. He looked at his arms and scratched at the torturous itching. "The woman is a sadistic witch."

"You're making it worse," Cass said. "You don't want to break the blisters and spread the poison ivy."

He stared at his hands. "How do I get rid of it?"

"I'll take care of it."

Her tone was deadpan as if a horrible task was in the future. The same matter-of-fact tone a doctor used before he amputated an arm or leg of a soldier. "What do you have to do?"

Cass let out a deep sigh. Her hazel eyes were filled with pain. "The cure can be worse than the disease."

He swallowed the lump in his throat. He needed to know how bad. "What do you mean?"

"Your skin is coated with the oil. I need to scrub hard enough to remove the oil but not break the blisters." She met his gaze. "I'm not giving you any opium. You'll feel everything, and the itching will be worse. For a while."

"Couldn't I take a bath instead?"

"A bath will spread the oil and the rash, but you can apply cold compresses to relieve the itching once I remove the oil." Cass wrapped the soapy cloth around the brush to remove the poison ivy but prevent tearing the skin. "This may feel good at first, like scratching, but the itching will return with a vengeance."

Zach planted his feet on the floor. He grabbed the covers with his fist. "I'm ready."

She handed him a pillow. "Scream into this."

"I won't scream."

"You will. I'll be lucky if you don't want to kill me when I'm through."

"Do your worst," he said. "It can't be as bad as a broken leg." He had screamed in jarring agony when the doctor had put the bones back in place.

Cass washed his face a section at a time. She scrubbed with the soap and brush, rinsed, rinsed again, and applied the tincture.

Zach tensed, his teeth grinding in a tight clench to prevent any outcry or movement. He needed to concentrate on anything but the pain. Cass leaned close to scrub his neck. Her long hair was in a loose braid, which fell forward as she bent to reach the blisters. The silky strands brushed against his face, the scent of lilac filled his nostrils.

She scrubbed his shoulders, and he grimaced. When he opened his eyes, her robe had parted enough to reveal the thin fabric of her nightgown beneath. The low-cut garment gaped as she worked, offering a brief glimpse of soft skin beneath. He had caressed the softness of her flesh, inhaled her scent, but the samplings made him hungry for more.

No stiff corset camouflaged the gentle curves of her body that made his hands ache to remove the clinging garments and discover the hidden treasures. He reached his hand forward and saw the blisters and rash covering his hideous skin. He bunched the covers in his lap to hide his growing desire. When he was healed, when she wouldn't be repulsed by his ugliness, he would show her how much he loved her.

He had heeded the advice of Logan and Blake to take his time courting Cass, but too many obstacles had interrupted their romance. He had planned to impress her with Ravenswood and woo her but had abandoned any future together after the fire, believing he would be disfigured. The loss had made him value Cass and her love more. But the current circumstances urged him to act. He couldn't wait and hope that providence would smile upon them for a normal courtship.

The pendulum beat of the grandfather clock in the hallway echoed the sound of his heart. His breath increased to rapid gasps as she applied the tingling lotion to offer soothing relief.

She tossed the water, scrubbed the bowl, and added fresh water. She lathered the cloth with the bar of lye soap and covered the scrub brush. She took his arm. "This is the worst part."

His muscles tensed as the brush scraped against his inflamed flesh. Cass was careful not to break the blisters, working carefully to remove the oils. Zach winced as she applied the last of the tincture to his raw flesh.

She examined the empty bottle and searched her bag. She removed the chipped jar of creamy lotion made with aloe she had used on her skin. "How do you feel?"

"Relieved I'm not going mad or disfigured." Zach examined his bare skin. "What should I tell Lucia when she sees the bandages gone?"

"I'll wrap you with clean bandages later. Mrs.

Graves said Seymour and Lucia don't rise until noon. You should sit in the sun when it comes up. It'll help dry the oil from your skin." She opened the curtains. The sky was lighter on the horizon. "Dawn will be here soon." She packed her bag, yawned, and stretched her shoulders.

"You need to sleep."

"I need to change the bedding. It's coated with poison ivy."

"I can do that," Zach said. "Besides I need to stretch my legs."

"Can you stand?"

Zach's legs were wobbly and weak. "I feel like a newborn foal." The blanket fell to the floor. He snatched empty air. All he wore were his short pants. Cass stared. The tight-fitting undergarment emphasized his ardor. "A lady wouldn't look."

"I've seen babies. The anatomy is the same." Her brows knit in puzzlement. "Isn't it supposed to hang down?"

He struggled not to laugh. Zach was as ignorant of her secret places as Cass was of his. He was eager to expand their knowledge when he was stronger. He took a tentative step.

Cass offered her arm. "Take hold. I don't want you falling and breaking your leg. Again."

He raised his arms. "I don't want you to get poison ivy."

"Too late, but we're healing from it."

His arm embraced her shoulders as he tested his legs. "Why am I so weak?"

"You've been in bed for four days."

He paced across the room and stopped. "This

wasn't a good idea."

"Why not?"

"I need to use the chamber pot."

She helped him reach the screen, and he disappeared behind it. He glanced over the top. Cass was turned away. He stared at the porcelain bowl. "It's too quiet. I don't need you hearing me piss."

"Like I haven't heard that noise before."

"Sing or something."

Cass laughed and hummed a lively Irish melody. She stripped the bed and replaced the sheet and blanket with a clean one.

He peered over the top of the screen. Her graceful movements restored his arousal. How did a man avoid bedding a woman when the tiniest behavior drove his desires? Her scent, her voice, her figure tormented him with unfulfilled release.

He turned away to gain control and saw his reflection in the mirror. He barely recognized the face staring at him with a shocked expression. Watery blisters covered his blotched skin and his eyes were puffy from lack of sleep. All thoughts of seduction vanished. Any suggestion of intimacy would be met with horror and repulsion. He groaned at his image.

She smoothed the bedding and turned. "Is something wrong?"

"There's a mirror on the wall." He needed to shave. He ran his hand over the bumpy surface of his jaw where blisters rose above the stubble. "I look like something left for weeks on the battlefield."

"I can't believe someone would do this over money," Cass said.

"It's not only greed," Zach said. "Seymour hates

me. My grandfather chose me over him. This is his revenge."

"I don't understand. Seymour talked about inheritance, but isn't he an employee?"

"No, he claims to be my grandfather's bastard son." Zach walked toward the bed where Cass stood. His footsteps were less hesitant. "He convinced Elijah to leave him half of Ravenswood in the old will, but he didn't receive anything but a job in the one Tyler wrote. Seymour only found out that I inherited all of Ravenswood after the will was read."

Cass pulled the blanket back. "But you had nothing to do with the change," Cass said. "Elijah chose you to inherit all of Ravenswood."

"Seymour can't fight a dead man." Zach relaxed against the clean sheet and examined his battered arms. "I can't wait to confront the old bat about his torture."

"Zach, they wanted to kill you."

"What do you mean?"

"Didn't you hear them talking about the fire?"

"Bits and pieces." He shook his head. "Everything is muddled. What did you hear?"

"They set the barn on fire hoping you would go in to rescue the horses and be killed."

Was Seymour capable of murder? He had seen him in the shadows by the burning barn, a rare smile on his face. If he hadn't been hit over the head, he would have rushed into the blaze and likely perished. "Who hit me over the head?"

"Major Edwards."

"I owe him my life."

"From what Seymour said, he won't try a second attempt on your life," Cass said. "He wanted to claim

Ravenswood, but he has to realize by now that we would never allow him to succeed."

He smiled. "Thank you for thwarting his plans."

Cass gathered her supplies. "He could still ruin you by selling all your horses while you're drugged."

"If he thinks I'm going to sign over any titles to my horses, he is in for a rude awakening."

"Let's not wake him until Saturday," Cass said. "Let him think he's going to succeed."

Zach lowered his voice. "Are you holding an ace?"

"You standing well and sane before Seymour and the buyers is how we'll beat him."

Zach examined his arms. "Do you think I'll be well enough to attend the sale?"

"You may not look pretty, but you'll be able to conduct the sale."

Zach turned on his side to face her. "How was Seymour going to sell the horses? Fred Kettler knows I'm here."

"All he'd have to do is show him how ill you are," Cass said. "The way Lucia was shoveling opium down your throat, you wouldn't be in any condition to conduct the sale."

"Mr. Kettler would sanction the sale for Seymour to supervise and collect the money," Zach said. "But then what? He would have to pay the bills or face collectors."

"Not if he left Ravenswood."

"But Ravenswood is the prize." Had been the prize. As long as Seymour had a chance to inherit, he wanted to be master of Ravenswood. The new will had created an obstacle, and Zach's survival had changed the objective. "Instead of claiming Ravenswood, he wants to ruin me."

Cass packed her supplies. "That's why I think once he has the money from the sale in his greedy hands, he'll flee. Lucia mentioned going to New York."

"Did Harry and Ethan bring any weapons?"

She was startled by his question. "No, do you have a gun?"

"I turned in my Enfield when I mustered out. I swore off killing. I had enough of it."

Her brow knitted in worry. "What about Seymour?"

"All he's ever armed himself with is a pen, and all my grandfather had was a muzzle-loading pistol."

"But the major and his men are armed," Cass said. "Do you know if they're part of Seymour's plan?"

"He hired them," Zach said. "The major may have stopped short of murder, but they're working for Seymour." He had survived the fire and so had the mares. But where were they? "I'm worried about the mares," Zach said. "Someone interested in starting a farm might not worry about paperwork, especially with the demand for horses so high. Do you know if they're still at Ravenswood?"

"We haven't seen any, but we've only been to the corral where they keep the older horses." Cass said. "Where are the best hiding places?"

"Do you have the map I drew of Ravenswood?"

"Yes, in my room."

"Bring it when you return. I'll show you the places to look."

"What if he's sold them?"

"Without the mares, I'd be ruined."

She placed her hand on his shoulder. "We'll

rebuild, Zach. Even if we have to do it from nothing."

Cass was no fortune seeker. He had wanted to impress her with Ravenswood and its wealth. "Be careful, Cassandra. I don't want anything to happen to you."

"It works both ways, Zach." Cass gathered her bag and the towel with the soiled bandages. "You didn't make it through the war to die now. You're more important than the horses, Ravenswood, or any amount of money. Promise me you won't risk your life."

Only for you. "Let's hope it doesn't come to that."

"I'm going to sleep, but I'll return to wrap your arms and chest before we look for the horses," Cass said. "Sit in the sun when it comes up and try not to scratch. I'll have Mrs. Graves make some cucumber paste to help with the itching. She placed the chipped jar of lotion on the table. "Put this on if you can't wait."

"Cassandra," he called as she approached the door. "I couldn't have survived their torture without you. Thank you."

"I'd kiss you, but you're not pretty enough...yet."

Chapter Twenty-Five

Cass awoke to someone lightly rapping on her door. She didn't want to wake up. She had dreamed of walking with Zach on the grounds of Ravenswood. His eyes had a look of desire in them. One she had recognized last night. She had welcomed his touch and returned his kisses. She was breathless, panting, wanting more.

The knock resumed. "Hey, Cassie. Aren't you awake by now?"

Ethan. She fought to steady her breathing as she grabbed her robe and answered the door. Ethan stood in the hallway. "What time is it?"

"The sun has been up for an hour. Aren't you feeling well? You're all flushed."

Cass touched her warm cheek. She glanced down the hall and pulled him inside. "I'm tired. I visited Zach during the night."

Ethan's eyes widened. "You can't do that."

"He's sick," Cass reminded him. "But he wasn't burned."

"He's covered in bandages."

Cass showed Ethan her arm. "This isn't sunburn. It's poison ivy. Zach was covered with it."

"Poison ivy?" Ethan backed away. "That would drive anyone crazy with scratching."

"Remember how Lucia panicked when I touched

the bandages?"

"What is she plotting?"

"Why do men think women do all the plotting? She has nothing to gain."

Ethan shrugged. "So who is the mastermind?"

"Zach said Seymour was planning the sale before he returned home. He's angry Zach inherited Ravenswood, and he didn't receive anything."

"Why would an accountant inherit Ravenswood?"

"He claims to be Elijah's illegitimate son," Cass said. "Seymour believed he was going to be master of Ravenswood, but Zach survived the war."

"The greedy bastard," Ethan said. "Sorry, Cousin."

Cass snickered. "It describes him aptly."

"Do you know Seymour's plan?"

"He wants to drug Zach enough to force him to sign the titles to the horses. Once the sale is complete, they'll run off with the money."

Ethan looked around. "How do we stop him?"

"By helping Zach recover for Saturday's sale." She gathered her clothes. "But we have another job today."

"What's that?"

"We need to locate the mares."

"Why? We know they aren't dead."

"Zach thinks Seymour may sell them privately."

"Off the books," Ethan said. "That's why Seymour said they were dead."

"Without the mares, Zach would have a hard time keeping Ravenswood." Cass retrieved the map Zach had drawn. "I think we should ride the horses today and search different parts of the farm."

They studied the drawing. "We have plenty of area to cover."

"There's three of us, and Zach can tell us the best places to search."

"I'll tell Harry."

"Wait." Cass searched her medical bag for the bottle of opium. "Take this to Mrs. Graves."

Ethan examined the bottle. "What is this?"

"Lucia left this bottle of opium on the table by Zach's bed."

"What is Mrs. Graves going to do with it?"

"Ask her if she has seasoning to match the powder," Cass said. "I'm going to replace the contents with something harmless."

Ethan clutched the bottle and grinned. "Then she won't be able to drug Zach."

"And Lucia and Seymour won't know we're onto their scheme."

"I can't wait for the sheriff to lock them up and throw away the key."

After Ethan left, Cass washed and treated her arm. Ethan's remark bothered her. What crime had Seymour committed? He could claim the barn burned by accident. The poison ivy infection was cruel but not worthy of jail. If they thwarted Seymour's plans to rob Zach, what would he attempt next? She needed to write Tyler for legal advice.

She dressed in a skirt, a cotton blouse, and short jacket. She pulled on her boots and grabbed her bonnet and medical bag.

Zach was seated in front of the open window soaking in the sun. She looked out the window. "Make sure no one sees you."

"No stables to clean. Everyone is on the other side of Ravenswood."

She examined his skin. "It already looks better. Did you wash?"

"I scrubbed anything red with the soap."

"I'll fill a pitcher with fresh water. You don't want to reuse it." She stared at his bare chest. Only a few blisters marred the smooth, molded muscles. Lucia had limited the poison ivy to his arms and shoulders. She had spared his face but wrapped it in bandages to frighten him with the thought of disfigurement. What sort of person took pleasure in another's pain?

Zach examined his arms. "The sun is helping, but my head feels like it's filled with cotton."

"It's the opium."

"What am I going to do when Lucia wants to drug me?"

"I have a solution."

She turned as the door opened. Ethan entered with a tray.

"Mrs. Graves sent breakfast." He handed her two bottles. "Is this what you wanted?"

Cass compared the two. Side by side there was an obvious difference, but alone, either one could pass for opium. She tasted the contents of the unmarked bottle. Her tongue burned. "She added pepper to color this one." She searched for an empty bottle in her medical bag and emptied the opium into it. Then she poured Mrs. Graves' mixture into the bottle with the label and placed it on the table by the bed. "Try to react as if it's opium and doze off afterward."

Ethan handed Zach the tray of food. "You are one ugly-looking blister."

He bit into a crisp strip of bacon. "Come a little closer, and I'll share my ugliness."

Ethan stole a biscuit from the tray.

Harry was in the hall calling their names.

Ethan backed away and opened the door. "We're over here."

Harry entered. "Hey, when are we going to look at the horses?" He stared at Zach. "Those aren't burns. What are you covered with?"

"Poison ivy," Cass said. "Lucia coated his bandages in it."

Harry gagged. "Can nuns do that?"

"You were right about her, Harry. She's no nun." Cass handed Zach the map. "Where do we look for the mares?"

Zach eliminated the woods and a swamp. "There's a road around the lake. It goes by several pastures and barns."

"I'll take that," Cass said.

"Harry can take the north pastures, and Ethan can take the southern section. If the mares are on Ravenswood property, you should be able to find them." He returned the map to Cass, who folded it and placed it in her pocket. She retrieved clean bandages from her bag. "I need to wrap Zach before Lucia visits."

"Why?" Harry asked.

"It's part of the plan to thwart their evil scheme," Ethan said.

Harry looked confused. "Are we playing a game?"

"No game." Zach said. "This is my future we're fighting for. Seymour wants to ruin me, and that fake nun would like to see me in an asylum." He finished the last bite.

Cass gave the tray of dirty dishes to Harry. "Can you return these to Mrs. Graves?" She added the empty bottle. "And thank her."

Harry paused at the door. "Do you want any breakfast, Miss Cassie?"

"Tell her I'm coming."

He waited for Ethan.

"I'm chaperoning," Ethan said. "Now that Zach is feeling better, I need to heed Dr. Beecher's words."

"What words?" Cass demanded.

"Not to leave you alone with high-spirited Zachary."

"I thought Dr. Beecher liked me," Zach said.

"And he'll continue to like you as long as you respect his daughter."

Ethan was going to prevent any romantic gestures. "Make yourself useful and toss the contents of the chamber pot out the window."

"Ew." Ethan made a face. "I don't think this is the duty of a chaperone." He opened the window and tossed the contents in the porcelain bowl to the ground below.

Cass applied lotion to Zach's bare arms to soothe his skin. Her fingers traced the swell and ebb of each muscle. Four days in bed hadn't eroded what years of marching and fighting had created. She grabbed a roll of bandages and wrapped his arms, starting at his hands. The bandages followed the hard muscles beneath the battered skin. The bandages absorbed the ointment she had applied and mimicked Lucia's poison ivy solution. She loosely wrapped his shoulders and face. "It's only temporary," she reminded him.

He jumped into bed and stared at the ropes. "Do you have to tie me?"

Cass looked at Ethan, who was washing his hands.

"Do you remember how Jake would tie a knot that appeared tight but could be loosened easily?"

"The robber's hitch." Ethan tied the ropes around Zach's wrist. "Pull this end of the rope with your teeth, and you can slip your hand out. Tug on the other end to tighten."

Zach tried each knot. It worked as Ethan instructed. "I should be out there helping you."

"You can find out more about their plans here," Cass said. "They talked freely in front of you when they believed you were drugged."

"What if I forget to act like a blubbering idiot?"

Ethan paused by the door. "Zach, they won't know the difference."

Zach freed his hand and grabbed a pillow. He tossed it, but Ethan escaped.

Cass returned the pillow. "Pretend to be sick," she reminded him before closing the door.

****

Bryce was waiting for them in the yard with their repaired buggy hitched to Black Knight. He helped Cass take the bench seat and joined her. Ethan and Harry climbed in the back. Cass tugged on her gloves. "Hand me the reins."

"Are you sure?"

"How am I going to know if I want to buy him?"

Cass slapped the reins on Black Knight's hindquarters, and he lurched forward. When they arrived at the barn and pasture, Harry and Ethan jumped to the ground. Bryce remained seated. "Don't you have chores to do?"

"You might need a guide." He was planning to accompany her.

"I can't ride in a buggy with a man who isn't a relative," Cass said. "It wouldn't be proper."

He tipped his hat and climbed down. "Stay on the path."

"Once I return, I'll want Peaches hitched to the buggy." She urged Black Knight forward. Cass followed the road along the lake. A split rail fence lined the opposite side and formed pastures for grazing. A barn rose into view with horses in the paddock. She pulled back on the reins. These were younger horses but not foals. They were being trained with long reins to take orders but weren't ready to be hitched to a buggy or saddle trained. Bidders wouldn't pay full price for them. Hopefully, Seymour wouldn't bother selling them.

She drove on. Black Knight pulled the buggy with ease and followed her instructions with a soft touch of the reins. She was on the far side of the lake when she arrived at another barn and attached paddock. A mare was being led inside and trotting beside her was a foal. Were the others inside? There was only one way to find out. She followed twin ruts in the grass that marked a path leading to a gate between the fence rails in front of the barn. Cass pulled on the reins to halt Black Knight. She looked around and headed for the building.

Flies buzzed in a droning circle, resting on a pile of fresh droppings near the opening that ran the length of the barn. The interior was cooler, and her vision adjusted to the darkness. A horse snorted. The nearest stall was home to a mare and foal. Another pair were in the next stall. She had found the missing horses.

Two men were looking inside a stall at the other end of the barn, their bodies outlined by the sunlight behind them. Could she slip out without being noticed? Cass turned.

"Hello," one of the men called as they walked toward her.

She turned and smiled. "Hello, gentlemen. I was riding by and my horse seemed hot. Is there a watering trough?" Horses needed plenty of water, so it was a logical excuse on a hot day.

The shorter man had a healthy middle and a broad smile. "I'm Ned Pike." He extended a chubby hand and shook hers before she could remove her gloves.

"Cassandra Beecher."

"Who?" The other man stared hard at her with dark eyes. His mustache and goatee drooped in a frown. Was he hard of hearing? Many of the men who had fought in battles had suffered hearing loss from the noise of the cannons and guns. Was this another of the major's men?

She spoke louder. "Miss Cassandra Beecher. I'm a guest of Zach Ravenswood."

"I'll be damned."

His profanity was unexpected. "What did you say?"

He tipped his hat. "Excuse me, Miss Beecher. I'm Vance Edwards."

"The major?"

He peered more intensely. "How do you know me?"

"Bryce told us about you."

"Us?"

"My cousin Ethan Donovan and our neighbor Harry Herbruck. We're buying horses from Zach."

His stare intensified. "Does Seymour know that?"

"Of course, but he gave us an ultimatum. We have to make our selections before Saturday, or we'll have to bid with the other buyers. I can't decide between Black Knight and Peaches." She waved toward her buggy. "What horse would you recommend?" She had spoken the words in a rush and ran out of breath.

"Are you nervous, Miss Beecher?"

"Me?" Her voice squeaked. "It must be the heat. It's a warm day. I should return Black Knight to the barn."

"You mentioned water," Vance said. "I'll haul a bucket."

"Thank you, Mr. Edwards." She turned to Ned, who had remained. "Have you chosen the horses you're going to bid on?"

"I'm working on a special deal," Ned whispered, looking at Vance, who was filling a bucket from the lake. "I'm buying broodmares for my own farm."

She pretended to be shocked. "I didn't know the mares were for sale."

"Elijah Ravenswood died this spring," Ned said. "His grandson isn't interested in the farm. Vance says I can have my pick of these mares."

"Then you're not bidding Saturday?"

"I'll be there. I have my eye on a young stallion."

Vance was returning. "It was a pleasure meeting you, Mr. Pike. I hope we see each other again on Saturday."

Vance placed the bucket on the ground in front of Black Knight. Cass joined him. "Seymour said Zach was ill. I hope he's feeling better by Saturday."

"He was burned in a fire. I doubt he'll be recovered so soon. Sister Lucia is taking care of him."

"You don't possess any nursing skills?"

What an odd thing for a stranger to ask. "I nursed soldiers in Washington City this spring."

"Where did you learn your skills?"

"My father is a doctor, but my sister taught me my midwife skills." Cass smiled. "There wasn't much of a demand for delivering babies during the war."

"I disagree," Vance said. "Plenty of babies were born during the war years. Many of them died."

Something in his voice indicated a deep loss. And anger.

"Vance, I'd like to take this mare out in the paddock and get a better look at what I'm buying," Ned said.

Vance met her gaze. Her cheeks burned under his scrutiny. She needed to dodge his suspicions. "Ned said he was starting a horse farm. He's lucky Seymour is authorizing the sale. I don't think Zach would agree to part with any of the broodmares."

He didn't challenge her explanation. "I see you're busy," Cass excused. "I'll be on my way."

Vance turned the buggy around and offered his hand to help her board. "Be careful, Miss Beecher."

Was it a friendly warning or something more sinister?

Chapter Twenty-Six

Cass headed around the lake. Ethan and Harry met her half way back to the pasture. They were eager to share their news.

"No mares," Ethan said. "But I found the three and four-year-olds."

"All I found was the manure piles and the fallow fields," Harry added.

"I found the mares." Cass gripped the reins so they wouldn't see her hands shaking. "In a barn on the other side of the lake."

"All of them?"

"I didn't have time to count," Cass said. "I met Major Vance Edwards."

Harry frowned. "What sort of man is he?"

"Fierce. I don't think he believed my story about watering my horse. He said the oddest things."

"Odd?"

"He guessed I was a nurse."

"Many women were nurses during the war," Ethan said. "It was a lucky hunch."

"Do you know what they're going to do with the mares?" Harry asked.

"They're selling them," Cass said. "A man named Ned Pike was selecting the ones he wanted."

Ethan rode beside the buggy. "How do we stop him from taking the mares?"

"Ned is staying for the auction. The horses won't leave the property until then."

"We should stop the sale," Harry suggested.

"No, Zach needs money for Ravenswood. He needs to take control of the sale and decide which horses are sold and which ones aren't. He can return Ned's money if necessary."

Harry looked worried. "Will he be well enough by Saturday?"

"He has no choice."

****

It was late by the time they returned to the main house. Cass washed, changed her clothes, and checked on Zach before dining. He had slipped his hands out of the ropes and removed the bandages on his face and neck. His thick blond hair was a scattered mess. She sat on the edge of the bed and stared as he slept. Even with the scabs, he had a handsome face. He needed a shave. The stubble on his face was forming a beard. It outlined his mouth. His parted lips invited her touch. Could she kiss him without waking him? "Poor baby." She leaned forward.

An arm wrapped around her body and pulled her against his chest. He rolled her onto the mattress and gazed at her with his sour apple green eyes. "I can't wait to become pretty." He kissed her. The surprise show of passion caught her off guard. She didn't have time to respond before he pulled away. The ropes creaked as he lifted his weight, but he didn't release her. She remained motionless, neither inviting him nor repulsing his eager attentions. His hand rested on her waist and moved along the curve accentuated by her corset. Her breathing accelerated in anticipation of another kiss. He complied, lingering on her lips, urging her to respond.

All the lessons her sisters had instilled in her rushed to mind. Set boundaries. Cry. Make him apologize. Keep both feet on the ground. How was she to set limits when she was sprawled out on his bed beneath him?

His fingertips poked beyond the wrappings covering his hands. He brushed a few strands of hair from her face, and gazed into her eyes. "You're so beautiful. You don't know my despair when I worried we could never be together. I believed I was going to be a monster trapped in these walls forever."

"You are a beast." She had meant to say the words in a serious reprimand, but her breathless voice gasped a seductive challenge. She was going to disappoint her sisters.

He nuzzled her neck. Her breath caught in her throat as he moved upward, tracing her jaw with his lips and nibbling on her ear.

Cass caressed his bare back, the skin smooth and hard beneath her fingertips. Her own spine arched against his body as he continued his assault on her senses. His manly scent was like an elixir stirring her passions to a boil. Her body throbbed with a rhythm that matched his.

His mouth captured hers. He plucked and plundered until her lips were bruised and swollen from the lovely assault. His hand fondled her breast and teased a nipple to a swollen peak beneath the thin fabric of her summer dress.

Cass groaned as her body responded in a wave of ecstasy. Her hips pressed upward in a mating rhythm, urging him to continue.

Zach needed no encouragement. His breathing broke with gasps of excitement. His hands had pushed her crinoline upward and with it, her skirt and petticoat. His fingers searched for the opening in her bloomers.

Sanity returned. "Zach!" She escaped, sliding out from under him and falling on the floor. She sat with her skirt bunched around her and her breast throbbing from his touch, taut against the fabric of her gown.

Zach stood and offered his hand. "Are you all right?" His short pants molded against his body, outlining every detail.

She batted his hand away and buried her face in her hands. "Didn't Logan have a talk with you?"

"Oh, that." The bed creaked, and she lifted her head. He was in bed, the covers pulled to his waist.

She stood. "Did you plan this?"

"No, I was asleep until you sat on the edge of the bed. You were staring at me, all warm and inviting. I couldn't resist."

She paced along the edge of the bed. "I promised my sisters I would set boundaries. You kissed me, and I forgot everything. A few more minutes and my virginity would have been a memory."

"I would have married you."

She leaned over him. "I haven't decided if I want to marry you, Zach Ravenswood."

He rose on his elbows. "Why not?"

"This passion we share may fade."

"How? It hasn't had a chance to peak."

"You were peaked high enough."

"Your nearness has that effect on me." He crossed his bandaged arms. "My passion is not waning."

"But is your physical desire a result of all the disasters that have happened around us and a desperate attempt to claim a normal life?" She resumed her pacing. "We need to discuss our future in a practical and logical manner."

"Now?" His chest shook beneath the covers.

She put her hands on her hips. "Are you laughing at me?"

"Sweetheart, you write any rules you want. I'll comply."

Cass sat on the chair by the dresser. Her heartbeat had returned to normal. She adjusted her dress. "No removing my clothes."

"Can I rearrange them?"

She glared. "Let's talk about something else. Did Lucia and Seymour visit?"

Zach rolled to his side. "They asked about the titles. I said they were in the safe like before. Then I begged for the opium."

"Did Lucia give you some?"

"A double dose. Wouldn't that be dangerous if the opium was real?"

"She only has two more days to guarantee your addiction."

"Then she'll probably return tonight for another dose." His brow wrinkled in thought. "What happened on your ride?"

"I found your mares."

Zach reached for her and stopped. "Where?"

"The barn on the north end of the lake. I didn't see all of them. I met Ned Pike and Vance Edwards at the barn."

"Ned Pike," Zach repeated. "He's bought horses in

the past. He'd visit during the summer to broker a private deal."

"He talked about starting a breeding farm of his own."

"With my mares, he could."

A knock turned their attention to the door. Ethan entered. "Good, you're awake. Did you tell him about the mares?"

"Yes." She turned to Zach "Ned said he was staying for the auction. He was interested in a stallion."

"Then I haven't lost them."

"Even if you make an appearance, there's still the major and his men," Ethan said. "We need to discover his role in Seymour's scheme."

"How do we do that?" Cass asked.

"Harry said Vance Edwards is downstairs, dressed for supper," Ethan said. "He was asking for you."

Cass took Ethan's arm. "I hope I can charm him into revealing his secrets."

"If anyone can, you can, Cousin."

"Not too much charming," Zach called.

Ethan escorted Cass to the dining hall. Harry was talking to Vance. The major had exchanged his work clothes for evening wear. The black frock coat and trousers were expensive but hadn't been worn for a long time. Creases remained where the fabric had been folded and stored. The suit needed pressing. When he turned, his coat was open to expose a silver embroidered vest. Colorful birds added splashes of color on the silk fabric.

His smile was eerily familiar. Why?

"Is that the man you met earlier?" Ethan asked.

She shook off the feeling of *déjà vu*. "Yes."

He gripped her arm. "You're shaking."

Seymour introduced the major, and they took their seats. Lucia was in her nun habit and remembered to wait until grace was said before buttering her bread.

Harry looked at Ethan. "I was telling the major about our service in the war. We may have crossed paths after Gettysburg."

"We crossed the paths of friend and foe," Ethan said. "I'm glad my years of war are over. Violence takes a toll on a man."

"It can rob him of his soul," Vance agreed.

"Greed can do that, too."

Cass kept her eyes downcast. Ethan was not being subtle, but his head-on attack might harvest some answers.

"No one can accuse Southerners of greed. While you were paid handsomely for your service, we were left with worthless paper currency," Vance said.

"The newspapers reported the Confederacy hid gold in Canada," Ethan said. "Did you profit from any of it?"

"If there was any gold, I never possessed any." He crumpled his napkin with his fist.

"I'm sure Zach will pay you fairly for your work at Ravenswood," Cass said.

"He promised us jobs," Harry added.

"Is that why you're here?" Seymour asked. "You said you were buying horses?"

"We are," Ethan said. "We'll finalize our choices tomorrow."

"I have mine picked out," Harry said. "Do you have the papers available?"

Cass wanted to kick Harry, but he was out of reach.

"I'll have them for the sale," Seymour said.

"What about you, Miss Beecher? Did you decide on a horse?"

"It's a difficult choice," Cass said. "Black Knight is strong, but Peaches has a sweet disposition. It would be easier if I was buying the horse for myself."

Seymour leaned close. "Who are you buying the horse for, Miss Beecher?"

"My father. He's a doctor and needs a reliable horse. The one we have now is old and frail."

"Do you come from a large family, Miss Beecher?"

"I have five sisters."

"Five!" Lucia shrieked. "How many brothers?"

"None, unless you count my brothers-in-law. Four of my sisters are married."

Vance played with the flaky fish on his plate. "Did they survive the war?"

"My sister Jennifer lost her first husband at Bull Run, but the others who served in the war, returned home."

Vance leaned toward her. "And those who didn't fight in the war?"

"They served the country in other ways. Logan Pierce worked as a secretary for the Treasury Department."

"He no longer works for the government?"

"No, they moved to Ohio." Why was Vance interested in her family?

"Did Tyler find him a job?" Harry asked.

"Yes, he's working for the mayor of Akron."

"Tyler Montgomery?" Vance asked.

"Yes," Cass said. "Do you know him?"

"Wait!" Seymour interrupted. "Tyler Montgomery

is the lawyer who wrote the new will." Lucia placed her hand on Seymour's arm. He jerked away, stared at those around him, and regained his composure.

Vance turned toward Seymour. "You don't seem to like this lawyer. Sordid fellow?"

"The worst," Seymour said. "Robbed me of what was rightfully mine."

"Tyler is not a thief," Cass defended. "And you are not the rightful…" She caught herself.

Seymour turned on her. "Why are you here?"

"I'm here to buy a horse for my father." She hesitated, but Seymour appeared vulnerable and continued. "There is one thing I would like for myself. I took care of the animals on our farm. I've raised puppies, kittens, chicks, and piglets. Even a few calves, but I always wanted to raise a foal. Are there any fillies for sale?" She turned to Vance. "One weaned."

"I explained earlier all the mares and foals were killed in the fire," Seymour said.

"The barn burned, but didn't any of the animals escape?" Cass waited for his reply.

"Not a one."

She looked at Vance. "But Ned Pike was looking at a mare and foal at the barn near the lake. He was anxious to buy several."

Seymour looked like he had swallowed a lemon. He stared daggers at Vance.

"Those must not have been the same horses that were in the barn Seymour is talking about," Vance lied.

"Yes, yes," Seymour agreed. "Those were set aside for Mr. Pike before the fire. All the other horses perished."

"What did you do with the horseshoes?" Harry

asked.

"What horseshoes?"

"The broodmares were shod, but there were no horseshoes in the ashes."

She had tipped her hand, but Harry had laid the cards on the table.

"I'm sure one of the hands gathered them," Seymour said.

"It must have been horrible to watch them die," Harry said. "Even as a vet, I hate to put an animal down. I had to shoot a horse at Gettysburg after a canister blew off his legs."

"I've seen worse," Vance said. "Dozens of horses wounded or broken during a battle."

"We were at Chancellorsville," Ethan said. "Wounded men were trapped in the inn when it burned."

"Soldiers were burned in the Wilderness," Cass added. "Or blown apart when the powder in their cartridge boxes exploded."

Vance frowned. "You couldn't have been there."

"My sister was. I listened to her nightmares when I stayed with her before she gave birth to her son."

"Miss Jenny?"

The hair on her arms stood on end. "No, my sister, Jessica. She married Major Morgan Mackinnon."

"Who did he serve under? Grant?" His voice was filled with hate.

"No. Morgan served under Jackson and Ewell. He was wounded at the Wilderness but recovered thanks to my sister's skill. He was with Lee when he surrendered at Appomattox Courthouse."

His eyebrows rose, and his eyes widened. "Your

sister married a Southerner?"

"Do you find that strange?"

"You're an abolitionist. A Beecher."

"Slavery is over. The war is over. Not every soldier fought about slavery. On both sides," she added. "Some in the Union believed in the inferiority of blacks and wouldn't let them serve in the army until the final years. Men like Morgan fought to defend Virginia where most of the fighting had occurred. As an officer, he worked to keep his men alive so they could go home after the war. He had barely fifty men left in a regiment that had once been a thousand strong when they surrendered at Appomattox. The war wanted to tear Morgan and Jess apart, but they beat it."

"Sometimes the war wins." Vance wiped his mouth with his napkin.

He was a cynic, but it was forged from reality. What tragedy had cast its dark shadow over Vance Edwards, and why did she feel sympathy for the stranger determined to ruin Zach?

Chapter Twenty-Seven

While the men smoked cigars and drank whiskey, Cass was isolated with Lucia in the library. Did the fake nun suspect something? She needed to discover the role of the major and his men in Seymour's plan.

Cass served tea and pie Mrs. Graves had left on the table. "This library has a lovely collection of old books."

"I don't read," Lucia said.

"Not even the Bible?"

She paused her fork in mid-air. "That one is required."

"What order do you belong to?"

"The Sisters of Mercy."

A bordello in New York City. They had already revealed too much about what they knew, but she needed to show interest. "Is it a strict order?"

"We believe in penance and the power of prayer." She put her fork down. "Now it's my turn. Is your heart set on marrying Zachary Ravenswood?"

"Of course. Why do you ask?"

"I couldn't help but notice that Vance Edwards was interested in you and your family."

"I don't know why he asked questions about them, but I have no feelings for Mr. Edwards. He's old."

"A mature man is often best for someone as young as yourself."

"I hardly think a nun is qualified to be a matchmaker." She stood and made her excuses to retire. Something about Vance nagged at the dark recesses of her memory.

****

Zach stared out the window. His friends and Cass had instilled a determination to stop Seymour in his plans to ruin him. Although the urge for the opium plagued him, he was determined to endure the itching without any medication.

When Cass entered his room late that night, she updated him on what had transpired during supper. "What are your impressions of Vance Edwards?"

"He seemed an honorable fellow. I reminded him we were veterans even if we were on opposite sides. Seymour was not."

"Lucia believes he's interested in me, but I've done nothing to encourage him."

"Sweetheart, all you have to do is smile to inspire a man to action."

She placed her hand on his chest. "How do I discourage a man?"

"You don't visit him in his bedroom in the middle of the night wearing your night clothes." The nightgown and robe clung to her natural curves and reminded him of what was beneath. He reached for her.

She stepped away. "Can you control your lust or should I leave?"

"I'll be a gentleman. I need you to rewrap my bandages," Zach said. "I'll be glad when I can take them off permanently."

"Do you think Seymour and Lucia will pay a visit tonight?"

"They always do. Lucia nearly emptied the bottle the last time she dosed me with opium."

Cass examined the container. "Don't let her give you anything from a different bottle."

Zach sat on the edge of the bed, the covers modestly placed as Cass wrapped his shoulders. Her nearness was a test of his self-control. "You should kiss me before wrapping my face."

She covered his mouth with a bandage.

He tugged on it. "That won't dissuade me." He put his arms around her and pulled her tight against his chest. "I'm feeling better each day."

"Good. We don't know Vance's role in this, but he's working for Seymour. He came to his defense when we made accusations."

How loyal was Vance? "Before you left Darrow Falls, did Tyler mention a letter from me?"

"No. Why?" She continued to wrap his face.

"When I arrived at Ravenswood, I was suspicious of Seymour. I have no will, and I wanted to know if Seymour could inherit. I wrote to Tyler asking him several questions. I wanted to know what would happen if I died without a will."

"They didn't succeed in killing you."

He touched the back of his head. "Death visited."

"Tyler should have sent a reply by now," Cass said. "He's efficient."

"I'm worried he didn't receive it. I gave the letter to Vance. He said he was going into town and would post it." Zach frowned. "When he saw the name, he was angry."

"He must know Tyler, and he doesn't like him." She chewed on her bottom lip.

Zach took her hand. "What's wrong?"

"I sent a letter to Tyler today."

"About what?"

"Legal advice."

He waited.

"I wanted to know if there was any crime we could prosecute Seymour for?"

"He tried to kill me." Zach waved his bandaged arms. "They gave me poison ivy."

She raised a pretty eyebrow.

Realization was like a punch in the gut. "If we prevent Seymour from stealing my money, he's not guilty of anything?"

"That's why I wrote Tyler. There has to be something he can prosecute Seymour for." Cass finished the final length across his forehead.

"And I can't fire him. My grandfather guaranteed him a job at Ravenswood."

"Even if we stop him this time, he may try something else. I don't trust him."

"Neither did my mother," Zach said. "We spent most of our time at the cabin by the lake. She was protecting Pax and me by keeping us away from Seymour."

"The cabin is beautiful."

He looked around. "You like it better than Ravens Roost?"

She nodded. "I know you wanted to impress me, but the cabin is warm and inviting. It feels like a home."

Zach turned toward the door. "They're coming." He climbed into bed.

Cass gathered her supplies. "How can you tell?"

"The floorboards in front of Elijah's room creak." He fell back against the mattress, arranged his covers, and slipped his bandaged wrists through the ropes. Cass took her position behind the thick draperies in front of the windows.

The door opened and a candle illuminated the room. Zach closed his eyes and remained motionless on the bed.

"He'll talk tonight, or you can dump the entire bottle of opium down his throat and make him gag on his silence," Seymour said.

"You're in a foul mood, my pet."

"Why didn't Vance tell me the girl had seen the mares and foals? I looked like an idiot when I said they were all dead."

"He covered for you."

"If he had let the boy run into the barn, I wouldn't have to offer explanations. I hired him to take care of any trouble."

"How much are you paying him?"

Seymour made a noise too dark to be a chuckle. "A lot less than he's expecting."

"He's a dangerous man. You need to be careful."

"I've calculated the steps of my plan even with the return of the boy and his pesky friends showing up. The rest of the buyers are arriving today and tomorrow morning. If I don't have the titles, Kettler won't authorize the sale even if he's convinced of Zachary's incompetence. Some of the men may pay for a horse without papers but not top dollar. It will be a fraction of what they're worth."

"What about forging the papers?"

"I asked Vance, but he said it would take time to

make passable forgeries, and the buyers are reputable horse traders, not back alley thieves. They'll recognize a sloppy counterfeit."

"I don't trust Vance."

"He's done his part. He arranged the sale, invited the buyers, and he'll collect the money."

"Why can't you collect the money?"

"Kettler will be present to record the sales. He's never liked me. A dozen years ago, he caught me drowning a cat and her litter in the creek below the lake and threatened to report my actions to Elijah."

"You drowned a bunch of kittens?"

"Worthless barn cats, but Pax and Zach had made pets of them." He chuckled. "They were heartbroken."

Zach clenched his fists. He and Pax had searched for the missing kittens and mother for weeks.

"No wonder their mother wanted them as far away from you as possible." She meant Allison. What had Seymour revealed to Lucia about his parents?

"You don't know half of what I did to keep my half-brother, Clayton, from endearing himself to Elijah. When he died, I was disappointed the game ended. But now Zach is playing for Ravenswood, and I always win."

"When we met, you said you were heir to a fortune. I don't like it when men lie to me."

"I was his firstborn son," Seymour said. "I wasn't going to be cheated from my inheritance. I'd spent too many years praising the old man and bowing to his wishes. How many years did I have to wait for him to die before I could claim what was mine? The wealth of Ravenswood was within my grasp until that snotty-nosed brat came home on furlough. Elijah was smitten with his tales of heroics. I never had any interest in horses, and the boy loved them. They spent hours touring Ravenswood."

Zach didn't dare look at them, but Seymour was getting angrier with each word.

"I didn't know the boy had hired a lawyer. When Tyler Montgomery visited, he talked Elijah into changing his will. He stole Ravenswood out from under me."

Elijah had ordered the new will, and Tyler had informed Zach later. Seymour was lying to Lucia. It was a life-long habit.

"Can't you claim Ravenswood if the boy is committed?"

"With his friends underfoot? Cassandra Beecher talked about her father examining Zachary. He'll see the truth. Then there's Tyler Montgomery. He'll fight me in court for Ravenswood. No, it's time to leave this place. Let the ravens have it. Besides, in my new plan I keep all the money for myself."

Lucia clapped her hands and giggled. "You are a clever man. I'm so glad you invited me to stay."

"Invited? You claimed to be a nun and then crawled into my bed. You're the most exciting thing that's happened to me since I finished my education and returned to this dreary place. All you have to do is keep the boy filled with opium. I want him so sick Saturday, no one will question my authority to conduct the sale." Seymour chuckled. "They'll all believe I'm raising the money for poor Zachary and Ravenswood."

Lucia cackled. "Of course."

Zach couldn't react outwardly, but inwardly he seethed. Seymour's whole life had been ruled by greed.

He would keep the fortune of Ravenswood out of his hands no matter what the cost.

"The boy is awfully still. You don't think you gave him too much opium earlier?"

A hand pressed against his neck. "He has a pulse," Lucia said.

"Wake up, boy!" Seymour slapped his face.

The bandages dulled the blow. Normally he would have taken the abuse, but he was supposed to be drugged and in pain. Zach cried out. "Don't hurt me. Please don't hurt me."

"Zachary, my boy. The sale is tomorrow. I need to know where you've put the titles to the horses."

"The safe," he gasped. "The safe."

"The safe in the study?"

"Yes," he gasped. "I need my medicine. Give me my medicine."

"I've checked the safe in the study a dozen times. It has nothing in it but the will," Seymour said. "Don't you want to save Ravenswood?"

"In the safe," Zach groaned.

"He gives you the same answer no matter how many times you ask," Lucia said. "When was the last time you saw the titles?"

"The boy was looking at them in the study, matching them against the inventory."

"Then they must be in that room," she said. "Is there a second safe? A secret box? A compartment in the floor?"

"Wait." Seymour paced across the floor. "When I first learned the combination, I would check on the contents of the safe regularly. I wanted to read through Elijah's correspondence. Once in a while papers would disappear, but I didn't think anything of it. But after Tyler Montgomery visited, I watched for any mail. Elijah received the will from him and placed it in the safe, but when I opened it later to read the document, it was gone. I thought he had taken it with him to his room, but we found nothing. I didn't know the contents until Kettler read it."

"So Elijah's copy was destroyed."

"No, after the boy arrived, the will was in the safe as if it had been there all along. Elijah had written some notes in the margin of the will. It was his original."

"You watched him put it in the safe, but when you opened it, the will was gone?"

Seymour snapped his fingers. "A secret compartment." Seymour headed for the door.

"What about the boy?"

"We don't need him anymore. Give him the whole bottle. Tomorrow I'll be rich, and the boy's addled thoughts will convince Kettler he's incompetent."

Lucia emptied the remaining powder into the bowel and mixed it with the honey. She forced a spoon in Zach's mouth. He fought it, but as soon as he tasted the hot powder mixed with honey, he recognized the concoction Mrs. Graves had created and relaxed. She gave him the remaining mixture followed by a drink of water. "Goodbye, you beautiful man."

As soon as the door closed, Zach sat. "Water, water." He struggled out of the ropes.

Lucia had left the empty bottle, spoon, and glass of water by the bed. Before Cass could reach the table, Zach downed the liquid. He waved his hand in front of his mouth. "Tell Mrs. Graves not so much pepper next time."

Cass poured water from the pitcher into his glass, and he emptied it. "There won't be a next time. He's going to find the papers."

Zach pulled on his trousers.

Cass blocked the door. "You can't fight him alone. We need to fetch Ethan and Harry."

He opened the door. "No confrontation, but I need to know what he does with the papers."

She followed him into the hall. "I can't be seen in my nightgown and robe."

"He won't see us."

"Why not?"

He lowered his voice. "We're going to use the secret passage."

Cass looked around. "What secret passage?"

He grabbed her hand and led her behind the tapestry to the servant's staircase. Moonlight illuminated the steps, but Cass placed her hand on Zach's shoulder as he led the way to the lower hallway.

He pushed open the secret door in the wooden paneling of the wall and entered the library. Zach held his hand in the air, a military signal for silence. Noise echoed from the study next door.

"Can we see what they're doing?" she whispered.

Zach touched his finger to her lips. He'd forgotten she wasn't a soldier. He turned a raven figure on a shelf, and a book shelf swung forward. He led the way into an opening that was the back of a matching bookcase in the study. He moved aside a panel that allowed them to see into the room. They stared through the slits that blended with the decorative woodwork.

Seymour had the safe open and had emptied the contents onto the desk. He was feeling around the interior. "I can't figure out how to open it."

"Is there a lever?"

"No. It's smooth."

"What about a spring release? Push down."

Silence was followed by a squeal of delight. Seymour turned, nearly facing them with the stack of titles in his hand. "The boy was telling the truth all along."

"I feel like celebrating." Lucia pushed Seymour into the chair. With Seymour's back to them, they couldn't see what Lucia was doing, but he was moaning and groaning in pleasure.

Cass gasped, and Zach put his hands over her eyes. She pulled them away.

They were done. Lucia pulled off her wimple and wiped her mouth with the cloth. Her straight brown hair was bobbed. "I hate this outfit."

"You can burn it after we convince Kettler that Zachary can't be responsible for the sale." Seymour gathered the titles from the desktop. "Do you know what this represents? Money. I had to put up with those smelly animals and the hordes of flies they attract. New York City is going to be a breath of fresh air."

"You've never been to New York, have you?" Her voice didn't conceal her sarcasm.

Seymour shoved the papers into the safe.

"Doesn't the boy know the combination?"

Seymour laughed. "The boy is in no condition to steal them."

"What about the signatures?"

"When Kettler sees how ill Zachary is, he'll authorize any scribble the boy can make. He won't dare cancel the sale with Ravenswood's future in the balance. With him notarizing the signature, it'll be perfectly legal."

Zach waited until they left the room and then pushed the secret passageway open. He opened the safe and retrieved the documents."

"What are you going to do with them?"

"Hide them. As long as I have the documents and not Seymour, I control the sale."

Chapter Twenty-Eight

The next day Harry and Ethan were given the task of keeping Seymour busy and out of the study. They didn't want him to discover the titles had been removed.

Cass spent the time washing her undergarments and ironing Zach's shirt and suit. They had decided to confront Seymour at supper and force him and Lucia to leave Ravenswood before the sale so they couldn't do any more mischief.

She carried his clothing to his room. He was applying aloe cream to his arms. "I'll buy a jar to replace this one."

"You still owe Colleen one."

"After the sale I'll buy each of your sisters a jar."

"You won't be embarrassed to buy a woman's cream?"

"Why should I be?"

"Then you can do all my shopping."

His eyes sparkled with mischief. "I have some ideas for camisoles and bloomers."

"Zachary!"

A smile played upon his lips. "You feign outrage when you're secretly pleased."

"I do not."

He chuckled and turned his head. "Did I cover all of it?"

She applied cream to his neck. "You are bold with your words but take my feelings for granted."

"Never. I covet the tenderness you offer this weary soldier."

"You look miserable, but your spirits have revived." She smoothed the lotion over his arms. "You sound like the Zach in your letters. I loved reading the description of your travels."

"I would rather describe you," he said. "Your fingertips play a song upon my flesh."

"Are you attempting to seduce me with poetic words?"

"Do I still repulse you with my hideousness? These past months have been dark and wearied my soul, but today, my heart is on wings. If my verbal eloquence doesn't inspire you, I can pen the words in a letter."

His letters had been filled with poetic phrases describing the countryside, the people, and his yearnings for home. Among the paragraphs had been tender words.

"I witness the sunrise and recall the light upon your soft cheeks, the feathery arch of your brow, and the look of love that inspires a weary soldier to continue the journey home."

"I wrote those words before leaving Atlanta," Zach said. "You remember them?"

"It was a long time before the next letter arrived. I memorized every word."

He embraced her. "When you are close, words fail me. How can I convey the depth of my feelings? I would sacrifice all for you, Cassandra. Command me, and I will obey."

His playfulness was contagious. "Now that you're

not so ugly, I wouldn't mind a kiss."

Zach took her in his arms, her body pressed against his, the heat building between them. He kissed her cheek, a chaste beginning. She offered her neck and he pressed warm lips against her tender flesh until a moan escaped.

His mouth silenced her as he devoured the fruit of her mouth. She gasped and his tongue found access. He plundered in a motion mimicking coupling. She grabbed onto his bare shoulders for support. He was half naked, and she was losing her resolve to remain upright. Her corset provided a thick barrier as his hands roamed her waist and moved upward, cupping her breast.

She pushed his hand away. "Behave."

"You shouldn't have allowed me to sample the sweets. Now I can think of nothing but satisfying my appetite."

She checked the bodice of her green silk gown. "You can satisfy your appetite at the dining table."

He grabbed his shirt. "I'll be there soon."

****

Seymour and his guests were seated at the table when she arrived. The men stood when she entered, and she took her seat next to Vance. "It's nice you could join us, Mr. Edwards."

"I couldn't pass on an opportunity to spend an evening with such a charming lady."

Lucia looked at each of them, a queer smile on her lips. "Have you ever been married?"

"Yes, but my wife and child died during the war."

"How awful," Lucia said. "But then you would value a spouse."

"I have no need to marry," Vance said.

"With so many war widows?" Lucia asked. "I would think it was your responsibility to wed."

Vance raised an eyebrow. "Are you playing matchmaker, Sister Lucia?"

Cass avoided eye contact with a grinning Lucia and turned to Vance. "Did your wife make your beautiful vest?"

"She did." He stroked the silk. "I haven't worn it since joining the service."

"She was talented." Why did the vest look familiar? Or was it the pattern? Jem had made Logan a similar vest with birds. The one he had worn the night of Lincoln's assassination. "Is the pattern a common one?"

"My wife designed it."

How did Jem have the same pattern? A crash of thunder echoed outside and interrupted her thoughts.

Harry jumped in the seat beside her. "I hope the storm doesn't ruin the sale."

"Most of the bidders have arrived and looked over the stock," Vance said. "They're eager to buy. A little rain won't change their minds."

Lucia raised her wine glass, froze, and dropped it.

"What's wrong with you?" Seymour demanded, dabbing at his coat where the wine had splattered.

She pointed toward the doorway.

Zach made his grand entrance. "Good evening, everyone. I'm sorry I'm late."

Ethan and Harry greeted him as if he was expected. "It's good to see you."

Cass stood. "I'm glad you could join us."

He hugged her. "It was time to rejoin the living."

"You shouldn't be out of bed," Lucia shrieked.

"Don't worry. My poison ivy is under control." He ran his fingers over a few blisters on the top of his hand. "Mostly."

She looked confused. "How?"

"Miss Beecher's father is a doctor. She recognized I had been infected using those bandages you claimed I needed for my burns." He frowned. "My imaginary burns."

"It's good to see you improved." Seymour glared at Lucia. "I was under the impression you were on death's door."

"I would have been if you had your way."

"I had no intention of harming you," Lucia said. "Seymour ordered me to give you the opium."

They were attempting to shift blame to each other. Zach stood by Seymour, who was seated at the head of the table. "I believe you're sitting in my chair."

Seymour stood and threw his napkin on the table.

Zach remained standing, facing his adversary. "Was it only greed, Seymour, or was there some other reason you betrayed me?"

"What do you know about being the bastard of the family? I obeyed the orders Elijah gave me. I graduated from college and handled his business affairs. What did it get me? Nothing but a promise to be employed as nothing better than a servant."

"Servant? Then you won't argue when I reduce your duties to cleaning the manure out of the horse stalls."

"Seymour is a gentleman," Lucia said. "He deserves better."

"You're nothing better than a horse thief."

"You agreed to the sale," Seymour said.

Zach turned to Vance. "Whatever agreement you had with Seymour, you can consider it null and void."

"You're canceling the sale?"

"It will continue on my terms. I'm only selling the horses on this list." Zach handed Vance a sheet of paper. "I know Ned Pike wants some mares. I've selected a few that are older and can spare to let go. The others are not for sale."

Vance studied the list. "What about the horses for your friends?"

"You can put their horses aside. I'll process the paperwork at the end of the sale."

"You have the papers?"

"Yes." Zach surveyed Seymour. "I removed them from the safe after you discovered the secret compartment."

He looked past Zach toward the study. "You stole the papers?"

"They were mine."

Seymour hurried from the room.

Lucia looked at the others. "Seymour was only trying to get what was rightfully his."

Zach took his seat at the head of the table. "Elijah chose me as his heir."

Seymour stomped into the room. "Vance, a word."

Vance excused himself.

"What about me?" Lucia followed them. "I won't be ignored."

They disappeared into the study.

Zach looked at his friends. "I couldn't have done it without you."

Ethan placed his fingers to his brow and saluted.

"All for one and one for all."

The violent thunderstorm had abated to a light rain. Cass burrowed into her covers, hoping the soft pitter-patter against the window pane would lull her to sleep. Seymour had admitted defeat and had retired to pack his bags. Lucia did the same.

Vance offered to stay and help show the horses. Zach had agreed to keep him and his men on against protest from Harry and Ethan.

After dessert, Vance had left for the cabin, and they had departed to their rooms in preparation for Saturday's sale.

Cass dozed off. She was awakened by a noise. Was someone in her room? A hand covered her mouth. She struggled. "Zach! Zach!"

"Keep her quiet." It was Vance.

"Yes, sir."

She recognized Bryce, who thrust a handkerchief into her mouth and tied another cloth around her face to secure it in place. He wrapped her in the blanket and hoisted her over his shoulder.

She could see the floor. They were heading along the hallway. Vance was following with her bag.

Cass worked to free her hands and arms, but they were trapped by her sides. She bounced on Bryce's shoulder as he ran downstairs. The cooler air outside hit her face. She was tossed over a saddle and had to endure the rough ride, praying she wouldn't fall off and meet her demise beneath the hooves of the horse.

When Bryce stopped, Vance pulled her from the saddle and set her on her feet. "Don't try anything, Miss Beecher."

They were in front of a small cabin she had never

seen. It wasn't on Zach's map.

"Put the horses away," Vance ordered. He removed the scarf covering her mouth and pulled out the gag.

She took a long draw of breath. "Have you gone mad? My friends will hunt you down."

"They're gentlemen. They won't discover you're gone until morning," Vance said. "By then it will be too late to rescue you."

Cass struggled free from the blanket. Vance cursed. Her nightgown was her only clothing. He snatched the cover from the ground and draped it around her. The ground was cold beneath her bare feet. She took a step into a puddle and jumped back.

Vance lifted her into his arms. She screamed. "There's no one to hear you but the coyotes."

The cabin was dark except for red and gold ashes smoldering in the fireplace. Vance carried her to a small bed in the corner and deposited her on the cornhusk-filled mattress. "Get some sleep before morning."

Cass scooted to the far side against the wall. She pulled the cover around her, huddling in its protective cocoon. Vance squatted in front of the fire and added a log. "This will take the chill off the damp air."

Bryce entered with her bag. "Where should I put this?"

Vance took it and dropped it near the bed where she cowered. "Be a good girl, and you'll be reunited with your friends tomorrow."

"Why are you doing this?"

"I'm getting paid to do it."

"I thought you were an honorable soldier, but you're nothing but a mercenary."

He bent near her face. "Don't talk to me about

honor. While Tyler Montgomery stayed safely home with his wife and son, I lost everything."

Why did he hate Tyler?

He turned and joined Bryce in front of the fire. "You take first watch. I'm getting some sleep."

Vance flopped onto another narrow bed across the small one-room cabin. The hewn logs were thick, and a small window provided the only light. Her only way to escape was through the door, and Bryce sat in a chair between her and freedom.

After watching her captors, hoping Bryce would fall asleep, her eyes closed.

****

Zach rose early for the sale and joined Ethan and Harry in the hallway. He knocked on the door for Cass. No answer.

"Hey, sleepy head, wake up!" Ethan called.

Zach opened the door. The bed was stripped of its blanket. A pillow was on the floor. Her bag was missing. "She's gone."

"She's been kidnapped," Harry said.

"No one would dare…"

Zach didn't hear the rest of Ethan's words. He rushed to Seymour's room. It was empty. He opened a drawer. His clothing was gone. They had ordered him to go. Did he take Cass with him?

He ran down the stairs. Seymour was seated at the head of the dining room table eating breakfast. "Beautiful day for a sale."

Zach grabbed Seymour by his coat and raised him off the chair. "Where is she?"

Seymour struggled from his grip. "No harm will come to Miss Beecher if you do exactly as I say."

Zach shoved him into his seat. "You want the papers."

"You're not as dumb as I thought."

Ethan and Harry stood beside him. "I'll turn them over to you when I know Miss Beecher is safe."

He tapped his fingertips together. "You'll see her at the auction. If you try anything, she'll be the first to suffer."

"You wouldn't dare harm an innocent woman. You couldn't hate me that much."

"Lucia mentioned Vance desires a wife," Seymour said. "He's had all night to convince Miss Beecher to marry him."

Zach punched Seymour. His head jerked with the blow, and his nose bled. Seymour grabbed his napkin and staunched the flow. "If he's touched her, you'll die by my hands."

Seymour examined the blood on the cloth. "You don't have it in you to murder a man."

He looked at Ethan and Harry and laughed. "We killed plenty of men in the war. When we ran out of cartridges, we used our bayonets. In close quarters we used knives, and when we were without weapons, we used our bare fists." Zach placed his hands on Seymour's neck. "When you choke the life out of man, he doesn't die quickly. He knows death is coming, but he can't stop it." Zach released him. "Cassandra would ask me to spare your life, but she's not here to stop me."

Seymour shook. "The war is over."

"You started this one." Zach sat. "And whether you live or die no longer matters to me."

Chapter Twenty-Nine

Cass spent a restless night in the strange cabin. As sunlight filtered through the lone window, she stirred. Vance was awake, dressed, and drinking coffee. Bryce was gone from his bed. She hesitated to rise. "I need to dress."

He turned his back. "Be quick."

The sparse furnishings didn't include a screen for privacy. "You could wait outside."

"I don't molest women, but if you don't hurry, you can attend the sale in your nightgown."

She threw off the cover and stood on the wooden plank floor. She glanced at Vance, his back toward her, and opened her bag. Her anger replaced her fear. "Don't you know how to pack?" Her clothes were clumped in a wadded mass. She sorted the undergarments from her dresses.

"I don't have time for you to sew an outfit," Vance said. "Pick something to wear."

Cold winters had taught her to dress quickly. She pulled her bloomers on beneath her nightgown and slipped on her stockings. She turned. He was standing at attention, facing the opposite direction. She turned away and pulled off her nightgown, replacing it with her camisole. She stepped into her corset and pulled it to her waist, struggling to tighten the strings.

"I don't have all day, Miss Beecher." Vance pulled

the lacings and tied off the strings.

"I don't need your help."

"Women say that and immediately find themselves in dire straits. Besides, you don't have anything I haven't seen before."

He'd been married, but Cass hurried to finish her wardrobe. She fastened the corset cover. "Where's my hoop?"

"Hoop?"

"For my skirt." Cass looked around. "Don't tell me you forgot the crinoline hoop."

"You can go without one," he growled.

Cass tied off her petticoat and slipped on a work dress. The sleeves were narrow and the collar high. The bodice buttoned in the front. The matching skirt hung in thick folds without a crinoline. She searched her bag.

"Now what?" Vance demanded.

"You forgot my boots."

"Go barefoot."

She found a pair of low-heeled slippers and put them on. "Next time you kidnap me, allow me to pack my bag."

"We're not holding you for ransom, Miss Beecher."

"I'm a bargaining chip to keep my friends in line while Seymour sells Zach's horses and steals his money."

"Precisely."

"That's blackmail, Mr. Edwards."

Bryce entered. "Zach has agreed to the sale."

"Of course he did." Cass didn't bother combing and arranging her hair. She tugged on her cloth bonnet and swiped at a stray tear. "You gave him no choice."

"Prepare the horse and buggy," Vance ordered.

Bryce looked at her, turned, and departed. He wouldn't help her. He was a soldier who followed orders first.

Vance offered her a cup of coffee. She declined. "I'm glad you understand the situation."

"What is your role in this?"

"Seymour hired me to manage the sale of all the horses on Ravenswood."

"All of them?"

"Except those we claim for ourselves as payment for the deed."

"That will ruin Zach."

He finished his coffee. "That's not my problem."

"How much is Seymour paying you? Zach will match it."

"With what? He won't have anything once Seymour leaves with his money," Vance said.

Zach would have her. Would her love be enough to sustain him through this treachery?

"Your smile worries me, Miss Beecher." Vance lifted her chin and examined her face. "What are you thinking?"

"You haven't stolen the most valuable thing to Zach."

His eyebrow rose, and a smile exposed crooked teeth. "You."

She tied the ribbons to her bonnet beneath her chin. "He's the man I plan to marry."

"You may want to reconsider when he's faced with poverty."

"I didn't fall in love with his money." She tilted her chin. "I love him."

"What do you know of love?"

"I know when it's real. You lost the person you loved. Can't you sympathize with my plight?"

His head jerked in her direction. "You haven't lost a wife and child."

His suffering could explain the coldness and harshness in his behavior. "What happened to them?"

"I don't know." He clanged the empty coffee cup against the table. "I was away fighting when death claimed them. I returned home to find two graves and an empty house. I should have spent the war sitting behind a desk like Tyler Montgomery."

Tyler again. "I understand why Seymour hates Tyler. He blames him for losing Ravenswood because of the will, but how do you know Tyler?"

He leaned against the edge of the table and scanned her figure. "You were a little girl in pigtails when I saw you on the square of Darrow Falls celebrating Independence Day. Tyler wasn't married to your sister then. He was stealing my property."

What was he talking about? "Tyler isn't a thief."

"He stole Tess even after the judge said she belonged to me."

Tess had been a runaway slave whom Tyler and Cory had helped in 1860. But her master had been Edward Vandal, owner of the Silver Pheasant plantation in Vandalia, Virginia. He had followed Tess to Darrow Falls with his chasers. Cass had seen him from a distance, but he had worn a colorful vest embroidered by his wife. "Did Reggie make your vest?"

"Regina," he corrected. "Tyler tried stealing Regina from me when we were younger. I made her the lady of the Silver Pheasant, but my home lies in ruins."

It had been five years, but Cass recognized the broken nose and fierce countenance that had fascinated and frightened her. His hair was darker, and the war had aged him, but it was the same man Tyler had fought in the town square and argued against in the courtroom. "Hello, Edward Vandal."

"You remember me?"

She packed her belongings. "Tyler has been searching for you."

"I know, that's why I changed my name."

She faced him. "I don't understand. Why don't you want to be found?"

"Tyler may not have fought in the war, but he's still my enemy. I don't trust him. And you can tell him he better not interfere with my plans to rebuild the Silver Pheasant."

"With stolen funds?" Cass shook her head. "You're not setting a good example for Jefferson."

He grabbed her arm. The tight grip made her cry out in pain. "How do you know my son's name?"

"My sister Jem helped Reggie after he was born." She smiled. "That's why you called her Miss Jenny. You were there."

"Regina. My wife's name is Regina." He turned away. "Was Regina."

"Jem explained how you were going to name him after the president, and she thought you meant Abraham Lincoln."

A slight smile appeared on Edward's face. "Stupid Yankee."

"My sister is not stupid."

"No?" Edward studied her. "She traveled to Richmond alone during a war. What woman does that?"

"She was searching for her husband."

"She had courage." His brows rose. "I see the same in you."

"Then you should understand I'll fight for Zach until my last breath."

Edward turned away. "I, on the other hand, have nothing to fight for."

"What about Jefferson?"

He turned, his hand raised to strike her. "I said not to mention my son's name."

"Why not? Don't you love him?"

"Of course. No one could love him more." He ran his fist across his cheek to swipe a tear.

"Our families have been tied together through the years," Cass said. "Because of Tyler, Tess, and Jefferson. The ties are too strong to break. We love him. Sterling loves him like a brother."

Edward looked confused. "Who is Sterling?"

"My nephew. Tyler's son."

"How could he have known Jefferson?"

"They're best friends. Jefferson has been living with Tyler since Reggie's death. I mean Regina," Cass corrected. "That's why he's been trying to find you."

Edward raised a clenched fist in the air. "Why do you torture me with lies? Jefferson is dead!"

Cass flinched, expecting him to hit her. He had turned his back. He cradled his head in his hands. "Why do you believe Jefferson is dead?"

"His grave was next to Regina's."

"That was the baby's grave," Cass said.

He spun to face her. "What baby?"

"Regina's maid, Esther, informed us your wife had a baby girl. They died within weeks of each other.

Those are the graves you saw."

He grabbed her arm and shook her. "What happened to Jefferson?"

"Esther delivered Jefferson to Washington City, and they traveled to Darrow Falls with my sisters two years ago. He's been living with Tyler and Cory at Glen Knolls."

"I don't believe you." Edward released his grip and paced across the room. "It can't be true."

"I'm not a liar." How did she prove Jefferson was alive? She turned toward her bag and searched through the contents. She withdrew her photograph album and flipped through the pages of family members. She stopped at a picture of two boys sitting side by side. She showed the book to Edward.

"Sterling Montgomery is on the right. I think you might recognize the boy sitting next to him in the photograph."

He grabbed the album from her hands and stared. His voice cracked when he spoke. "When was this taken?"

"In June when all the family was together."

His voice was soft, a whisper. "The last time I was home he was still wearing a gown and bonnet."

Jake's age. "Sterling and Jefferson are inseparable," Cass said. "They share everything. They had the chicken pox together. Of course, they shared it with Olivia…" A sob stopped her words.

Edward sat in the chair in front of the fireplace, his head bowed over the album. He brushed away tears. "I thought he was dead." His voice broke in pain. He turned toward her. "You swear he's alive?"

Cass shook her head. "I swear. Jefferson Vandal is

alive in Darrow Falls."

"You said he was living with Tyler Montgomery."

"Regina wrote him before she died. She asked Cory and Tyler to take care of Jefferson in case you didn't survive the war. That's the only reason Tyler has been searching for you. He wants to reunite you with your son."

Edward snapped the album shut. "This doesn't change anything. I'm selling the horses."

Cass reached for the album. "You can't. You've made a deal with the devil. Seymour doesn't own those horses. They belong to Zach."

"I don't care about Zach Ravenswood. I need money to rebuild the Silver Pheasant. Now, more than ever."

"You can't rebuild your home with stolen money," Cass said. "If you commit this crime, Tyler will prosecute you, and he's an excellent lawyer. Jefferson will be a grown man by the time you see him."

Edward put the album in his pocket. "You're going to do exactly as I say. You will follow my instructions without question, or Zach will lose his horses, home, and you."

Cass swallowed. A threat by Edward Vandal needed to be heeded. "Yes, sir."

Bryce opened the door. "It's time for the sale, Major."

"Take her bag." Edward offered his arm. "Come along, Miss Beecher. We're going to an auction."

Cass loosened the drawstring on her reticule and examined the money inside. "At least let me buy a broodmare."

"Keep your money, Miss Beecher."

Edward escorted her to a buggy. A wooden box with metal reinforced corners was loaded in the back behind the single seat. It was the one she had seen in the room in the cabin. The broken handle had been repaired. Bryce placed her travel bag on top.

"Everything is packed," Bryce said. "We can head out as soon as the sale is completed."

"You'll be wanted men on the run," Cass said.

Bryce looked shocked. "What does she know?"

"Nothing," Edward said. "I'll take her in the buggy. Tie my horse to the back.

"Is that Black Knight?" The familiar gelding grazed under a nearby tree. "I was going to buy him."

"You'll be happier with Peaches," Edward said. "She's gentler."

Cass didn't hesitate. She ran to Black Knight, stroking his neck and speaking gentle words to keep from spooking him. Then she put her foot in the stirrup and straddled his back. She kicked her heels into his sides and urged the horse along the overgrown path.

The element of surprise wouldn't last long, but if she could reach Zach, show him she was safe, she could prevent Seymour and Edward from robbing him.

It had been years since she rode astride, but she hadn't forgotten the skills that had made her one of the best riders in Summit County. She directed Black Knight forward along the little-used trail, hoping it led to a familiar site or landmark from her earlier trips on the property.

She glanced back, expecting Bryce to be pursuing her, but it was Edward. He was angry. She urged Black Knight into a run to distance herself from her pursuer.

"Pull up, Miss Beecher!" Edward shouted. "Do you

want to break your foolish neck?"

Cass had been riding horses since she was five. She was the best rider in the Beecher family. Only Edward didn't know that. She should thank him for forgetting her crinoline. It made her ride easier. She looked back. No one was behind her. She had lost Edward.

Ahead of her, she could see the blue waters of the lake through the gaps in the trees.

As she broke out of the woods into the clearing, she recognized the large cabin by the lake to her left and headed for it. Edward broke out of the woods in front of her escape. He had taken a different path. He grabbed her off the horse and pulled her against his chest. Cass fought for her freedom.

"What did you think you were doing?"

His grip was too firm. His hands bruised her arms. She ceased struggling. "I was never in danger. I'm a good rider."

"Even the best rider can make a mistake." Edward pulled her to the ground and shook her, knocking her bonnet back. "You could have been thrown or a branch could have knocked you off." He examined her for any injuries.

Edward appeared genuinely concerned. Where had this slice of kindness come from?

His hand brushed back her hair where it had escaped her braid. He cupped her cheek. "You scratched your face."

Her hand touched her cheek. She hadn't felt the twig smack her. "I'm fine."

His mouth covered hers. His kiss was so surprising, Cass stood still, unable to react. Why were men always kissing her? And why couldn't she think of ways to stop them?

When he released her, she found her courage. She wiped her mouth with the back of her hand and spat on the ground to rid the taste of him. "I did not give you permission to kiss me, you cad!"

"You could pretend you liked it," he said. "Seduce me into thinking you were in love with me to save Zach."

Cass hadn't considered anything so deceptive and repulsive.

"No, you're not the type to pretend. The Beecher women are lousy liars."

"Some people would consider that a virtue."

"Not to a man who is considering making an honorable proposal of marriage."

"What?" He couldn't be serious.

"Lucia mistook my interest in your family and hinted about a liaison. Seymour wanted me to defile you. Another revenge against Zach, but I consider myself a gentleman. I am serious about my proposal. Jefferson will need a mother. You talked fondly of my son. Do you like him?"

A marriage of convenience? "I love Jefferson, but I don't love you." She stepped away, worried he might try to change her mind. "Don't you know anyone who might make a good stepmother?"

"I wasn't looking until now, but you've given me hope. I'm not as dead as I thought, and there are plenty of women looking for a husband. One of them might fall in love with me."

"Thievery and deception are hardly admirable traits in a husband."

"Regina recognized good in me when others did

not. I need you to see what she did."

"Why? I have no intention of marrying you."

He grimaced. "I understood your rejection clearly. What I'm asking is for faith. I always admired your sisters for their lack of hysterics during a crisis. I expect the same of you during the sale."

She bit back any tears and glared. "I won't cry."

He lowered his voice. "I need you to do exactly what I say."

"Is it dishonest?"

"No. It will save the man you love."

Was he still hopeful? "You do understand, that's not you."

He laughed. "Do you always decide so quickly?"

"Your kiss doomed you. Harry kissed me, too, and I had the same reaction."

"Has Zach kissed you?"

She didn't answer.

"Keep smiling like you are now. We don't want anyone to think you're attending this event against your will." He retrieved the horses.

Chapter Thirty

Edward helped her mount Black Knight but kept the reins in his control as he rode beside her.

Cass tried to sway Edward. "Seymour is not an honest man."

"I'm counting on it."

What did he mean? "If you don't trust him, why make a bargain with him?"

"The bargain was tilted in my favor until Zach arrived. Seymour tried to kill him."

"With the barn fire, but you kept him from going inside." Cass studied him. "Why did you do that?"

"I don't murder innocent men, but others don't share my scruples. Do you want Seymour gone and out of Zach's life?"

"Yes. He's a dangerous man."

"Then we're on the same side."

She looked at the gun on his hip. "Are you planning to shoot Seymour?"

"Miss Beecher, you have an active imagination."

"None of the horrible events in the last few months have been a result of my imagination."

He shook his head and snorted. "What has been so tragic in your young life?"

"Zach and I were at Ford's Theater when Lincoln was shot."

He studied her. "Then you understand that even

with precise plans, something could go wrong. Booth thought he would escape to the South and be hailed a hero, but he broke his leg when he jumped from the balcony and was trapped because of his injury. If I give you an order, you must promise to obey me. I would like to keep everyone alive."

Cass nodded. She wasn't sure she could trust Edward, but his plan was better than none.

They arrived at the paddock where the buyers were gathered around to view the horses for the auction. A large tent was placed to one side with a table and chairs arranged beneath the canvas. Edward helped her down. She made sure to keep her face turned from his. "Don't worry. I won't kiss you again."

"Zach is a jealous man. He tussled with Harry for kissing me, and your nose has been broken enough times."

He touched the crooked ridge. "Thanks to Tyler."

Bryce arrived with the buggy and stopped at the tent. "Everything all right, Major?" He handed him the hat he'd lost in the chase.

"Miss Beecher won't give us any trouble." He helped Bryce with the chest, and they placed it on the table. He placed her travel bag beneath on the ground. "Take these horses to the barn and save Black Knight for Miss Beecher. He isn't too much for her to handle."

"What about Peaches?" Bryce asked.

"I'm sure her future husband will want to present her with a gift."

"Aren't you selling them?" she whispered after Bryce left.

"Please don't act like a woman and talk too much," Edward said.

"I'm the least talkative of all my sisters," Cass defended.

Edward pointed. "There's Zach."

Cass turned. Zach jumped from the seat before Ethan stopped the wagon. He ran to her and took her in his arms. He kissed her long and deep, and she returned his passion. He held her, refusing to release her. "Are you all right?"

"You're a lucky man," Edward said.

"If you touched her…" Zach threatened.

"Miss Beecher is a lady, and although it's been years since I've enjoyed the company of the gentler sex, I fancy myself a gentleman."

"I ought to kill you for kidnapping her."

"No killing," Cass said, placing her hand on Zach's chest. "We're no longer enemies."

Zach frowned, puzzled by her words. "Are you sure?"

"Trust me."

"Heed her words," Edward said. "And we'll avoid any complications."

Ethan and Harry joined them. She hugged them. "I'm fine."

Harry gave Cass her basket. "Mrs. Graves thought you might be hungry."

Ethan pointed at Edward. "I'll deal with you later concerning my cousin."

"I'm sure you will, but for now, you'll do exactly as you're told. Two of my men have rifles, and I don't need to tell you they're sharpshooters."

The men looked around.

"You won't spot them." Edward turned to Cass. "Convince them they should do what I say for their best interest."

"Everything will work out if we do as he says. No heroics. Promise me," she begged.

"Heed her advice, gentlemen." Edward brushed back his coat to reveal his Colt revolver. Zach offered Cass a chair and sat beside her.

Edward removed papers from his jacket. He gave one copy to Ethan. "This is a list of the horses for sale. You and your friend can help Bryce show them to the buyers."

"I think I should stay here."

"Miss Beecher is perfectly safe with Zach present," Edward said.

Zach nodded to Ethan and Harry. "Go ahead. Do as he says."

"Don't worry, Zach," Ethan said. "We'll help you rebuild Ravenswood."

Seymour arrived with Lucia in a buggy. Lucia had transformed from nun to flamboyant mistress in a figure-hugging gown of salmon. A matching bonnet covered her short hair. The bodice barely contained her breasts, pushed upward by a stiff corset. Rice powder covered her face to give her a pale complexion, and her red-dyed lips contrasted like a bloody wound on a corpse. She twirled her lace-covered parasol. Lucia sat next to Zach and batted her darkened lashes. "It's good to see you've recovered."

"No thanks to your medicine," Zach said.

"I sincerely regretted marring such an attractive body. It was a pity I had already attached myself to Seymour."

"Like a bloodsucking leech," Cass said.

"I do believe the kitten has claws," Lucia said.

"Did you enjoy spending the night with Vance?"

"I slept soundly, alone in my bed," Cass said.

She closed her parasol. "Pity. Horses aren't the only things meant to be ridden hard and long."

Lucia's crude remark was meant to shock her. "You and Seymour appeared to keep your encounters brief."

Lucia's smile widened. "You watched?"

"It was unavoidable," Zach said.

"I hope it was educational. At the Sisters of Mercy customers paid to witness the deflowering of a virgin. I lost mine fourteen times."

"How…" Cass caught herself. Lucia had conned men for a long time. She almost felt sorry for Seymour. But he deserved everything Lucia took from him.

Seymour placed his hand on Lucia's shoulder. "Are our guests behaving?"

"We're having a lovely chat," Lucia said.

Seymour looked at Edward. "Did you make sure all the men are disarmed?"

He moved his jacket aside. "I have a gun, but the rest are unarmed."

Zach and Cass exchanged glances. What about the sharpshooters?

Seymour frowned. "Even your men?"

Edward never changed expression. "Those were your orders."

"Good, you can hand over your gun to me." Seymour held out his hand.

Edward rested his hand on the handle of his revolver. "That wasn't part of our agreement."

Lucia pulled a derringer from her handbag. "Do as Seymour says. A derringer at close range can be effective."

Cass grabbed Zach's hand. "Lincoln was shot with a derringer."

"A bit theatrical, but John Wilkes Booth was an actor," Lucia said. "I also consider myself a student of the arts."

Edward handed over his revolver. "So you're not only robbing Zach, you're leaving without paying me or my men."

"Sorry. You did an excellent job, but I need as much cash as possible to support this lovely creature." He stroked Lucia's cheek.

Zach looked at Edward. "It seems they have no respect for veterans. But we can be patient." He turned to Seymour. "How far do you think you can run before the law catches you? Remember, they hang thieves."

Lucia pointed the derringer at them. "They don't hang women."

"Tell that to Mary Surrat," Cass said. Mary was the lone woman who had hanged with the other conspirators of Lincoln's assassination. "She wasn't even part of the conspiracy. She had the misfortune of owning the inn where they met."

Lucia's hand shook.

"Be careful her finger doesn't shake against the trigger accidentally." Edward pointed. "Fred Kettler and the auctioneer are arriving."

"Put it away," Seymour ordered Lucia. He waved the gun at Zach. "I hope you understand the role you are to play. Do not give me any reason to shoot you." Seymour placed Edward's heavy revolver on the table, his hand resting on top. "I'd hate to put a bullet in the lovely Miss Beecher, but she will be the first to go."

"She's done nothing against you," Zach said. "If you're going to shoot someone, kill me. Then Ravenswood will be yours."

"I don't want a barren horse farm. The Ravens Roost kept Elijah a poor man. The sale of the horses barely paid the expenses from year to year. Your grandfather was stingy for a reason. All I want is the money. You can drown in Ravenswood's debts."

Cass grabbed Zach's arm. "I don't want to lose you. Don't do anything foolish." He nodded, but the muscles beneath his sleeve remained taut.

"Smart decision, Zach," Edward said. "Let's finish this sale as quickly as possible so we can resume our lives."

They greeted Fred who sat at the end of the table. He opened his portable desk and arranged his record book and official seal.

"Do you have the titles?" Seymour asked Zach.

Zach withdrew a large envelope from his coat. "In here."

"Let Miss Beecher match them to the inventory." Edward placed the inventory list between them and pointed to the first horse. Zach handed her the envelope, and she found the corresponding title.

Edward signaled Bryce to show the first horse for sale.

Lucia clapped her hands. "Isn't she a pretty horsey?"

"It's a gelding," Zach corrected.

"It's money," Seymour said.

The auctioneer took bids, his voice trilling the numbers in rapid succession until he hit a gavel against a block of wood and shouted, "Sold!"

The bid ended at one-hundred-eighty dollars. The buyer paid Zach. Edward handed him the title and took the money. He opened the money chest and stacked it inside. "I better keep the lid closed. The wind is picking up."

Zach put the inkwell on top of the paper and signed over ownership. Fred recorded the sale, and Seymour handed the title to the new owner.

"See, that wasn't so painful," Seymour remarked. "He was a bit reluctant to part with the horses, Mr. Kettler."

"I've supervised Elijah Ravenswood's sales in the past. You have a fine turnout."

"I expect Zachary will sell a large number of his stock today," Seymour said. "I hope you can keep up."

"Don't worry about me. Do you have a guard for the money box?"

Seymour patted Edward's revolver. "I don't expect any trouble with my friend here."

Ethan and Harry helped Bryce show off the horses. The auctioneer took his time extoling the traits of each horse before he began the bidding. The hours wore on into the hot afternoon.

The older horses were easy to let go, but when the first mare and foal were led out, Zach turned on Seymour. "Ghost horses?"

"Ghost?" Fred repeated. "Your grandfather rarely sold the broodmares."

"With the loss of so many horses during the war, Zachary wanted to help other horse breeders by parting with a few of his mares," Seymour said. "Isn't that right, Zachary?"

Zach looked at Cass and turned to Fred. "I'm

obligated to help my fellow soldiers."

"Veterans should stick together, even those on opposite sides," Cass said.

"A man who has fought in a war knows what is worth dying for," Edward said. "And he knows what is worth living for." He patted his coat pocket. The one containing her photo album.

Ned paid Zach. "I was hoping for a special deal, but I didn't have to bid too high for that beauty."

"You're lucky I was willing to part with her." Zach handed the money to Edward, who stacked the bills inside the strongbox.

It was late in the day. Many of the buyers had already taken possession of their horses and left. Edward checked his watch and nodded toward Bryce. He approached the table, the list in his hand. "That's the last one."

Seymour grabbed the paper from him. "I thought there were more."

"The younger ones won't fetch anything," Edward said.

Zach had been tracking the numbers in his record book. He looked at the envelope Cass was holding on her lap. She opened it to reveal more titles inside before folding the envelope and shoving it into his coat pocket. "You have to let them go, Zach. They're all gone."

He met her gaze. She couldn't explain why Edward had kept some of the horses back from the sale. The inventory sheet in front of Seymour accounted for all of those sold. But he had to know some were missing. Or would he? Seymour had shown little interest in the animals except for the money they could net. Lucia was restless and had distracted him through much of the proceedings.

Edward removed his watch. "The train will be leaving soon, or do you plan to spend the night at Ravens Roost?"

Seymour stood. "The trunk is full?"

Edward opened the lid to the cashbox; the bills were stacked neatly inside to the top.

Seymour removed a handful of bills, a rare smile on his face.

Fred finished the paperwork and packed his supplies. He coughed and signaled the auctioneer he was ready to leave. "Our pay."

Seymour counted the money, paid Fred, and tossed the remaining bills back in the box. He shook hands with Fred and the auctioneer and hurried them on their way.

As soon they rode off, Seymour pointed the revolver at Edward. "Load the chest in my buggy."

Edward locked the lid and went to the front of the table to lift the box. The handle broke, and it crashed to the ground.

Everyone hurried to the overturned chest. Seymour examined the broken handle. "How am I going to carry this?"

Zach helped Edward lift the trunk to the table. "Why don't you put your money in Miss Beecher's travel bag?" Edward suggested. "It would be less conspicuous than this trunk."

Cass wanted to protest, but Edward nodded slightly at her and looked at her bag beneath the table. Had he placed it there on purpose? He lifted it and plopped it next to the trunk. She removed her clothing and stacked it on the table.

Seymour waved the Colt revolver toward the trunk. "Open it and make sure the wind doesn't blow any of it away."

Edward opened the lid. The bills were a bit messed, but that was expected after the trunk tumbled to the ground. He handed Zach the empty travel bag. "Do you mind holding it open?" Edward transferred the bills to the travel bag in large clumps.

"We're rich!" Lucia cooed. She grabbed several bills from the bag and tucked them into her bodice.

"Get in the buggy, Lucia."

Seymour glanced into the empty trunk as he reached into the bag. "Is this all of it?"

Edward nodded and closed the lid to the trunk. "What about my pay?"

Seymour handed ten dollars to Edward and closed the cloth valise. "Thank you for all your help. I couldn't have done it without you."

Edward examined the single bill. "This is not the price we agreed upon."

"You can take your payment from what is left of Ravenswood." He gripped the bag. "I need a hostage to guarantee no one follows." He waved the gun at Cass. "You're coming with me."

Cass looked at Zach and Edward. Was this part of his plan?

Edward threw his arm to block Zach from attacking Seymour. "Put the derringer away, you fool woman. You might hit Seymour."

Lucia stood in the buggy, the derringer in her hand. Seymour shoved the bag into the buggy. "Do as he says. I don't need a hole in the back of my head."

Ford's Theater. A shot in the balcony. Lincoln

assassinated. Cass clutched her stomach, nauseated by the memories. She stumbled.

Seymour grabbed her arm in a tight clench. She struggled to escape. She looked over her shoulder for help.

"Let her go!" Zach lunged for Seymour, who fired the revolver. The noise echoed as the powder exploded, and the man she loved fell back, hit full in the chest.

Edward tackled Zach to the ground. Cass screamed, wrenching her arm free and hitting Seymour in the face. The gun discharged in her direction, and she stumbled backward. Seymour stared in horror as she fell to the ground.

"What have you done?" Lucia slapped the reins against the horses' hindquarters.

Seymour dropped the gun as he lunged for the moving vehicle and scrambled onto the seat.

Cass watched the buggy fade into the distance. She clutched her burning chest and closed her eyes.

Chapter Thirty-One

Cass didn't feel dead. The sun was warm on her face. She opened her eyes. The clouds floated overhead in soft shapes against a blue sky. She looked for Zach, who was on the ground nearby. Edward was on top of him pounding on his chest. He jumped toward her, tore off his jacket, and covered her. Why wasn't she dead? The booms of the shots rang in her ears. She struggled to hear the bits and pieces of conversation around her.

"What are you doing?" Zach shouted.

"Putting out the fire," Edward said.

"We're going after them," Harry said.

"I'll get the horses," Ethan said.

"Don't waste your time," Edward said. "Bryce, go after them."

"Are you sure, sir?"

"Go."

She batted the coat away. Zach knelt beside her. His coat was burned, and a hole was in his vest. "Are we dead?"

"Just singed." Edward reclaimed his coat. "I needed to put out the flames."

Cass examined her dress. It had caught on fire, and holes were surrounded by black circles. Her corset had protected her from skin burns, but her gown had several revealing holes in it.

"Seymour shot us. Why aren't we dead?"

Edward retrieved his revolver from the ground. "When Seymour wanted me to disarm the men, I figured he'd disarm me as well. Vermin are predictable. I loaded black powder in the cylinder but no bullets."

Zach helped Cass to her feet. He draped his coat over her damaged gown. The wool fabric smelled of sulfur and smoke. "Then we weren't in any real danger."

Edward shook his head as he put on his coat. "You forget Lucia's derringer. I hadn't counted on that."

"She still has it."

"Which is why I sent Bryce to stop your friends."

Zach looked toward the hillside. "What about your sharpshooters?"

"They were given orders not to shoot unless I gave the signal. I didn't want a bullet flying if Seymour fired *my* revolver." Edward raised his arms in the air, crossed them twice, and lowered them.

Zach picked his hat off the ground. "But if Seymour's gun wasn't loaded, why didn't you stop him?"

"Shoot a man I knew wasn't armed?" Edward shook his head. "That would be murder. Besides, we want Seymour to run. The coward thinks he killed you. That's why I knocked you to the ground." He turned to Cass. His eyes were worried, and his voice shook. "I didn't expect him to shoot you. I hope you weren't hurt."

"Get away from her!"

It was Tyler's voice. She looked beyond Edward. A carriage had pulled to the spot Seymour's buggy had vacated. What was her brother-in-law doing at Ravenswood?

Tyler jumped from the carriage and grabbed Edward by his coat collar. "I saw you assault Zach and Cassie." He pulled back his arm to hit him and froze. "You're not Seymour." His blue eyes widened. "You're Edward Vandal."

Cass wedged herself between them. "He was saving us."

Tyler released Edward and backed away. He looked from Zach to Cass. "You smell like smoke."

"A gun misfired." Zach brushed at his vest. "I got scorched a bit."

Cass pulled Zach's coat around her. "What are you doing here?"

He pointed at Zach. "I received your letter and was worried. I figured I better visit."

Cass stepped forward. "What about my letter?"

"That's the one that made me drop everything and rush here." Tyler frowned. "What has Seymour done that could be criminal?"

"He stole Zach's money." She pointed toward the west. "He's escaping on the train. Ethan and Harry went after him."

Zach put his arm around her shoulders, offering comfort. "They had a head start, and I heard a train whistle. It's too late to stop them."

Tyler turned toward the carriage. "Don't bother getting out." It was too late. The boys jumped to the ground, and Cory carried Olivia.

"You brought my sister and the children?"

Tyler removed his hat and brushed his fingers through his hair. "They insisted upon joining me."

Cass hugged Cory.

"Stinky." Olivia held her nose.

Cory pulled back Zach's coat. "What happened to your dress?"

"An accident. I have my clothes on the table." She turned. Her clothes had blown off the top and were scattered around the yard. "Oh, no!"

"Boys, gather Aunt Cassie's clothes before they blow away!" Cory ordered.

They watched the boys chase her garments. Olivia pointed at Zach. "Chick pox."

"Did you catch the chicken pox from Olivia?" Cory examined Zach's neck.

"Poison ivy."

She jerked her hand away and turned to Edward. A smile played on her lips. "Edward Vandal. My husband has been looking for you."

"I know," Edward said. "I feared you wanted to throw me in jail."

Zach stared. "But Seymour introduced you as Vance Edwards."

"I changed my name so Tyler couldn't find me."

"Why didn't you want to be found?" Cory asked.

"I didn't know about Jefferson." Edward removed the photo album from his pocket and turned to Jefferson's photograph. "Until your sister showed me this, I believed he had died with Regina."

"Oh, Edward," Cory said. "It must have been awful to believe you lost both of them."

Jefferson and Sterling ran toward them, their hands full of clothes. "We can't hold any more."

They had dragged several items through the mud. "Let me take those," Cass said.

Jefferson's straight blond hair blew in the breeze. He stared at his father. Tears brimmed in Edward's eyes, and he choked, unable to speak.

"There's some more!" Sterling pointed toward the corral.

"Race you," Jefferson said.

"Jefferson!" Cory called as they dashed off.

"Let him go." Edward watched him run toward the fence. "That's him." Edward swiped a few tears away. "My boy."

"Don't you want to meet him?" Cass asked.

"How could he possibly remember me? He was so little, and it's been too long." He returned her album. "Knowing he's alive is enough."

"We spoke about you," Tyler said.

Edward didn't look pleased.

"Only good things," Cory said. "He knows his father is a soldier, and he's coming home someday, like his mother promised."

"Regina." He brushed away a few tears. "The Silver Pheasant is in ruins. What sort of home can I offer him?"

"It isn't the house or land," Cass said. "It's the love that makes a home." She rested her head against Zach's shoulder. "That's why it doesn't matter about the money."

The boys returned with the remaining garments. "We found all of them," Jefferson said.

"Good job, son." Tyler patted Sterling on the head.

"What about me?" Jefferson asked.

"We have a surprise for you," Tyler said. "Do you remember we said your father was a soldier?"

"He fought in the war." Jefferson puffed out his chest. "He was brave."

"I wrote letters to find him, and I did."

A smile lit up his face. "You found my daddy?"

"Jefferson," Tyler knelt to his level. "This man is your father, Edward Vandal. He's an old and dear friend of the family."

Edward looked surprised by Tyler's kind words. They had been enemies most of their lives. He knelt on the ground. "I don't think you remember me, Jefferson, but I remember you."

Jefferson stared. "Why are you cryin'?"

Edward choked back tears. "I didn't think I would ever see you again."

Jefferson cupped his face with his hands. "Don't cry, Daddy. I'm right here."

He pulled his son to his chest. Cass searched for her handkerchief.

Ethan and Bryce returned with a horse in tow. Harry was driving the buggy Seymour had taken. "The train left before we reached them." Ethan looked at the guests. "Tyler, Cory, what are you doing here?"

"I was worried Seymour might cause trouble for Zach."

"Did he ever," Ethan said. "He stole all of Zach's money and shot him."

Cory examined Zach. "Are you hurt?"

"Vance, I mean Edward loaded the gun with black powder. No bullets. We have a few holes in our clothes."

"He shot Cassie!" Cory looked at her sister closer. "What sort of monster would shoot a woman?"

Zach put his arm around Cass. "I'm grateful we're all alive."

"There are some horses left," Harry said.

Zach withdrew the envelope and pulled out the

papers. "Edward saved these."

"I only sold the ones on the inventory list you gave me," he said.

Zach extended his hand. "Thank you. I'll have to sell more stock. Maybe even parts of Ravenswood." He looked at his friends. "But we'll survive."

"Well, we better leave." Bryce lifted the broken strongbox by lifting the bottom. "Leave these folks to their visit."

"Put it down, Bryce. We're not taking it," Edward said.

"But Major, what about the plan?"

"The plan has changed. We aren't thieves."

"Thieves? The trunk is empty." Zach opened the lid and stuck his hand inside. "Hey, it's shallow." He knocked on the bottom. "The trunk has a false floor."

Edward closed the lid and flipped the chest. He opened the bottom which was identical to the other side. Inside were neatly stacked bills. "Here's your money."

"I watched as you packed the money into the bag," Zach said.

Edward withdrew the ten-dollar bill Seymour had paid him with from his coat pocket. "This is what Seymour took."

Zach examined the bill. He lifted it toward the sunlight. "It's counterfeit."

"Oh, he'll fool a few people, but once the news spreads he's passing counterfeit bills, he'll have to hide or go to jail," Edward said. "Seymour ought to be safely out of the area and your life by the time he realizes he has a bag full of worthless paper."

"Was this your plan all along?" Cass asked.

"No. The Silver Pheasant was in shambles, and my family dead when I returned after the war ended," Edward said. "The only thing I had was a trunk of Confederate bills. Payroll for my men that wasn't worth the paper it was printed on."

"Do I want to know how they turned into Union greenbacks?" Tyler asked.

"Probably not," Edward said. "We traveled north to pass off the fakes for real greenbacks, but Fred Kettler has a keen eye. He thwarted our plan. Then Seymour offered me a job. He wanted a sale arranged as quickly as possible. We were going to be paid after the horses were sold. That didn't sit well with me or my men. We'd been double-crossed too many times. So we figured we'd con the con man."

"What changed your mind?"

"Zach showed up, all bright-eyed and full of dreams for a future," Edward said. "Even though you were a Yankee, I liked you. It didn't sit well when Seymour wanted you dead."

Zach touched the back of his head. "Thanks for saving my life."

"Then Miss Beecher arrived and unraveled everyone's plans." He turned to Cory. "You and your sisters should come with warnings."

"You were going to collect the money for the sale, let Seymour run off with the counterfeit bills, and leave with the real cash," Zach summarized.

"But Jefferson was alive," Cass added.

"A little boy with his mother's smile made me an honest man."

"I could use you and your men at Ravenswood," Zach said.

"We'll stay long enough to rebuild the barn we burned, but I have to rebuild the Silver Pheasant." He looked at Jefferson. "I hate to separate the boys, but…"

"He's your son," Cory said. "We'll visit."

"I was raised in Vandalia," Tyler said. "I think I can remember the way back."

"You have to promise to visit Glen Knolls." Cory turned to Cass. "Did you ever buy a horse for Papa?"

She withdrew her money from her reticule. "No."

"Black Knight is in the barn," Bryce said. "Along with the horses your friends chose."

"Could you ask Mr. Kettler to return and finalize the sales?" Zach said.

Bryce nodded and rode off.

Cass placed her stack of clothes and album inside the trunk on the back of the carriage with Cory and Tyler's belongings. Ethan loaded the money chest next to it, and Edward helped the boys board the carriage.

"I'll need to send a telegram warning authorities about the counterfeit bills," Tyler said.

Zach waved the fake ten dollars in the air. "I'll show this to Mr. Kettler. He'll send word."

"Why don't I show your guest to Ravens Roost?" Edward climbed into the back of the carriage with the boys.

Cory turned to her sister. "We're full, but we could squeeze you in."

Cass pointed at the buggy Harry had retrieved. "I have a ride." She looked around. "Where are Harry and Ethan?"

"Must be in the barn," Zach said. They stepped into the dark coolness and looked around. Black Knight was in a stall like Bryce had said, but his friends were nowhere in sight.

Cass rubbed the gelding's nose. "I've been thinking about the horses and how your grandfather struggled to pay the bills."

"Maybe Seymour was a lousy accountant."

"I have a feeling that was the only thing he was good at."

Zach looked around the barn. "Do you want me to sell Ravenswood?"

"No, I want you to open a hotel."

He paused. "What?"

"The railroad is nearby. You have plenty of rooms at Ravens Roost, and it's grand enough to impress guests. Blake could help you start the business."

A smile creased his handsome face. "That's a brilliant idea. Instead of living year to year, the extra income would make Ravenswood profitable. We could rent carriages or horses for those who need to travel. And we could rent rooms in the cabin by the lake."

"No," Cass said. "Your mother made the cabin a home."

"I enjoyed growing up there." Zach leaned into her, pressing her against the stall door. "And hotels don't allow much privacy." He traced the edge of her jaw with his fingertips and lifted her chin. "People coming and going. It's difficult to find time to be alone."

"We've had little of that with chaperones and mad men." She poked her finger through a hole in his vest. "Papa expects me to return home with a horse tomorrow."

"Tomorrow?" He gently brushed her hair back from her face. "Would he be upset if you returned home engaged?"

Her heart raced, but she steadied her voice before speaking. "Didn't you bargain two geldings and a carriage for my hand?"

"I could give him all of Ravenswood, and it wouldn't be enough. I thought I had lost you twice. Once to Harry and then to Seymour's treachery. You're my heart and my soul, the very breath that gives me life. I love you, Cassandra. Will you marry me?"

She caressed his cheek. "Yes."

Zach lowered his mouth, capturing her lips and sealing their promise.

A sharp whistle broke them apart. Harry and Ethan were standing in the stall opposite them, leaning over the half-door. "It's about time." Black Knight shook his head in agreement.

A word about the author…

Laura Freeman has been a reporter for the past thirteen years and covers the MyTown NEO beat for Summit County in Ohio. She has won the Press Club of Cleveland's Ohio Excellence in Journalism award twice and the Ohio Newspaper Association award several times. Her novel, *Impending Love and Madness*, is the sequel to *Impending Love and War*, *Impending Love and Death*, *Impending Love and Lies*, and *Impending Love and Capture*.

Madness takes place in 1865 when Cassandra Beecher and Sergeant Zach Ravenswood attend a play at Ford's Theater. Lincoln's assassination is followed by a series of events that threaten to destroy the young couple's love.

Laura lives in Ohio, where she is working on her final book in the series, *Impending Love and Promise*.

Thank you for purchasing
this publication of The Wild Rose Press, Inc.

If you enjoyed the story, we would appreciate your
letting others know by leaving a review.

For other wonderful stories,
please visit our on-line bookstore at
www.thewildrosepress.com.

For questions or more information
contact us at
info@thewildrosepress.com.

The Wild Rose Press, Inc.
www.thewildrosepress.com

Stay current with The Wild Rose Press, Inc.

Like us on Facebook

https://www.facebook.com/TheWildRosePress

And Follow us on Twitter
https://twitter.com/WildRosePress